Bad Boy

A Jason Davey Mystery

Winona Kent

Winona Kent / Blue Devil Books

Preface

Please be aware that this novel contains details of a suicide.

For help and support and when life is difficult, in the UK and Republic of Ireland, please call the Samaritans–day or night, 365 days a year. You can call them for free on 116 123, email them at jo@samaritans.org or visit samaritans.org to find your nearest branch.

Outside the UK and ROI, or for additional resources in the UK, please consult this worldwide list:

https://en.wikipedia.org/wiki/List_of_suicide_crisis_lines

ACKNOWLEDGEMENTS

I'd like to thank my husband Jim Goddard and my sister Stella Kent, who put up with me while I embarked on sometimes strange but always intriguing strands of research to write this novel. Writers tend to be solitary, focused creatures who function extremely well in their own company. Stella and Jim are hardy souls who understand, accept and assist this aberrant behaviour with good cheer and infinite patience. They also allowed the necessary "me-time" to get all six drafts written. Thank you, both!

I'd like to thank Brian Richmond for his continuing enthusiasm, wonderful story sense and clever suggestions (and he designs my covers, too).

It's often been said that if the police were to investigate mystery writers' online searches, we'd end up looking very dodgy indeed. *What kind of damage is caused by ripping out a pierced earring? Can a body be completely incinerated in a very hot fire? Can you mummify a body by burying it in sand?*

But we also rely on the assistance of real individuals, and some of our query letters might raise curious eyebrows there, too. I'd like to thank the following people who helped with my research:

Cousins Martin and Deborah Hofman, for their hospitality, advice and excellent guidance to all of the places Jason visits in Derbyshire; cousins Nick and Jenny Tidman for a lovely lunch in Sutton; and cousin Andrew Wilson for his musical knowledge, suggestions and introductions.

Music industry veterans Ken Nicol and David Stark, and the late (and much missed) Mo Foster, for their helpful reminiscences.

The late Jake Kutarna, who heard many of my confessions when I was a child and he was a priest, in Regina.

Author and walking-tour guide Paul Talling, the undisputed expert on London's lost music venues.

The British Library's Chris Scobie (Lead Curator, Music Manuscripts, Music Collections), and Darren (Customer Services).

My friend and writing colleague Shoshona Freedman, for her first-hand PI knowledge.

The Samaritans.

Andrew Humphries at Paradise Road publishers, and Peter Watts, author, for their most fabulous book, *Denmark Street.*

And finally, the late John Hammond, friend and handyman, who inspired the character of Marcus Merritt.

Thank you all!

Note: Wikipedia entries which are quoted in this novel, regarding Sir Edward Elgar and his works, can be found here: https://en.wikipedia.org/wiki/Enigma_Variations

These are shared under the Text of the Creative Commons Attribution-ShareAlike 4.0 International License.

CHAPTER ONE

Classical music should never take itself too seriously.

Case in point: *Aria Sopra la Bergamasca* by Marco Uccellini. Composed in 1642. Traditionally performed with two violins and a basso continuo. And very definitely not a Gretsch solid body G5135 CVT, with a harpsichord patch on a Roland XP-80, a tenor sax wailing out the baroque melody line, and a polite little snare drum keeping us all well-behaved.

My band and I had taken over the main studio at Ardwick House, a rambling 18th-century cottage in NW3 that had been owned by successive generations of a local musical family. Around the time I was born, in 1968, the last of them—a pair of elderly spinster sisters who'd kept cats and nearly everything else their ancestors had accumulated since 1794—died within a month of each other. The property and its antique-cluttered rooms were left to some distantly-related and financially-savvy cousins, who were also musically-inclined. The cats were dispatched to a leafy estate in Dorset. The antiques were dusted off. And the rooms they occupied were converted into rehearsal spaces.

I knew one of the cousins, so we were enjoying a "mate's rate" on that quiet Sunday afternoon. We'd set up in the main hall, which the musically-inclined cousins had created by demolishing a couple of interior walls and removing part of the second floor. It had a high ceiling with a pitched roof embedded with skylights. It had a wonderful old fireplace set into oak panelling and a sprung maple floor that bore the comfortable scars and scuffs of instruments, music stands, amps, and flight cases. A beautiful concert piano occupied one of the corners, near an abundance of large green houseplants, and the entire south wall had been knocked out and replaced with floor-to-ceiling windows—which overlooked an untidy, overgrown, and completely secluded back garden.

"Once again," Rudy said, with a gentle final brush on his Zildjian cymbals, "invoking the perfect synthesis of the unnatural with the bizarre."

It was true. We're a jazz combo—guitar, sax, keyboards and drums—with a permanent residency upstairs at The Blue Devil in Soho. We're the after-hours Late Show's main act. I'm notorious for my everything-goes audio-fusion. You can do it with food, so why not with music?

"I can't wait for your very special arrangement of Handel's *Messiah* on Guy Fawkes Day," Dave replied, giving us the triumphant orchestral violin intro to the "Hallelujah" Chorus on his keyboard.

"You're on," I said. "'Last Train Home' next?"

One of my favourites by Pat Metheny. We'd been playing it since our very first gig at The Blue Devil.

Ken gave his sax a little polish. "Our current version?" he inquired. "Or your heavily-sampled re-imagining of the original Klingon?"

***

It was Sunday, October 14, 2018. I'd just come off a thirty-four-day, eighteen-city tour of Wales and southern England with my mum's band, Figgis Green. I'd taken a leave of absence from The Blue Devil while Rudy, Ken and Dave had carried on with a series of guest acts taking over my chair.

And now I was back. We'd just run through half of our first set, mostly to make sure I still remembered where my fingers were meant to be after more than a month on the road with the Celtic-folky-pop Figs.

Dave had gone into the little blue and white Dutch-tiled kitchen to make us some tea. Rudy and Ken were expecting me to wander out to the overgrown garden for a quick ciggie. I surprised them.

"Gave it up in Tunbridge Wells," I said, returning my Gretsch to its stand so I could share out the chocolate digestive biscuits I'd brought in a sustainable shopping bag from a homeopathic health care shop in Lincoln.

"My sister quit last year," Ken replied. "She put on two stone."

"Thanks very much," I said.

I was fifty and I was lucky. I'd inherited my dad's lean build. He was fifty-four when he died—struck by lightning while he was caddying for a mate on a golf course. I never got to see him grow old. But I knew what he'd been handed down by way of his own father. Noah Figgis was fit and healthy well into his senior years. He'd cycled to the village shop every morning for his *Daily Express*, a pint of milk, and an apple for his afternoon tea. He'd been to the shop on the day he died in 2005. It wasn't old age that killed him—it was a careless driver. He was taken away too soon—aged eighty-five. We all thought he'd carry on until he was at least one hundred.

I'm aiming for that myself, in spite of my addiction to Maltesers, chocolate digestives, and an utter lack of any kind of physical fitness—other than a daily walk, which, admittedly, does usually cover a couple of miles. Giving up smoking was something I'd been wanting to do for a long time. In the end, it was easy. Well, easy compared to what had led up to it—someone had tried to do me in with an overdose of insulin. I'd recovered in hospital in Tunbridge Wells, and after I was discharged, I suddenly found I no longer had the urge.

"I honestly wouldn't recommend it as a Stop Smoking strategy," I said, to Dave, as we joined him in the little kitchen to recharge on his Yorkshire tea and my chocolate digestives.

I'd had my phone switched off while we were rehearsing. I took it out of my pocket now and skimmed through the usual collection of checking-ins, reminders, and shared memes and jokes.

A text from my son, Dom, telling me about an upcoming film festival. He was nearly twenty, and he was doing his BA (Hons) in Film and Television Practice at London South Bank University.

You'd love it, he wrote. *It's all crime thrillers, detectives, mystery, and suspense. Chinatown. Night Moves. Very Raymond Chandler. Very noir.*

No amateur sleuths? I texted back. *Send it on to your aunt—she'll be there with bells on.*

Angie, my sister, writes best-selling cozy mysteries under the pen name Taylor Feldspar. Her main character, Jemima Fielding, is a chef who solves murders which always seem to happen when she's called on to cater a function. But, in spite of the professed lighter side to her writing, Angie's a voracious fan of hard-boiled gumshoes.

I'm on it, said Dom.

A text from my daughter, Jennifer—a professional photographer—who'd flown home to Vancouver to cover the launch of a quirky new cafe featuring coffee, pastries, and wildly bizarre decorations thought up by a couple of her fashion-designer friends. She'd attached photos. They looked like something that had escaped from a Tim Burton film.

An email from Katey, my independently-faithful girlfriend. She wasn't in London, either. She'd jetted off to California for a sixteen-night repositioning cruise, San Diego to Tampa, by way of the Panama Canal. All expenses paid by the travel agency where she worked.

We're approaching Puntarenas. It's in Costa Rica. I bought you some hand-blown Christmas tree ornaments that look like musical notes from a glass factory in Cabo. I'll stuff them into my socks so they don't break. Love you. PS the WiFi's atrocious.

I knew all about the atrocious WiFi on cruise ships. It had been just as bad when I was an entertainer on board the *Star Sapphire* in 2012. Six years later and they still hadn't solved the problem with satellites, at-sea internet connections, maritime communications and dodgy bandwidth.

Love you too, I emailed back. *Though you probably won't get this until yesterday.*

There were three voice messages from someone named Marcus Merritt. Follow-ups to the two voice messages he'd left yesterday, and the five texts.

"Hello Jason. You don't know me. I was at Figgis Green's last show in Hammersmith."

He was right—his name didn't ring any bells.

"I bought a program that I wanted you to sign, but I just missed you."

Every night, after each show, we'd gone out into the foyer to mingle with the fans and sign things: programs, tea towels, posters. Our venues weren't huge—Hammersmith Apollo, case in point—and the audiences—some of whom had travelled quite a distance—appreciated us for giving them the chance to say hello.

But the tour was over.

"I wonder if we might meet somewhere so I can get that signature."

I don't hide my telephone number—I'm easily found. But he was assuming a lot.

Dave slid a mug of Yorkshire tea with plenty of milk and sugar across the table to me and then went back to the messages on his own phone.

My phone chimed. Marcus Merritt. Of course.

I let it ring.

Dave glanced up at me.

Ken and Rudy decided to consult a news feed on Rudy's phone.

"Eleven badly-decomposed infant bodies discovered inside the ceiling of a former funeral home in Detroit," Ken read, aloud.

"New research," Rudy added, "suggests Europa, one of Jupiter's moons, may be covered in tall, jagged ice spikes. Are you going to answer that, Jason?"

"No," I said, drinking my tea.

Marcus Merritt's call went to my voicemail.

I helped myself to another biccie.

I really didn't want to have to block him. But he was testing my patience.

And, evidently, my voicemail was testing his.

There he was again.

"Points for persistence," Dave said.

I put the phone on speaker.

"Jason Figgis."

"Ah," he said. "You are there."

"I was rehearsing," I said.

"I assume you got my messages."

I didn't say anything.

Rudy, Ken and Dave were all looking at me, fingers poised over their screens, waiting.

"I wonder if we might meet," Marcus said.

"I'm afraid I'm busy for the rest of today," I replied.

"Tomorrow, then. I think you'll find it worth your while. There's something I'd like to discuss with you. A possible job. Investigative."

A few years earlier, I'd tracked down a legendary musician—Ben Quigley—who'd dropped off the face of the earth after attending a music festival in northern Canada. I'd rescued him from certain death and brought him home. His story had ended up in all the papers, and my second-string career as a PI had been launched. I'd solved a few more mysteries since then, on a bespoke basis only. I wasn't licensed—you don't have to be in the UK. I'd done the course, answered the questions, submitted the exercises. I actually had a certificate that said I'd successfully achieved the requirements for the SFJ Level 3 Award. I'd just never got round to sitting the actual exam.

I wasn't sure I wanted to. Everything I investigated had a habit of landing me in trouble. Often to the detriment of my health. And occasionally, my life.

And, I was tired. I still needed time to decompress.

"Could we meet tomorrow, half past one, Level 72 at the top of The Shard?" Marcus inquired.

"A soulless spike skewering the beating heart of historic London," Dave muttered. (Dave was not a fan of the city's new architecture, and shared Prince Charles's opinion of an early design for an extension to the National Gallery as being "a carbuncle on the face of a much-loved friend".)

"A glass facade equal in size to almost eight Wembley football pitches," Ken supplied.

"Fabulous views from the public toilets," Rudy added.

"I'm not really able to take on any new cases right now," I said. "I'm very sorry."

"It has to do with Elgar," Marcus replied.

"The composer?" I asked.

"The very same."

"Do it," Ken mouthed, silently, daring me.

"A new musical adventure," Rudy added, his eyes filled with mischief.

"Just go and talk to him," Dave suggested. "You don't have to accept his offer."

I gave in. "How will I recognize you?"

"Don't worry," Marcus replied. "I know who you are. I'll find you. See you there."

CHAPTER TWO

MY FLAT'S IN ANGEL, on Pentonville Road. N1. On the first floor of a Georgian-era conversion near the tube station. The people who lived there when it was first built occupied all four floors: kitchen in the cellar, servants in the attic, 18th-century family discourse conducted everywhere in between. My open plan kitchen and lounge were created out of what used to be the main drawing room at the front of the house, and my bedroom at the back constitutes most of what used to be a second drawing room. The former ante-room between the two is now a very compact but functional toilet. It's a tiny place—less than 500 square feet—but it's perfect for what I want and what I need. And I have all the mod-cons. USB wall chargers in the lounge and bedroom. One of those contraptions attached to the kitchen tap that delivers scalding hot water at the push of a button.

I popped my teabag into the pot and summoned the water and made myself a late breakfast—scrambled eggs with some chopped up cheese and ham, and a slice of toast with butter and Marmite. I love Marmite. My daughter thinks it's vile. But she was raised in Vancouver, without my gastronomic influences.

Four days earlier, I'd been on top form at the Hammersmith Apollo. Two days before that, I was onstage in Ipswich, and two days before that, Southend.

In total, I'd been away for nearly two months, first rehearsing and then, touring.

The most striking sensation of walking back into my flat, after it was all over, had been the absence of connection. I'd had a strange, suspended feeling of familiarity—but I was observing it all from a distance. And I was alone.

I'd had two months of not having to look after myself. Eating in cafes and restaurants and, just as often, my hotel room. Leaving my bed unmade and my towels on the floor.

I'd enjoyed our 50th Anniversary Reunion tour. The constant change of scenery, the shows—I loved the shows. I loved—and still do love—performing. But it had all depended on a constant supply of adrenaline, and, in the end, when it was all done and dusted, I missed that rush.

I was a little surprised that what I didn't miss was the camaraderie. It was lovely working with the other Figs—mum, my uncle Mitch and my cousin Rolly, Beth and Bob—and most of the crew. But, after weeks of sharing a tour bus and enduring constant and close proximity with people you're fond of (but who have some of the most overbearing idiosyncrasies you could ever imagine), saying goodbye actually felt like a relief.

There's a song by Duran Duran—"Ordinary World"—which I think really captures a lot of what I was feeling on that Monday morning in October.

I'd woken up feeling restless and detached. And I really and truly didn't feel much like going out to meet Marcus Merritt. The offer of an investigative job aside, he'd probably want to sit me down to discuss chord progressions in "Roving Minstrel". Or take issue with the fact that we'd added a new bass line and strings to "One Summer Day". And he'd very probably want to argue about the absolute heresy of switching lead singers at the end of "The Whistling Gypsy".

I'd really meant it when I'd told him I wasn't able to take on any new cases. In fact, I was seriously considering giving it up altogether. A couple of weeks earlier, in Tunbridge Wells, I'd very nearly died. My heart had actually stopped—twice. But I'd been brought back by the paramedics. It's quite a sobering experience. It gives you some perspective on what's important, and what isn't. But when I'd told Katey I was thinking of giving up investigative work, she'd said, "Are you thinking of giving up sinning, too?"

She knows me entirely too well.

***

It was drizzling as I walked along Islington High Street towards Angel tube station. I had my umbrella up. And I wasn't at all optimistic about the view from the top of the tallest building in western Europe, with the highest habitable floor in the UK.

I rode down the Underground's longest escalator and waited on the platform—the one that used to be a terrifying twelve-foot island with trains blasting past in opposite directions on either side, but which is now—since the station was rebuilt in 1992—double that width and only has tracks going in one direction.

My mood improved somewhat on the journey to London Bridge, four stops south. The tube wasn't busy and the carriage was half-empty. I didn't have to be in charge of anything. I just had to sit there, and be conveyed. And, once I got to my destination, I didn't have to agree to anything. I just had to listen.

London Bridge's mainline tracks sit on top of a wonderful Victorian red brick viaduct, and the tube exit landed me underneath one of its arches in a cross-passage that led straight to The Shard's entrance.

I was fascinated by those arches when I was a kid. The area used to be very grim, and the London Dungeon—as gruesome a museum as you could ever hope to explore as a twelve-year-old—used to be housed in one of the arches on Tooley Street. It's an anonymous shuttered entrance to something else now, with a Starbucks on one side and an FCB Coffee place on the other. And the London Dungeon itself is long gone, having relocated to the more lucrative lure of the South Bank, next to the London Eye.

There weren't a lot of people going up The Shard that day, mostly because of the weather. But then again, it was mid-October, and not the busiest time for tourists anyway.

I looked around as I went through the airport-style security, wondering if any of the other visitors was Marcus Merritt. Evidently not. He'd said he would recognize me—and nobody had.

There was a bloke doing a commentary into his phone while he filmed his "experience" for YouTube, but he was the only one who seemed remotely interested in me—and that was only because I was standing in the way of a shot he wanted.

Getting to the top of The Shard involves two lifts. The first shoots you up to Level 33 while you peruse ceiling panels that project a pre-recorded glimpse of what the view would be like if it was a perfectly sunny day, and not wet and grey with rain that couldn't make up its mind whether it wanted to fall or just annoy you by threatening to.

Then you have to walk around to the next lift, which takes you up to Level 68. And then it's around once more, this time to some stairs—and Level 69 (the enclosed view)—and Level 72 (the one that's open-air).

I'd been to The Shard exactly four times since its opening in 2012. Had a glorious dinner at Aqua on Level 31, spent an extremely interesting weekend with Katey at the Shangri-la Hotel (and had a swim in the highest hotel pool in Western Europe)—and I'd done both versions of The View, inside and out.

It was cold and damp on that day—about 12C, according to the weather app on my phone—and I was glad I was wearing my lined weatherproof jacket. Everything on Level 72 looks very functional—exposed pipes and steel frames and rivets, with fake green turf underfoot and, if you look up, a fabulous perspective of the minimalist maintenance floors.

There are also CCTV cameras. London has nearly a million of them, one for every ten people in the city. You're likely to be captured up to seventy times a day if you live here.

I saluted the camera that was aimed at me, and had another look for anyone that might had been Marcus Merritt. I walked all the way around the central core, past the stairs and the bar, but nobody approached me.

I stopped and had a look at the view to the west but, to be honest, everything disappeared into a grey smudge roundabout Blackfriars Bridge, and well before the curve in the river leading to Waterloo and the London Eye and Dungeon.

I sent Marcus a text to let him know I was there. He wasn't doing himself any favours being late.

I walked along to the north view—the money shot—the Walkie-Talkie building, the Tower of London, the HMS *Belfast,* and Tower Bridge. At least I could still see those.

And then, on the east side, I stopped to have a look down at the railway tracks. I know it's a cliche, but we were so high up—800 feet—that the trains speeding in from the suburbs were like toys, inching under the undulating white roofs of London Bridge Station.

"Jason?"

The voice belonged to a tall, lean man with a shock of untidy white hair. He had a large nose and a long, angular face and chin. He looked to be in his mid-sixties, and he was wearing black: jacket, high-necked pullover, jeans.

"Marcus?"

I'm good at remembering faces, and he suddenly seemed familiar, though I couldn't think why. I supposed I might have seen him loitering in the foyer after that last show in Hammersmith.

"I'm sorry," he said.

"No problem," I replied, even though it was nearly half an hour past the time we'd arranged to meet.

"You don't recognize me, do you?"

"I don't," I said. "Should I?"

He smiled.

"First things first," he said. "Before we discuss Elgar. I've brought the program."

I had a terrible thought. Had I remembered to bring my black Sharpie? I checked my jacket pocket. I had.

"I want you to remember something for me, Jason. Newlydale. It's in Derbyshire."

"OK," I said. "Why?"

He handed me the program. "Please."

As programs go, it was pretty good. A glossy book filled with photos of Figgis Green through the years, all of the people who'd played in the band, right the way through to the lineup my mum had assembled for our 50th Anniversary tour. Posters from past gigs, album covers. Bios of everyone. Set lists and credits, right the way down to our production team, suppliers and management. 12" x 12", forty pages in full colour, heavyweight paper, £10 well spent.

"Marcus with a 'c'?" I checked.

"Marcus with a 'c'," he confirmed.

I looked for somewhere to sit so I could sign it, and spotted some resin-wicker chairs corralling a small cube coffee table near the bar.

I appropriated one of the chairs and opened the front cover.

There was a little envelope with my name on it, tucked into the binding. Something to do with his proposed investigation? I popped it into my jacket pocket.

It was while I was making sure my *To Marcus with a 'c'. Hope you enjoyed the show!* scrawl was legible that I caught movement out of the corner of my eye.

I glanced up in time to see Marcus taking a run at the window at the southeast corner of the floor.

On Level 72, the tall glass walls are open at the top. Each of the four corners has panels that are shorter—probably only about eleven or twelve feet high—with a decorative pipe running horizontally about two feet below the top edge.

I'm not sure what the designers were thinking when they created those four corners, but I know for a fact that at least one illegal BASE jumper's filmed himself hiking up and over that exact same spot without too much difficulty at all.

Marcus had grabbed the horizontal pipe and was in the process of kicking and hauling himself the rest of the way to the top of the open-air window.

He wasn't a BASE jumper.

He didn't have a parachute.

"Wait!" I yelled, leaping to my feet and running towards him. "Stop!"

I knew what he was going to do. I *knew*.

"What the fuck are you doing? Please—no!"

It all happened very quickly, though in my head, afterwards, it was slowed down to a frame-by-frame snail's pace, like the trains crawling into London Bridge Station 800 feet below.

I got to the glass wall just as Marcus was tipping himself over. His face was turned to me. Our eyes met momentarily. And then, he let go.

I heard a woman shrieking. It was one of the waitresses from the bar.

I remember looking down, stupidly. But I couldn't see much because of The Shard's outward slope. And I remember thinking, also rather stupidly, that he was probably going to smash right through one of the glass canopies at the bottom and crash onto St Thomas Street, directly outside Guy's Hospital.

And that's all I remember, because after that I'm pretty sure I went into shock.

I still had Marcus's program in one hand and my black Sharpie in the other.

I walked back to the little table where I'd left my umbrella.

I sat down.

***

Someone came to talk to me. I think he must have been one of the other visitors. He had a neatly trimmed grey beard and unusual eyes—hazel-brown in the centre, fading to a halo of green, but finishing with a outline of bluish-black. He was older than me.

"I'm Craig," he said. His voice was calm and kind. "I used to work with the railways, though I'm retired now. I've witnessed a few suicides in my time. What's your name?"

"Jason," I said. I was shaking. I put down the program but I couldn't make my fingers let go of the pen. Inside, I was numb, the way your ankle goes after you've stupidly misjudged a curb and twisted it badly, and with a sickening crunch, on your way down.

"I didn't actually see what happened, but I gather you did."

I nodded.

"Do you feel like talking about what you saw?"

I didn't.

And then I did.

I tried to organize my thoughts but they wouldn't cooperate and it all came out in a jumble. I think I must have ended up telling him my entire life story, up until the point where Marcus called me at Ardwick House. And then it all became crystal clear. Every detail, every thought, every word.

"If only I'd been quicker. I could have grabbed his legs. I could have stopped him from going over. I could have pulled him back."

Craig was listening. He didn't interrupt. He didn't try to hurry me.

"And I don't know why he did it," I said. "He went to all the trouble of arranging to meet me here, to bring me the program..."

I picked it up and showed it to him.

Craig took it, and opened it, deliberately, not a casual flip-through. He paused to read what I'd written inside the cover.

"Why did he jump while I was signing it? Was he blaming me for something? Was it something I said? Something I did?"

Craig was still holding the program. "Had you met him at all before today?"

I shook my head.

"Then I don't think he could have been blaming you for anything, really, Jason. You had no way of knowing how his mind was working, or what had gone wrong in his life, how he was feeling about things..."

"He asked me if I recognized him. The way he said it, he was surprised I didn't."

"You're a performer," Craig said. "You must know, from all of your experiences, that people will think of you as being familiar—possibly on the same level as one of their best friends—even though you haven't got a clue who they are."

He was right, of course. And I did know that.

"And then he apologized," I said.

"Why do you suppose he did that?" Craig asked.

"He'd made up his mind about what he was going to do next."

"There you are," Craig said. "And by turning up here, to sign his program, perhaps you showed you cared. At a time when, possibly, no one else did."

"He wanted me to remember Newlydale."

"In Derbyshire?"

I nodded.

"Have you ever been there?" Craig asked.

"Never."

I don't know how long we talked. But I was gradually aware that things were happening around us. Everyone who'd been present when Marcus had kicked himself over the glass wall had been asked to stay put, to sit down and wait for the police. And now the police were arriving.

"They'll likely want to take a statement from you," Craig said. "Since you were the last person to speak to him before he jumped. Just a routine investigation. Nothing to be worried about."

He took something out of his wallet. "I'll give you this card," he said. The Samaritans.

"I'm a volunteer. If you feel you need to talk more, give us a ring. Always there to listen."

"Thank you," I said, meaning it. I put the card in my pocket. "Which way's the Gents?"

"That way," Craig said, gesturing with his head. "Down the stairs. You'll see the signs."

The toilets were one floor down and along a passageway. I went into the one at the end and found myself in a room with a floor to ceiling view of that money shot: HMS *Belfast*, the Tower of London, the Thames. Drenched in rain. The opposite side to the one Marcus had chosen when he jumped.

I remembered the little envelope that he'd tucked inside the program. I took it out of my jacket pocket.

Inside was a First Class train ticket from London St Pancras to Matlock for Tuesday, October 16. There was a printed itinerary pointing out that I needed to change trains in Derby. And a single piece of note paper, the size of an A4 sheet cut into quarters, with handwriting scribbled on one side.

The scribble was a single name—*Judy*—and an address—*Wensley Manor, Market Street, Newlydale*.

CHAPTER THREE

"I WANT YOU TO remember something for me," Marcus had said. "Newlydale. It's in Derbyshire."

It was half past six on the morning after Marcus had tumbled off the top of The Shard and I hadn't slept. My imagination wouldn't let me.

If only I'd looked up sooner. If only I'd been two seconds faster. If only I could have got there, grabbed his feet and pulled him back from the brink.

If only our eyes hadn't met through the glass.

My mind kept going back to that. Marcus's eyes. They were grey and they were intense. And in that frozen moment, those eyes had drilled right through to my soul. *Remember me.*

Sometimes, when it's the middle of the night and sleep eludes me, I put the TV on and watch something mindless until my brain surrenders to boredom and decides it's time to go back to bed. Or I get out one of my guitars and cue up some music and play along to the track.

Sometimes it's jazz, my stock in trade at The Blue Devil.

Sometimes it's something altogether different.

That long night, it was "Diamonds". What The Blue Devil was called when it was still a shabby old rock and roll club. Named after a tune written by Jerry Lordan for Tony Meehan and Jet Harris, who'd released it in January 1963. The best version I'd ever heard, though, was from 2007, when Jet was invited to appear onstage with Marty Wilde for his 50th Anniversary Tour at the Palladium. I had the DVD and that was what I was playing along to.

The danger of listening to a favourite piece of music when something traumatic's happened is that it becomes forever burned in your memory as an intrinsic part of that unhappy event. I risked it—four or five times. I risked it another five times for the second tune Jet and Tony were best known for—"Scarlet O'Hara"—even though it was common knowledge Jet never actually played on the single Decca released.

And then I went to bed and had a nightmare that a big boom mic was crashing down from the ceiling and landing on top of me and I woke up on the floor, drenched in sweat, my heart pounding.

I surrendered to the insomnia. I made myself a chaotic breakfast with two mugs of very strong tea, a fried egg with bacon, and two slices of toast and butter with far too much Marmite.

And then I packed a bag. I locked my door. And I got a taxi to St Pancras station.

***

Elton John once gave a performance at St Pancras. It was February 2016, and he did a four-minute piano recital in the Lower Arcade to celebrate the release of his thirtieth studio album. When he was finished, he donated the piano to the station. It's still there and anyone can have a play. It's just across from The White Company, in front of the lift.

My train wasn't due to leave for another hour. I got a coffee from Starbucks and walked back to Elton John's upright black Yamaha.

Plenty of people, famous and not, amateur and professional, have played that piano, entertaining passers-by with an impromptu recital. I never had.

I put my bag on the floor and placed my coffee cup on top of the piano, and sat down on the bench. I knew what I wanted to play. "Bumble Boogie." Up and down the keyboard, rapid-fire in A Minor, left hand outdoing the right, my party-piece. Pure insanity.

My fingers hovered over the keys.

My brain went blank.

Absolutely blank. It wasn't that I didn't know how to play the thing—I did. With my eyes closed. It was that my hands and my head had stopped talking to each other.

And not even my Venti coffee with three sugars, extra cream and White Chocolate Mocha Sauce could kick my brain back into gear.

I sat there, dumbfounded, half-aware that another song was worming its way into my mind. The complete opposite of the organized chaos that was "Bumble Boogie". A simple thing that Marty Wilde had made famous in 1959. "Bad Boy".

It was a simple lament. A breathless and almost-whispering teenage boy complaining that everyone considers him a bad boy for staying out late with his girlfriend, with whom he is very much in love.

Perhaps it was just the simplicity of the composition. And the fact that I could pick out the melody with one finger.

I finished, and was enthusiastically applauded by a five-year-old girl who had stopped to listen with her mum. I felt like Richard E. Grant at the end of *Withnail & I*, flawlessly delivering *Hamlet* to a couple of wolves in the rain at the zoo.

What a piece of work is man.

***

I had wandered into the Boots at the north end of the station arcade, not really sure what, if anything, I was actually looking for. Perhaps nothing. Perhaps I was just killing time.

I was on my way out when I spotted some bottles of Radox shower gel on sale for 99p on a shelf beside the Self-Serve tills. Citrus Oils and Eucalyptus. Brilliant green. An encouraging scent: wake up, seize the day. It occurred to me that I hadn't actually thought of packing any shower stuff. I bought a bottle, and a large packet of Maltesers, tucked them both into my bag, and went across to Starbucks. I bought a second cup of coffee and a little package of dried mixed fruit and nuts. And then I went upstairs and found a seat near the domestic platform gates.

St Pancras station was built in 1867 to accommodate trains coming into London from the Midlands and the North. The railway tracks were twenty feet above the ground—a characteristic which exists to this day—which resulted in the creation of an under-croft supported by 688 cast iron columns.

That underneath bit, the Lower Arcade, was where I'd picked out Marty Wilde's piece on Elton John's piano. You can still see the original Victorian iron columns when you're down there. You can see them when you're upstairs, too, looking down through the cutaway floor, while you're waiting to catch your EMR train to Derbyshire.

I'd avoided watching or reading the news that morning, just as, when I'd finally been allowed to leave The Shard, after I'd given my statement, I'd avoided looking at the road where Marcus had crash-landed. I couldn't have got near it anyway. St Thomas Street was cordoned off with blue and white tape and there were a lot of emergency vehicles blocking the way.

I hadn't gone home on the tube. I'd really needed to be up on the surface, breathing London's fresh October air, surrounded by life—workday people, visitors, taxis and cars and motorbikes—and not trapped under the ground, burrowing through the city's veins and arteries.

I'd deliberately walked north and then west, my umbrella shielding me from the worst of the drizzle. I'd crossed over the Thames at London Bridge. The river was alive with water taxis and fast clippers, growling tugs and work boats and the marine police.

I'd walked all the way up King William Street to Bank. And then, on Princes Street, I'd caught a 43 bus and climbed to the top and ridden along London's business streets, the roads the tourists rarely saw. I'd got off at Angel tube station and walked the rest of the way home.

I still had Marcus's voice messages on my phone. I hadn't deleted them. Couldn't. I listened to each of them again, trying to find anything, any clue at all, that might have alerted me to what he had planned. Nothing. His voice was ordinary, matter-of-fact. I recalled the actual conversation I'd had with him at Ardwick House when he'd rung me back. No hint.

I looked again at his note. Was there anything there? My Granny Vera—mum's mother—had many talents, and one of them was graphology. She'd have been able to tell me, surely.

But Granny Vera was ancient, and she lived in a private care home in Hertfordshire, and I was on my way to Newlydale.

And anyway, the note was printed. It wasn't cursive. Marcus had used a blue pen. It contained six words:

Judy
Wensley Manor
Market Street
Newlydale

And that was all.

***

My train was boarding. I went through the gate.

I walked down the platform and found my carriage.

One of the perks of First Class on East Midlands is single seating with a table. I was grateful. I really didn't feel like talking to anyone. The chair was like something you'd find on a plane, black leather with a head cushion. There was a plug socket for recharging phones and laptops, and there was free WiFi. And the promise of complimentary food—a hot breakfast roll, a mug of Earl Grey tea and whatever biscuits and pastries they had on offer.

I stowed my bag and leaned my head against the window.

It was an hour-and-a-half ride north through the English countryside to Derby. Once there, I had a quick change onto a local shuttle which would get me into Matlock by noon.

As we set out from St Pancras, I watched London's northern suburbs slip away. Intercity trains hurtle you through too fast to catch station names. A platform appears and then *whoosh*, it's gone. You just have to know it was West Hampstead or Cricklewood and that was the Royal Air Force Museum at Hendon. And then, after Mill Hill, the houses and depots fall away, and you're thrown into green countryside.

I watched until we'd got past Elstree, Borehamwood, and St Albans and then, as we approached Luton, my eyelids got heavy and I tried to make myself comfortable in my corner. The quiet *shhhh* of the train was soothing. I set an alarm on my phone for one hour—just in case—and then...I dropped off to sleep.

CHAPTER FOUR

I DIDN'T END UP needing my phone alarm. My brain snapped me awake after about forty minutes. And I wasn't quite sure where I was.

"We've just passed Kettering," said the young lady who was wheeling a trolley of snacks down the aisle. She handed me a packet of biscuits and a cup of tea. "And we'll be in Leicester in about ten minutes. Milk? Sugar?"

"Both, please," I said. "Thanks."

I felt like I'd tumbled down a rabbit hole. It was surreal. How the hell had I ended up on a train hurtling through the East Midlands? I could barely remember getting up that morning. A taxi ride. A vague recollection of the Lower Arcade at St Pancras and Elton John's piano. And, strangely, a vivid memory of buying a bright green bottle of Radox shower gel.

I still had that slip of paper. The scrawled blue pen note from Marcus Merritt. I read it again.

Judy
Wensley Manor
Market Street
Newlydale

I put the note back in my bag, and watched through the window as the train glided past Leicester's outlying neighbourhoods, big box stores, and storage facilities and parking lots, and then, rows of houses.

The station. A one-minute stop while passengers got on and off. And we were away again.

Ten minutes later, Derby.

I picked up my bag, disembarked, and consulted the indicator boards. And then I made my way over to a quiet secondary platform where the regional shuttle would take me up to Matlock.

Emotionally, I was completely at sea.

Physically, I felt like I'd flown halfway around the world and woken up during the afternoon rush while my half-asleep body was screaming that it was still the middle of the night at home.

The little diesel shuttle had two cars and one class of service. I sat down in a group of four seats with a table between them. I put my bag on the seat beside me, but I needn't have worried. There were only about a dozen other passengers on the entire train, and none of them wanted anything to do with me. I hadn't showered when I'd left my flat in London, and I hadn't bothered to shave. I was the poster boy for anti-social.

The little railway ran north from Derby, meandering to and fro over the River Derwent, stopping at stations with lovely imaginative-sounding names...Duffield, Belper, Ambergate. After Whatstandwell, the track ran alongside a stretch of the historic little Cromford Canal. It then disappeared into a series of tunnels, emerging at Matlock Bath (which had a curious aerial tramway going up to the top of a nearby hill), before it reached the end of the line at Matlock itself.

It was a quiet little stone block station, opened during Queen Victoria's reign in 1850, with canopy trim and columns painted in EMR's distinctive cream and dark red livery.

I heard birds as I stood on the platform.

And very little else.

There were no gates. No one checking tickets.

It was a long way from the bustle and noise of London.

I walked through to the parking lot and realized I had no idea how I was going to get to Newlydale.

I got out my phone and found the village website, which informed me there was a bus, adding that the service was "pretty good" (up to five trips a day, though not on Sundays or Bank Holidays) but subject to a "relaxed view of timekeeping" when it came to the published schedule.

The bus wasn't due for another hour. Give or take forty minutes.

Was there a taxi?

I searched again and rang the first firm that came up.

The rate was a flat £10.75 to Newlydale in a four-seater saloon and my driver's name was Reggie. He told me he'd meet me in front of the station in ten minutes.

***

The drive from Matlock to Newlydale was along a two-lane country road that meandered through rock-walled fields and thickets of trees. Every now and then, the fields gave way to surprising little clusters of cottages plainly-built from square-cut bricks of local limestone.

Newlydale (pop. approx. 600) appeared suddenly, a Victorian primary school with three peaked roofs looming on the left, followed by some modern houses, and then, just as quickly, its historic centre.

"Here you are, mate. Market Street. And Wensley Manor."

It didn't look much like a manor. You know the kind of place I'm talking about—*Downton Abbey* being at the very grand end of the scale (along with Highclere Castle, where it was actually filmed)—and then, at the other end, Stoneford Manor, on Hampshire's south coast, a ramshackle old place notorious for excessive partying in the 1960s, bed-and-breakfasting in the 1980s, and finally, in the 21st century, a rehearsal space. That was where we'd prepped for our 50th Anniversary Tour a couple of months earlier.

That tour felt like a lifetime ago.

A manor, to me, meant a building with an excessive number of bedrooms and drawing rooms, sitting on privately-owned land which was often stocked with pheasants and the occasional deer and sometimes sheep.

Wensley Manor was not that.

In fact, it looked very ordinary.

And I could see, without getting out of the car, that rather than being one house, it was actually five. I counted five front doors, anyway, and none of them had numbers.

"Thanks," I said, handing over a cash tip—I'd paid the tariff in advance on my credit card. "I don't suppose you'd have any idea where I could buy lunch."

"You'll be lucky," Reggie replied, humorously. "Nearest Pret's back in Derby."

Pret A Manger, for the internationally uninitiated, is a UK-based sandwich chain. Two-thirds of their shops are in London. If you want a quick Chicken Salad Baguette to go, Pret's your place.

"Try the Village Shop," he added. "Just up the road."

"Thanks," I said again, getting out.

"Enjoy your stay. And your lunch."

The Village Shop was a two-storey limestone building with a sloping roof. It had large picture windows on either side of its open door, and, providentially, it also had an awning, which was open and providing shelter from the on-and-off-rain.

Under the awning were a small metal table with two chairs and a slightly worse-for-wear wooden bench seat.

I went inside and discovered a selection of breads and buns and some interesting cheeses. Some of the bread was sliced. The Double Gloucester wasn't.

"Hello," I said, to the lady behind the counter.

She had greyish hair cut into a sort of bowl and she was wearing a black bib apron with a name tag. Mavis.

"Do you sell knives?" I asked.

"We don't," Mavis replied, taking a step back. I guessed she was alarmed by my appearance, which, by that point, was somewhere between unshaven swarthy rock god and partied-out roadie who'd spent a rough night on the tiles. More the latter than the former.

"For eating," I said. "Not murdering anyone. Plastic forks? Spoons?"

"I'm terribly sorry, no."

I gave it one last try. "Tin opener?"

"I'm afraid not."

What kind of a village shop didn't sell tin openers?

Mavis's hand was hovering near her mobile, which was recharging next to the till. I wondered who looked after policing in Newlydale—the

Derbyshire Constabulary?—and where their nearest station was, and whether I was going to meet up with a suspicious constable, intercepting me with, "Who's been making a nuisance of themselves in the Village Shop, then?" the moment I stepped outside.

I went back to hunting down the makings of my lunch. I walked past a small table with a book on display. The book itself was a rather posh-looking hardbound, *Newlydale: A Village History*. I picked it up and had a look at what was inside. Interviews with people whose families had always lived there. Historical photos. Anecdotes about life in the "old days".

"Newly published," Mavis supplied. "£14.00."

I tucked it under my arm, and then picked up a small package of butter and tried to find some Branston pickle. No luck. But there was some tomato chutney in a glass jar that didn't look too difficult to open. That would do. I added a bottle of Fairy washing up liquid to my bread, cheese, butter and chutney, a roll of kitchen foil, a bottle of sparkling water, a tin of Red Bull, a little plastic pot of black cherry yogurt and a packet of chocolate digestives.

"Amex OK?" I checked, holding up my card.

"Yes, of course," Mavis replied, convinced, I'm sure, that it was stolen.

"Thanks. Have you got a bag I can put this all in?"

"I'm sorry, no."

I supposed most people in the village brought their own, due to carbon neutral footprints and not wishing to contribute to the floating rubbish island in the middle of the Pacific. They probably kept their reusable bags in the same place as their highly-sought-after limited edition tin openers.

I paid, and carried everything outside balanced on the flat cover of the book. I sat down on the wooden bench under the awning. No sign of the local plod. I tore off a large sheet of the kitchen foil and made a workspace.

I poured a little of the washing up liquid onto my Amex card and slid it around with my finger. I rinsed it clean with the sparkling water, gave it an extra splash, just to be on the safe side, then used its hard plastic edge to cut the Double Gloucester into manageable, sandwich-sized slices. My card then did double-duty as a butter knife and a spreader for the tomato chutney. I washed it again in the Fairy liquid, rinsed it off with another splash of sparkling water, and set it aside on the bench to dry while I ate my sandwich and drank the tin of Red Bull.

While I ate, I paged through the *Village History*. Nobody named Judy there, although there was an entire page devoted to Wensley Manor which had, in its past, variously been a town hall, a private hotel, and a den of iniquity.

Dessert was the little pot of black cherry yogurt, with half a chocolate digestive making quite a good improvised spoon.

I swigged the last of my sparkling water, wrapped everything up in a very long, fresh sheet of kitchen foil, popped the book into my bag's side pocket and then went back inside the shop.

I could literally feel Mavis cringing, even though she was doing her best not to show it.

"I wonder," I said, "whether you know a woman named Judy who lives at Wensley Manor."

Now I was a stalker as well as a washed-up rock roadie.

"My name's Jason Figgis," I added. "And I'm a private investigator from London."

"Are you," Mavis replied, unimpressed. "You'd better have a look inside the book for her, then, hadn't you."

"I have," I said. "And she's not there. I'd like to have a chat with her about a case I'm working on."

Stalker, washed-up roadie, and squalid PI.

"And Judy's last name is...?"

"I don't know. I'm sorry."

Squalid PI with completely deficient investigative skills. What was I doing here?

"And I'm terribly sorry, but I have no idea who she might be," Mavis replied.

I usually know when people aren't telling me the truth. Amateurs, anyway. Professional liars are a bit trickier. But people who aren't used to lying give themselves away with their body language, their eyes, often just their voices. Mavis was not being honest with me.

"Thank you," I said.

"Do come again," Mavis replied, definitely not meaning it.

I walked back along Market Street to the five-doored stone manor. A gravel driveway led to a small parking area and a path that went past everyone's back gardens.

There was a vintage brass knocker in the shape of a woodpecker fixed to the first door. I used it.

I heard excited barks from inside, and then the door was opened by a little woman who looked about seventy, with grey-blonde hair cut into a short bob and friendly wrinkles at the corners of her eyes. I immediately thought of Helen Mirren.

"Hello," I said. "My name's Jason Figgis. I'm looking for Judy."

"I'm Judy," the woman replied. "And you'd better come in."

***

The two dogs were called Peter and Gordon ("Yes, of course, after the singers, who else?") and both of them were elderly and mostly Border Collie. They herded me past a little room containing a washing machine and a dryer and collections of rubber boots, dog leashes and brown cardboard boxes, and rather a lot of plastic bins, and into a very large kitchen.

"Please, sit down," Judy said, indicating the table, which was also very large and made out of rough-hewn wood. "My last name's Galpin, by the way. Pleased to meet you."

"Likewise," I said.

I sat.

Peter and Gordon retired to matching beds beside a sliding glass door which opened onto a paved patio. Beyond the patio was a spacious garden, and a set of stone steps leading up a grassy hill, at the top of which were two sheep, a donkey, and a llama, all happily grazing.

"I've been expecting you. Tea? I'm afraid I've only got Yorkshire."

"Perfect," I said.

"Milk?"

"And two sugars," I said. "Sorry, but how long, exactly, have you been expecting me? And, more to the point, why?"

"Since last week," Judy said, from the other side of the immense kitchen, which contained cupboards, drawers, and pantries, and the requisite fridge, cooker, built-in microwave, and dishwasher, and which was bigger than my entire flat in London. "In answer to your first question."

She filled up an old-fashioned kettle from the tap and set it on the stove and lit the gas. No boiling water on demand.

"And to answer the second, I don't know. But this came in the post on Friday." She picked a large brown envelope out of a collection of papers in a wicker tray on the counter, and brought it over to me.

The envelope was open. Inside was a hand-scrawled note in what I recognized as Marcus's messy printing.

Judy: Please give the enclosed to Jason Davey. Or Figgis. He answers to both. He's a musician and he'll be coming to see you. Thanks. Marc.

There were two further envelopes, both sealed and both addressed to me. One of them had a large Alice-in-Wonderland-like invitation scrawled across its front: OPEN ME FIRST.

I did. Inside was another note, and it was much longer.

Hello Jason. The fact that you're reading this confirms that you took advantage of the ticket I left you in the program. I apologize for not elaborating on the details of the Elgar investigation we discussed on the phone. It was time to go.

I promise you will be paid in full for your services. If you look in the second envelope, you'll find a cash retainer which will function as a deposit. I trust it meets with your approval.

I opened the second envelope, which contained rather a lot of pound sterling notes in various denominations bundled together with an elastic band.

Please go to Tissington, Marcus continued. Once you arrive, proceed north along Chapel Lane, until you see a red telephone kiosk. Beside it, you'll see a barrow, which belongs to a friend who crafts pots and bowls. Behind the barrow is a stone wall. One particular stone in the wall is stained black. Remove the stone, and you'll find further instructions.

"Where's Tissington?" I said.

"It's not too far away," Judy replied. She retrieved a large leather handbag from a chair beside the window. From it, she withdrew a very old, well-thumbed, spiral-bound *Geographers' A-Z Road Atlas of Great Britain*. The date on the front was 1996.

She put on a pair of spectacles and peered at the Index at the back of the book.

"5F 85."

She flipped to page eighty-five, found the square where the horizontal row 5 and the vertical row F intersected, and showed me where Tissington was.

It had literally been decades since I'd consulted an actual paperback *A-Z* of anything...I didn't even know they still sold the damned things.

"Of course they do," Judy said, taking off her spectacles. "Collins prints them. Not everyone trusts their phone. And not every phone will actually work when you need it in an emergency. Paper batteries never run down."

I didn't disagree. But there was a lot to be said for a map app. I consulted my mobile. Tissington was about twenty minutes away from Newlydale by car. The app showed me the route, outlined in blue.

"Why does he want you to go to Tissington?" Judy asked.

"He wants me to look for a stone in a wall beside a telephone kiosk and a barrow."

Judy rolled her eyes. "Typical," she said.

"You sound like you know him well..."

"Once upon a time," Judy said, "I was married to him."

She got up to rescue the kettle, which was whistling furiously on the stove.

"Shall we at least enjoy our tea before we go haring off on another one of his insane wild goose chases?"

CHAPTER FIVE

I'D GIVEN JUDY THE detritus of my lunch—butter, Double Gloucester cheese and the remnants of my wholemeal sliced loaf. Not the chocolate digestives, though. I was keeping those.

And now we were on our way to Tissington.

Her car was an impeccably-maintained white 1985 Ford Escort. It had a cassette tape player in the driver's console. A push-button radio. Plush bucket seats in the front, a folded paper road map of Derbyshire in the plastic well between the seats, and an old flannel blanket in the back, smelling of dog.

"It's an RS Turbo S1," Judy said. "It's the same vintage and make as Princess Diana's. Hers was custom-painted black, of course. It's been my faithful runabout for the past thirty years."

"I've got a ten-year-old Volvo V70 back in London," I said. "I bought it second-hand from the police after a tip from my sister. She's married to an ex-copper."

"That's handy," Judy replied, though I wasn't sure if she was referring to my car or my brother-in-law.

I'd put off mentioning Marcus was dead, dreading having to deal with it all over again in my mind. Dreading having to deal with her possible reaction. But, it turned out she already knew.

"I found out late last night," she said. "Julie rang me. Our daughter. She lives in Battersea. I suppose she was the only family member the police could locate, under the circumstances."

We were driving through green country fields punctuated by intermittent farmhouses, grazing sheep and noncommittal cows. The road was narrow—but paved—with just enough room for two small cars to pass safely, if they were going slow.

"I could say I was sad," Judy said. "I'm sad when anyone dies, especially like that. But he belongs to a different part of my life, before I met Tim. Marc and I were married for five years, starting in 1975. He was a musician—amongst his many occupations. He was also a long-distance lorry driver. And he did a stint managing a block of flats. He had some very dodgy ways of making money. I know he consorted with criminals. He always assured me he was going to give up those associations. But he never did."

If I'd been at home and things had been normal, I'd have worked up a dossier on the guy. Where he'd come from, where he'd been before and after he'd met Judy, all the jobs he'd had and who his friends were. But I wasn't at home and nothing was normal.

"Why did it end?" I asked.

"Because he was emotionally unwell and he was off his meds more often than he was on them," Judy said. "And he had other demons he couldn't control. He drank too much. He womanized too much. The final straw was on a Saturday in August in 1980. He'd been out all night and he came home smelling of smoke."

"Cigarette smoke?" I said.

"No. Smoke from a fire. Burnt wood. His hair, his clothes. He wouldn't say where he'd been. He wouldn't talk to me at all about it. We were living in a flat in Marylebone—wretched place, the lift never worked. There was a fire station down the road and the sirens had woken me up in the middle of the night. I knew he had to have been involved. He and his Soho pals. I rang my mum. And I packed up Julie and two suitcases, and I left."

"Do you think he had something to do with the fire?" I asked, carefully.

"I thought a lot of things," Judy replied. "God knows what he'd got up to. I just knew I needed to leave. And he never really owned that it was due to him that we had to go. But that was typical of him, too."

"Did you stay in touch?" I asked.

"On and off. He'd show up for important events—school things, birthdays, Julie's wedding—and then he'd disappear again. I finally lost touch with him for good about eight years ago. I had no idea where he was, how he was…nothing. Until Friday, when that envelope arrived. Out of the blue."

"You don't really strike me as the sort of person who'd end up married to a guy like Marcus."

Judy smiled. "You're giving me too much credit. I used to be a singer. Adverts and jingles. You've probably heard me more times than you realize. Instant coffee. Washing up liquid. Incontinence pads."

I laughed.

"All your favourite independent broadcasting top-of-the-hour ident's."

She sang something I recognized from Capital Radio many years earlier.

"That was you?"

"That was me," Judy confirmed, turning off the main road and onto a narrow avenue lined with lime trees which, I discovered, upon consulting my map app, was called Rakes Lane. "We were in the studio recording one day, and Marc was one of the musicians. He was playing his guitar. I was, of course, immediately smitten."

"I used to be a busker in Covent Garden," I said. And I sang her the first verse and chorus of the theme song from *Fireball XL5*.

"That was you?" she asked.

"No," I said, "it was Don Spencer. An Australian. His daughter married Russell Crowe."

"Wasn't *Fireball XL5* one of those Supermarionation kids' shows from the early 1960s?"

"It was," I said. "Bad puppet science fiction. Neil Gaiman."

"Neil Gaiman wrote it?"

"No, he said it."

We'd arrived.

***

Tissington is a tiny picture-book village that's been the home of the FitzHerbert family for 500 years. They actually own the entire village (a rarity in England these days), and live in a hall that dates from 1609. Most of the little cottages are occupied by renters, and there are tenant farmers on the 2,000 surrounding acres.

Rakes Lane became The Green, which took us to a tranquil duck pond worthy of any posh toffee-tin cover. Judy turned left, and there was Chapel Lane. She turned left again.

"The iconic red call box," she said.

"And the barrow," I confirmed.

Judy parked the car by the side of the road and, as I got out, I recognized a piece of music drifting over from a nearby cottage. "Cantaloupe Island." A live recording from the 1990 Mellon Jazz Festival, with Herbie Hancock on keyboards, Dave Holland on bass, Jack DeJohnette on drums and, my perennial favourite, Pat Metheny, on guitar.

And one extra musician. Someone in the cottage was playing along with Herbie Hancock on a slightly out-of-tune piano. They were partly improvising, partly sticking to what was on the recording.

I listened with appreciation, then made my way over to the little cart, where there were handmade glazed pots and bowls for sale for £5. It was on the honour system—there was a slotted box where you could leave your money, and black and white striped paper bags if you needed something to carry your purchase home in. I looked at the wall behind the barrow. There it was. A smoky black stone. I jiggled it out.

Tucked into the cavity was, of course, another envelope. And something in a striped black and white paper bag.

It was starting to rain. And I hadn't brought my umbrella. I grabbed the envelope and the paper bag, shoved the stone back into the wall, and ran back to the car.

I looked inside the bag first. It was a tiny bowl with an aquamarine blue crackled glaze.

Inside the envelope was a single sheet of paper, both sides crammed with Marcus's untidy printing.

Hello again, Jason. And thank you for following my instructions. The raku bowl is a gift. Please accept it as a peace offering. I know I probably shocked you with my sudden departure.

That, I thought, was the understatement of the year.

I presume you know something about Sir Edward Elgar.

I did, of course, know something about the greatest English classical music composer since Henry Purcell. Even if you recognize nothing else about Elgar, you'll have heard of his most famous piece: "Pomp and Circumstance March No. 1", otherwise known as "Land of Hope and Glory". Especially if you're a yearly regular at the last night of the Proms at London's Royal Albert Hall.

Sir Edward Elgar was also one of the first composers to fully embrace recorded music and to take the gramophone seriously and, for that, he was a man close to my heart.

You may also know about Elgar's birthplace at The Firs, in Broadheath, Worcestershire. And that it was turned into a museum and repository for his works, at the behest of his daughter, Carice.

I did know that as well, although I'd never been there. The National Trust had taken over the museum's administration two years earlier, in 2016.

In July of this year, the majority of the Elgar archives were transferred from The Firs to the British Library in London. During the transfer, it was discovered that one important piece of the collection was missing—a folder containing original sketches, drafts, and revisions to one of his best-known works, The Enigma Variations.

An exhaustive search of The Firs turned up nothing. The police were notified. The press were not.

The folder had, of course, been stolen.

I know it was stolen because I was the one who took it.

I had to put the sheet of paper down, briefly, in order to process what I'd just read.

I was well paid for my efforts.
And now, in turn, I'm offering you a very generous amount of money, in the hope that you'll fulfill my last wish, and return the collection to the Elgar Foundation.

I looked at Judy. I showed her the message, with its cramped blue-ink block printing.
She read it, with thought.
She handed it back to me.
I knew what she was thinking.
Typical.

Of course, Marcus had written, *first you'll have to find it.*
Here's something that will help: A courtesan skilled in the culinary arts. Ask for Tricia.

CHAPTER SIX

"HE'S INSANE," I SAID.

We were still sitting in Judy's Escort, across from the red telephone kiosk and the barrow with the little fired pots for sale. Fat raindrops were running steeplechases down the car windows.

"Yes," said Judy, "well, that's a given, isn't it? Off his meds and embracing yet one more fantastic and completely imaginary quest."

"He's done this kind of thing before?"

"So many times, I lost count. Even after I left him. On those rare occasions when we did meet up, he was full of it. If something dodgy was in the news, he was the driving force behind it, he'd planned the caper, he'd got away with it, or, he was trying to make it right, or, he hadn't done the deed himself but he was assisting the police with their inquiries, they were relying on him to identify the real crooks because he knew them all personally and he had inside knowledge...it just went on and on, Jason. I learned never to believe a word of it. He couldn't help himself."

I studied the piece of paper with the cramped, controlled, blue-ink printing.

The police were notified. The press were not.

I got out my phone and googled for info about missing or stolen works by Elgar.

Antiques Roadshow caught in legal row over rare £100k manuscript

It seemed that, a few months earlier, a woman had appeared on an episode of the popular TV series, with a manuscript containing some original drafts and revisions to Elgar's *Enigma Variations*. She'd claimed the manuscript had belonged to her late husband, a music scholar and lay clerk at Worcester Cathedral. After the program was filmed, she'd approached Christie's auction house to sell the work. The only trouble was, the manuscript had gone missing from the Elgar Foundation in Worcester in 1994. And the Elgar Foundation had, that past July, asked for it to be returned to the archive at the British Library.

"See what I mean?" Judy said. "An utter and complete invention. I'm so sorry Marc's involved you, Jason. I don't know what else to say."

***

We were on our way back to Newlydale. I'd been dozing with my head propped against the passenger-side window, and I jerked awake at the clicking sound of the turn indicator.

"It's a cryptic crossword clue, isn't it?" I said. "A courtesan skilled in the culinary arts."

"A pie-making prostitute?" Judy mused. "That was another of his habits. *The Times* crosswords."

"I wouldn't say that was a bad habit to have. I've been known to occasionally tackle those. You need a keen creative mind."

"Well, he had that in spades, didn't he."

"A cooking concubine," I said.

"A percolating paramour," she said.

All that made me think of was Norrie Paramor, a British record producer and composer best known for steering the careers of Cliff Richard and the Shadows. In 1968, he'd conducted the UK entry in the Eurovision Song Contest, which was "Congratulations". It had a perky orchestral intro and four bass drum kicks that were now embedding themselves in my exhausted brain.

Boom boom boom boom.

Judy's *A-Z* was open in the little well between the two front seats. I picked it up to see where we were.

"Bakewell," I said. "Tart."

"Sorry?"

"A courtesan skilled in the culinary arts. Tart. Bakes well."

I showed her the map.

"Bakewell."

Judy glanced down briefly, then returned her eyes to the road.

I looked it up on my phone.

"The Bakewell tart and pudding," I said. "One's a derivative of the other but they're both historically famous. Attributed to a Mrs. Greaves who ran the White Horse Inn in the mid-19th century."

"Do you actually want me to drive to Bakewell, then?" Judy asked.

***

We motored past fields, meadows and copses, and sheep, and places with names like Middleton-by-Youlgrave, Conksbury and Over Haddon.

Bakewell's considerably larger than both Tissington and Newlydale. It's an old market town with about 4,000 inhabitants, a parish church dating from 920 AD, a 13th-century bridge over the River Wye, and the aforementioned pastry, which is either a pudding or a tart, depending on which particular history you've been reading.

There were several different bakeries in the town centre, each claiming to offer the original confection. But only one actually had "Bakewell Tart" incorporated into its name.

It was nestled between a tailor shop and one selling outdoor clothing, its frontage painted dark brown and its big display window offering samples of the delectables to be found within. Puddings *and* tarts. With helpful signs explaining the difference. Savoury pies and homemade scones, Eccles cakes and shortbreads, and little jars of jams and spreads and packages of biscuits. And the most amazing scent of freshly-baked bread, wafting out through the open door.

"Hello," I said, to the lady behind the counter. My life was starting to be defined by women standing behind counters. "I'm looking for Tricia."

The lady seemed momentarily surprised. Then: "I'm so sorry but we haven't got anyone named Tricia working here."

"Are you sure?" I asked.

"Reasonably sure, yes. I'm the owner."

An elderly lady with a little plaid shopping cart and a see-through plastic rain cap tied under her chin had followed us into the shop. "Tricia," she said, "That's my nephew's lass. She's at the other Bakewell Tart."

"The frock shop," said the lady behind the counter. "Up the road and around the corner. You can't miss it."

At least it had stopped raining. Judy and I walked up the road and around the corner.

It was true. You couldn't miss it. The shopfront and door were painted a brilliant scarlet. Occupying the big display window was a mannequin dressed in a slinky black strapless cocktail dress from the 1950s, pencil thin and impossibly revealing. Next to it, a helpful sign: *Vintage Frocks, Bought and Sold. Do come in and tart yourself up.*

"You'd need some double-sided tape to keep that frock from tarting up your vintage," Judy said, humorously, with a nod at the mannequin's barely-concealed breasts.

I held the door open for her, and followed her inside.

"Hello! Hello! Welcome to my boudoir!"

The young lady issuing the enthusiastic welcome had brilliant blue hair cut into a Mary Quant-Vidal Sassoon geometric bob. She was wearing black velvet shorts, a black lace camisole, a pink silk dressing gown printed with stylized Japanese maple trees, black sheer stockings with suspenders and bright red platform-soled sandals.

"Tricia?" I said.

"Tricia!" she confirmed.

"My name's Jason Figgis," I said. "And I've been told to ask for you."

"Me!" the young woman exclaimed. "And you!"

"I gather you've been expecting me...?"

"Of course!" Tricia paused. "Do you have some identification?"

I pulled out my wallet. "Amex and driving license. OK?"

Tricia scrutinized them both carefully, holding up my atrocious-looking mug shot to compare it with the equally atrocious-looking me. She handed them back.

And then she took my arm and dragged me over to a rack of hats, picking out a beige flat cap with a red and black hounds tooth pattern. "Dents. Authentic 1970s. It's *you*."

She placed it on top of my head and adjusted my hair and gave me a large mirror with a long handle.

"I look like a serial killer," I said.

"Sixty-two pounds," Tricia said. "A positive steal."

"Extortionate," Judy agreed.

"But for you, Mr. Figgis, no charge. It's a gift."

I glanced at Judy, who shrugged, and gave me a bemused smile back.

"Hang on!" Tricia exclaimed.

She swept into the rear of the shop and returned with—of course—a large brown envelope. I pulled the flap open.

There was—of course—the mandatory hand-scrawled message, and it was—of course—from Marcus. But while the other messages had all been straightforward, this one was written in what looked like code. A series of "c"'s, all in different positions: vertical, horizontal, backwards and on an angle, stacked two-up, and three-up, and sitting upside down.

The squiggles took up an entire page.

And there was a second piece of paper, this one containing a hand-drawn circle. Around the rim of the circle were a series of pie-shaped compartments, and inside each of the compartments, at the top, was the letter "c"—in its various iterations—that matched the coded "c" squiggles on the previous sheet.

Printed underneath the circle was a URL, and underneath the URL, Marcus had written "c = 17". The "c" in question was three-up and backwards, and was lying at a forty-five-degree angle.

I showed the pages to Judy.

"Typical?" I guessed.

"Rather more convoluted and entangled than his usual efforts," Judy sighed, "but yes. Typical."

The upside-down and angled "c"'s reminded me of something I'd seen before. But I couldn't quite put my finger on what.

There was no address on the front of the envelope, and there were no stamps or courier labels.

"When was this delivered to you?" I asked. "And how?"

"Last week," said Tricia. "Tuesday—no, Wednesday. And it was Marc Merritt who dropped it off. In person."

"Tall fellow? White hair, late sixties?"

"That's him!" said Tricia, amused. "He's one of my dad's oldest friends. They were in a band together in the 1960s. Marc played guitar and my dad played the piano. Sadly, the band never got anywhere, so my dad decided to focus on his pottery instead. He still kept up with his music, though."

"Your dad lives in Tissington," I said.

"That's right! How did you know?"

"Jason's very good at connecting dots," Judy replied.

I'd left my little turquoise dish in its striped paper bag in the car. Otherwise, I'd have shown it to her. "'Cantaloupe Island'," I said.

"One of dad's favourites. Marc bought Herbie Hancock's original 1964 *Empyrean Isles* album for him a couple of years ago—for no reason at all. He just showed up with it. Worth about two hundred quid these days. I had a look online."

"Generous to a fault, my ex," Judy said. "If he had money, he spent it."

"Oh! Were you married to him?"

"Centuries ago," Judy replied.

"Well," said Tricia, "I have to say, he's one of the kindest, most caring gentlemen I've ever met."

I glanced at Judy.

And then Judy told her about Marcus's leap from the top of The Shard.

Tricia's face fell. She looked truly devastated.

"Oh," she said, quietly. "No..."

***

We emerged from the shop twenty minutes later. After she'd recovered from the news of Marcus's death, Tricia had offered us a little pamphlet.

The Derbyshire Players. An upcoming tour of *The Buddy Holly Story*. Select performances throughout the Peak District. "I'm in it," she said. "Amateur theatrics only, I'm afraid. But I was quite involved with Student Drama when I was at Oxford."

"Ambitious," I said. "Especially with blue hair."

"Would you like to buy a ticket?"

"I'll take two," Judy replied. "Tim and I love to support local talent."

We walked back towards the bakery.

"You do look rather shifty," Judy said, peering at me humorously. "I'll just pop in and get one of those famous tarts for our tea."

As I waited outside, thinking I'd have another look at Marcus's coded message, a car stopped on the road in front of me.

It was a Mercedes E Class Saloon. Lunar Blue. And there were two occupants: a female driver in front, and, in the back, someone I'd met before, but hoped I'd never see again.

The rear curbside door opened.

"Mr. Figgis. Please join me."

There was no point in running away.

I got in.

Arthur Braskey looked much the same as the last time I'd seen him, outside The Blue Devil, a year and a half earlier. Back then, I'd thought he was about seventy. I was more than ten years out. Arthur Braskey was eighty-three, with thinning grey hair combed gracefully back from his forehead, carefully-tended eyebrows and a dimple in his chin that belied the cruelty that lurked behind his thin rubber-band lips.

He was wearing an expensive camel overcoat.

"Let me have the envelope, Mr. Figgis."

I gave it to him.

He removed the pages and looked at them. Then he handed the two sheets of paper back to me.

"What is this?"

"I have no idea," I said. "But I'm guessing you have an interest in finding out?"

"A collection of scores by Sir Edward Elgar, Mr. Figgis. *The Enigma Variations*. The current value, at auction, would be close to £500,000. Do you know where that folio might be?"

"The manuscript went missing in 1994," I said. "It disappeared from the Elgar Museum in Worcester. It showed up on *Antiques Roadshow* in July. I believe it's now been quietly returned."

"I'm surprised at your lack of knowledge, Mr. Figgis. I was given to believe you had a degree of intelligence dancing around inside that musical brain of yours. You disappoint me. That's not the collection I'm talking about."

"I didn't know there was another one."

"Let me enlighten you, then. The particular collection I'm talking about also contains original sketches, drafts, and revisions to *The Enigma Variations*. But it predates the items that turned up on *Antiques Roadshow*. It's also twice as extensive. It was stolen to order some years ago, Mr. Figgis. The individual who took it was Marcus Merritt. At my request."

My heart stopped. And then started again.

I didn't say anything.

For the first and last time in his life, had Marcus actually been telling the truth?

"Mr. Merritt was my employee, Mr. Figgis. His duties were varied. Most recently, you may recall, he was my driver."

That was where I'd seen Marcus Merritt before.

That was why he'd seemed familiar to me.

I'd first met Arthur Braskey in February 2017, after I'd been asked to look into the theft of £10,000 from a locker belonging to a dancer at a gentlemen's club in Soho. Arthur Braskey, I was reliably informed by the owner of the club, was not someone I was likely to be acquainted with.

"You have a respectable bank account," I was told.

It was further confirmed to me, by my brother-in-law Tom (the ex-copper), that Braskey was one of Soho's better-known crime bosses. And that I really ought to steer clear.

And I would have, except that Arthur Braskey had rather a large stake in the missing money, and I'd promised to try and help the dancer with her problem. Within a short amount of time, I was coerced into taking part in a charity firewalk that Braskey was sponsoring, after which I was informed by the gentleman himself that he wished very fervently to locate the dancer in question. Being the chivalrous guy that I am, I declined the opportunity to tell him—which led to all kinds of complications, not the least of which led to me being hung up by my arms and beaten half to death by a small-time thug. I was rescued from that predicament by Braskey's driver, but instead of releasing me, he'd delivered me into an even worse hell where the soles of my feet really were burned—by Braskey, assisted by that same driver—after which I was abandoned, tied to a chair, in a derelict warehouse.

I could be forgiven for not remembering Marcus Merritt. I'd never really got a clear look at his face. Only glimpses, muddled with pain. And after that, I'd done my very best to forget him.

"Last month, my Elgar folio went missing, Mr. Figgis. As did Mr. Merritt."

"And you think he took it?" I said.

"I know he took it. He was one of a very small number of people with access to the locked vault in which it was kept. He disabled the motion sensor alarm but was captured on several security cameras entering the room, removing the documents, and leaving. Whereupon he went to ground."

I didn't say anything. I valued the soles of my feet.

"Yesterday, I received a text from Mr. Merritt. He requested my presence at the base of The Shard, on St Thomas Street, at half past one in the afternoon. I arrived in time to witness his...disembarkation."

Braskey's face betrayed a sudden, brief flash of emotion. But it was only a flash. And it was probably only annoyance.

"It's not something I wish to dwell upon. His act was deliberate and he meant me to witness it. But if Mr. Merritt believed I would cease my efforts to locate my Elgar collection with his death, he was very much mistaken. I know you met him at The Top of the Shard."

"How do you know that?"

"His mobile survived the fall. Your last message to him was visible on its Lock Screen."

"You saw his phone?"

"I took his phone, Mr. Figgis. Not something for the faint of heart, under the circumstances."

He reached into an inside pocket in his camel overcoat, and brought out a mobile. It was dented in several places but its glass face had survived intact. I didn't want to speculate about the brown stains on its side.

Braskey switched Marcus's phone on. My message was still there.

"You must have been seen on CCTV when you took that," I said. "And there had to have been witnesses."

Braskey appeared unconcerned.

"I believe Mr. Merritt may have told you where you would find my folio."

"You believe wrong," I said.

"I've been following you, Mr. Figgis. From your home to St Pancras. Then, to Matlock and Newlydale, which is where Mr. Merritt's former wife lives. Then Tissington. And now, Bakewell. Where is it, Mr. Figgis?"

"I don't know," I said. "He did ask me to return the collection to the Elgar Foundation. But he's hidden it somewhere. All he's given me is clues and games. This is the latest instalment."

"Very well," Braskey replied. "I tolerated his eccentricities while he proved to be a faithful, if flawed, employee. That trust was broken when he removed the collection from the vault. I will exercise patience. Once you've located the collection, you will, of course, return it to me."

"And if I decide to just walk away, go back to London and forget about the whole thing?"

"Let me be clear. Your failure to locate my Elgar folio—and return it to me—would not be in your best personal interests, Mr. Figgis. You may exit the car."

I slid the two pieces of paper back inside their envelope. I climbed out of the car.

"Shut the door, Mr. Figgis."

I closed it, with care.

There was a momentary pause and then, as Judy came out of the bakery with a freshly-baked tart in a cardboard box, the Mercedes sped away.

"Are you all right, Jason?" Judy said. "You don't look at all well."

CHAPTER SEVEN

I WASN'T FEELING AT all well.

I told Judy about Arthur Braskey as we drove back to Newlydale.

"Yes," she said, thoughtfully. "I remember that name. Marc mentioned it a few times. But he didn't elaborate. And I didn't really want to know, to be honest."

The road we were on was wide enough for two lanes—one in either direction—with a white dividing line down the middle, but absolutely nowhere to stop in the event of an emergency. The overgrown green countryside began where the sides of the road ended. Judy overtook a slow-moving maintenance truck.

"What do you think you'll do, now?" she asked.

"I don't really have a lot of choice," I said. "I'm assuming all these codes are going to tell me where Marcus hid the folio. So I'll figure them out, and then I'll go and collect the damned thing."

"And then what? Give it back to Arthur Braskey?"

"What do you think?" I said.

***

I was using up the last twenty-three percent of my phone's battery hunting online for Sir Edward Elgar.

The Enigma Variations—otherwise known as *Variations on an Original Theme, Op. 36,* had been composed between October 1898 and February 1899.

Elgar had been known for his playfulness and for his love of hidden messages, and all fourteen of the compositions that made up the collection (plus the introduction) were widely recognized as representing fond musical caricatures of his friends, his family members, and even himself.

I'd once arranged one of those pieces into something I thought Ken, Rudy, Dave and I could offer our fusion-appreciative audiences at The Blue Devil.

It was Variation X, "Dorabella".

After two performances, I was unceremoniously informed by my band that if I was going to subject them to much more of my "idiosyncratic wankery" (as Dave put it), I might consider continuing my gig at the club as a solo act.

But that tenth variation was what had jiggled my memory. The piece was inspired by Dora Penny, a young woman whose step-mother was friends with Elgar's wife, Alice. In 1897, Elgar had sent a playful message to Dora, all in code.

And there it was, on my phone: a series of eighty-seven characters spread over six lines, using twenty-four semi-circular squiggles oriented in one of eight directions, upright and angled, upside down and on their sides.

It was easy to see how Marcus had borrowed the idea for his own encrypted message to me.

And, just like Dora Penny, I had no idea how to even begin to decipher it.

Except that Marcus had provided me with what looked like a clue: a link to a website.

It turned out to be a fan-run blog for *Lollygobble*, a kids' TV program I remembered watching when I was about eight: a frenetic half hour of large puppets and small jokes, twirly-moustached villains, insanely silly contests and a serial drama involving a group of unsupervised children living in a derelict castle, solving mysteries that always had the local adults baffled.

Lollygobble had a fan club, and one of the perks of membership was a secret decoder wheel that you had to assemble yourself once it arrived in the post. At the end of each program, the amiable hosts would send out a "secret message" to the faithful, who would then use their decoder wheels to solve it.

And there it was, on the website. A downloadable PDF which contained a put-it-together-yourself three-piece replica of that very famous wheel.

I made Judy stop the car so I could show it to her.

Its outermost circle was the same size and shape as the hand-drawn circle that Marcus had left me. But while *Lollygobble's* outer circle contained the twenty-six letters of the alphabet, the one Marcus had provided contained twenty-six "c"'s.

"I assume you have a working printer back at Wensley Manor...?" I inquired.

***

"It's Tim's computer," Judy said, as she fed Peter and Gordon. "And I'm afraid I don't know the password."

The two dogs suddenly perked up their ears and ran to the front door, barking excitedly.

"That'll be him now."

Tim Galpin walked into the kitchen accompanied by the dogs, who danced around his legs like breathless four year olds, anxious to tell him everything about their day.

Tim was my height and looked about the same age as Judy. He was, like his wife, in very good shape for someone in his late sixties. No hint of any loss of muscle tone or surreptitious sagging. His hair was starting to thin out and it was a nondescript grey-brown, untidy and on the long side. He had crinkles in the corners of his eyes. Fond of laughter, I thought. He was wearing a V-necked woolly pullover, a white shirt, and very battered jeans.

"And you must be Jason," he said, extending his hand.

***

Tim had a workspace set up in the lounge, with an immense antique mahogany campaign desk and a swivelling purser chair.

He logged on to his computer.

"We were based in Sheffield for yonks' years," Judy said, hovering. "Tim was a professor of chemistry at the uni. Recently retired. We've only been here a few months."

"Though I can't think why Mavis claimed not to know us," Tim said. "We were both in the shop yesterday, stocking up on tea."

I gave Tim the URL for the *Lollygobble* site and waited while he called up the PDF and printed it out. I'd already explained the Elgar connection to him, and the Dorabella Cipher.

"And nobody's ever been able to crack it?" Tim asked.

"Nobody," I replied. "They've held competitions."

"Perhaps they just never bothered to consult *Lollygobble's* secret decoder wheel," Judy said, humorously.

"My favourite theory," I said, "is that the Dorabella Cipher's not text at all. It's a melody. Twenty-four individual symbols representing all of the notes over two octaves, including sharps and flats."

Judy retrieved the printout from a laser printer in the corner.

I cut out the three components and consulted the instructions for assembly.

The first circle—the smallest—was the hub of the wheel, and it had a cutout slot that could be rotated around.

The second circle, in the middle, contained the letters of the alphabet on a shaded background, and below each of them, a number. X was 1, Y was 2, Z was 3 and A was 4. And so on, all around the wheel, to W, which was 26.

The third circle, the largest, was designed to sit at the back. I tossed it away and substituted the one Marcus had included in his message to me.

I fastened the three wheels together with a push pin stuck through the centre, so that they could all rotate independently.

On Marcus's circle, I found the "key" that he'd given me in his note—the three-up, backwards, forty-five-degree-angled "c".

According to Marcus, "c" equalled 17.

I lined up the number 17, revealed by the slot on the innermost wheel, with the squiggly "c" on the outermost wheel. I popped a paperclip onto the three wheels so they wouldn't move. Then I looked at Marcus's squiggled secret message and located each figure according to its corresponding letter in the shaded middle section of the wheel.

PAST MUSIC HAUNTS OF SOHO
THURSDAY OCTOBER EIGHTEEN
MEET AT THE MONTAGU PYKE
ELEVEN AM
PICK UP TICKET IN NEWLYDALE
FROM BEATRIX THE BAKER

"We haven't got a baker named Beatrix in Newlydale," Tim said. "Have we?"

"I don't even think we've got a bakery," Judy replied.

"You used to," I said.

I pulled *The Village History* out of my bag.

"Chapter Two. 'Shops and Businesses'. The author's listed all of the past owners of the village's shops, and where they were located. There used to be a little bakery on Newlydale Path. It's now a private residence owned by Mrs. Beatrix Cummings."

"Clever clogs," said Judy. "Who knew?"

"And there's a picture," I said.

It was a tiny stone cottage, standing off on its own, at the end of an equally diminutive lane.

Tim checked the time.

"It's a bit late to be calling on Beatrix now," he said. "But we can go up that way tomorrow morning, with the dogs."

"And what's a 'Past Music Haunts of Soho' when it's at home?" Judy inquired.

Tim consulted Google on his computer. "It's a walking tour," he said.

We gathered in front of the screen. The itinerary took in the former sites of clubs and coffee bars, recording studios and watering holes, record sleeve photos and memorials—official and otherwise. It was four hours long and it was offered on the third Thursday of every month, guided by one Lesley Wharton.

***

I hadn't given a lot of thought to where I was going to spend the night when I'd packed my bag that morning and set out for St Pancras.

I'm a scheduler. Everything's in my calendar. Days in advance. Weeks. But it had all come apart after that one horrendous night with no sleep. Nothing in my brain had been working properly. And it still wasn't operating at one hundred percent.

"There's a pub up the hill," Tim said, "and I think they have extra rooms..."

"But so do we," Judy said. "Two, in fact. Upstairs. You can have the one with the bed in it."

"As opposed to the one with the three dozen moving boxes that still need to be unpacked," Tim added, humorously.

I'm not crazy about being a guest in another person's house. I'd have been hopeless in that era when the titled classes all trekked over to each other's estates for drink-fuelled weekends and shooting parties. I'd much rather stay in a hotel, where you can do what you like at four o'clock in the morning and not have to worry about disturbing the children or the dogs or your host who, God-forbid, suffers from PTSD and jerks awake convinced you're about to attack him when you tiptoe across the landing to use the toilet.

There weren't any children at Judy and Tim's, and I was on decent terms with the dogs. I wasn't going to ask about PTSD and, in any case, their spare room came equipped with its own little ensuite bathroom. And it was only for one night.

"Breakfast's at seven," Judy said, delivering an armload of sheets and pillowcases and a duvet. "And we do walkies at eight. But if you're fast asleep, no need to worry. Come down when you wake up. Night night."

I unzipped my bag and discovered that the lid of the bottle of Radox I'd bought at Boots in St Pancras had popped open and coated my chocolate digestives in bright green citrus-and-eucalyptus-smelling shower gel.

I went into the bathroom and rinsed off the bottle and stood it up on a shelf in the shower. I threw away the cardboard biscuit box and most of what was inside, but rescued the ones that had escaped the Radox and stacked them up on the bedside table.

I'd brought along a change of pants, some socks and a t-shirt and my shaving stuff, a toothbrush, and some toothpaste. I unpacked them all, then placed my little blue raku bowl from Tissington on the table beside the biscuits and my flat cap from Bakewell.

And then I checked my phone.

Which was dead.

Because, of course, the battery had run out somewhere between Bakewell and Newlydale.

I had remembered to pack my charger. I plugged it in, and up popped everything I'd missed.

Three texts and two voice messages from Rudy, wanting to know where the hell I was and did I remember we were booked to rehearse the second half of our set tomorrow afternoon at Ardwick House?

Shit.

Ardwick had a seventy-two-hour minimum notice for cancellations, and inside the minimum you were on the hook for the full amount. Which was £44 an hour. For three hours.

I texted Rudy back, apologizing.

I'm in Derbyshire. Can you get them to move it to Friday? I'll cover the fee.

We can make it any day you like, Rudy texted back, almost immediately. *See you Friday.*

Well. I'd assumed Marcus's clues were going to tell me where he'd hidden the folio. I was evidently wrong. Marcus's clues were now pointing me back to London where, presumably, at some point on that walking tour, I would be further enlightened.

Perhaps Mrs. Beatrix Cummings, who lived in the old bakery, would have some insights to offer.

I used my phone to make a reservation to London on East Midlands for the following afternoon, leaving Matlock at 1.14 pm, changing in

Derby, then catching a fast train that had me arriving in St Pancras at 3.38 pm.

They don't let you pick specific seats on EMR, even in First Class, so I noted my preferences—forward facing, single, window—and, guessing how busy that route between Derby and London was going to be at that time of day—and how last-minute my request was—crossed my fingers.

Coach G, Seat 14. Aisle.

I looked up the seating plan. Well, it was forward-facing, anyway.

It was only about 10 pm, and I was exhausted. I really, really needed to sleep.

But I dreaded what I was going to see, in my mind, the moment I closed my eyes. Marcus's face. And that split-second of eternity before he fell…

I picked up my phone, still tethered to its charging cable, and consulted YouTube. I found Elgar's *Variations*. I clicked on the first of them, the Theme. "Enigma". *Andante.* A G minor opening. The composer's sense of loneliness and searching introspection.

I laid back on my freshly-made bed.

I slipped off my shoes…and listened.

CHAPTER EIGHT

I opened my eyes.

The bedroom light was still on.

My phone had dropped off to sleep.

As, apparently, had I.

The house was quiet.

I checked the time. It was one o'clock in the morning.

I was wide awake.

And hungry.

My little collection of Radox-rescued chocolate digestives was where I'd left it, stacked on the bedside table. I finished half of them, washing them down with a glass of cold water from the tap in the bathroom.

I hunted through my bag and found the packet of Maltesers I'd bought at Boots, and the mixed fruit and nuts from Starbucks.

I munched on them as I glanced out of the window, at a dark and deserted Market Street, and at the car that didn't belong there—Arthur Braskey's dark blue Mercedes saloon.

There hadn't been a lot of traffic on the road as Judy and I had driven back to Newlydale from Bakewell. If Braskey had wanted to maintain a low profile, he'd have needed to put quite a distance behind us to avoid being obvious.

He didn't seem to care.

I'd got Judy to pull over so I could show her the *Lollygobble* decoder wheel on my phone. That had caught Braskey off-guard. His driver had overtaken us, then turned off onto a little country lane, where they'd waited until we'd caught up.

After we'd driven past, Braskey's driver had slid in behind us again and followed us all the way into Newlydale.

And now, that same car was parked up the road, facing the Manor, and his driver was killing time on her phone—I could see the glow from her screen illuminating her face.

I hadn't noticed any interior motion detectors inside Judy and Tim's house. I'd looked. And I hadn't remembered Judy setting any alarms when we'd left to go to Tissington. She hadn't disarmed anything when we'd got back, either.

The house was vulnerable. But, right at that moment, that was to my advantage.

I wrapped the last of my chocolate digestives in a wad of toilet paper, put on my shoes and, very quietly, went downstairs. I was met at the bottom by Peter and Gordon, greeting me with curiosity and an abundance of wagging tails but, thankfully, none of the frantic barking they'd presumably have employed had I been an unwelcome intruder.

I collected my jacket from the rack in the front hall, then went back to the kitchen, where I quietly opened the sliding glass door and slipped outside.

I walked along the entire length of the backside of the manor to its opposite end, and then doubled back onto Market Street, so that I could approach the Mercedes from behind.

Arthur Braskey's driver was so intent on whatever she was doing on her phone, she didn't see me amble up and pull open the passenger door.

"What the hell!" she exclaimed, as I seated myself beside her.

She was in her late thirties, I guessed, with a face like a young Joni Mitchell and hair that belonged to Jane Fonda in *Klute*.

"You're not very good," I said. "First off, you're parked too close to your target. You should be further down the road." I indicated the gap where I'd emerged from the manor's back gardens. "Thatta way."

She didn't say anything.

"And if you'd done your homework you'd have clocked all my means of escape. I could have been halfway to Derby before you'd even realized you'd lost me."

"I'm calling Mr. Braskey."

"Go ahead," I said. "And, pro tip, always keep your doors locked when you're doing surveillance. Especially the passenger side and especially when it's the middle of the night."

I dug the three chocolate digestives out of my jacket pocket and unwrapped them as she made her call.

"Hungry?" I inquired.

No response.

I placed the biscuits on the front centre console, beside an open tin of Red Bull and a packet of caffeine tablets.

"Jason," I said, offering my hand.

"Matilda," she replied, not taking it.

"Not your real name, of course."

"It is."

"Where's your boss? In a room at the pub up the hill?"

That was, obviously, where he'd opted to spend the night, in the absence of anything approximating the sort of five-star, over-the-top glitz-and-glam accommodations favoured by London's crime lords.

Some moments later, the man himself appeared, striding purposefully towards the car in his camel coat, impeccably groomed and unaccountably unruffled after being roused from his bed.

He opened the passenger door.

"Please join me in the back, Mr. Figgis."

I did.

"I dislike having my sleep interrupted, Mr. Figgis."

"Sorry," I said, feeling reckless. "I dislike being followed."

"A matter of routine diligence."

"Don't you trust me?"

"I don't trust anyone, Mr. Figgis. Did you learn anything from your coded message?"

"I've been invited to join a walking tour," I said. "Thursday morning in London. *Past Music Haunts of Soho.*"

"That's all?"

"Afraid so," I said. I leaned forward and retrieved one of the chocolate digestives. "Biccie?"

Braskey accepted it, unlike Matilda, who remained impassive and silent in the front.

"Whatever possessed Marcus to go to work for you?" I wondered.

"It was more a case of whatever possessed me to take him on, Mr. Figgis. The answer, which you may or may not believe, is that I acted out of a sense of charity. Mr. Merritt was, as you may know, a profoundly flawed character. He was mentally unstable. He also suffered from a significant injury sustained when he was driving his lorry in Spain. This resulted in his being addicted to medication for the pain, and contributed to his being chronically unemployable. I felt sorry for him."

"Uncharacteristic charity on your part," I said.

"I took him under my wing. I shepherded him through his withdrawal from the unhelpful pharmaceuticals. I ensured he received superlative care from my private physician. I encouraged his adherence to a proper regimen of drugs designed to stabilize his mental health. I was not always successful. But, in spite of his emotional challenges, he became one of my most trusted and indelible employees."

"Until he decided to make off with your stolen Elgar collection."

"I'm afraid to say that Mr. Merritt, did, in the end, prove to be singularly...feckless."

"Why did he jump?"

"I have no idea, Mr. Figgis."

I didn't believe that.

"Perhaps you threatened him in some way?"

Braskey gave me a thin-lipped smile. "I issued no threats."

"Largely because you couldn't find him to deliver them," I guessed.

"In another life, Mr. Figgis, I would find you unfathomably irritating. If you were following me on certain social media accounts, I would have you blocked."

"In another life," I said, "you wouldn't need me to track down that collection. But in this life, you do, because Marcus seems to have ensured whatever clues he's left behind can only be recovered by me."

I opened the car door.

"Feel free to block me," I said, getting out of the car.

***

I managed to get another couple of hours of sleep, but it was shallow and troubled. At least by the time I ventured downstairs for breakfast, I looked less like a serial killer and more like my normal, tousled rock god self. I'd put the Radox to good use in the shower, given myself a shave and towelled my hair dry.

For breakfast, there was hot oatmeal with cream and a selection of nuts and berries and seeds, and slices of excellent toast from home-made bread, and butter and three kinds of jam, and two kinds of marmalade. And there was tea and coffee and freshly-squeezed orange juice.

I love it when other people do the cooking. It's just like being on tour.

Then, after breakfast, Judy, Tim, Peter and Gordon and I set out to find Mrs. Beatrix Cummings.

Our walk took us up a twisting, paved lane, populated on both sides with very old but well-maintained cottages built out of local limestone blocks and grey gritstone. The little lane meandered here and there, past pitched roofs and tall chimneys and names on plates over cottage doors that featured an abiding fondness for flowers—Jasmine, Ivy, Lavender.

"This was a prosperous little town in the mid-18th century," Judy said. "Population up around 2,000 or so. Because of the lead mines."

I could see the wealth. The restorations were meticulous and discriminating. The cars nestled outside in endlessly creative parking arrangements were high-end and as scrupulously maintained as the cottages and their little manicured gardens.

Halfway up the hill, the paved lane became even narrower. A sign identified it as Newlydale Path, and the cottages were much plainer and smaller. These had once been the homes of lead miners, quarrymen, and ag labs.

"There," I said, pointing out the little building that we'd identified by its picture and write-up in *The Village History*. "The former bakery."

It was tiny and had no front garden. Its brown-painted front door opened straight onto the lane. A small wooden table had been set up just to the right of the door, featuring an interesting collection of glass bottles and jars and mismatched cups and saucers. A handwritten sign:

50p each.

Kindly leave cash in the teapot.

I knocked on the door.

No answer.

I tried again, and a little woman who looked about eighty bustled around the corner from the cottage's rear.

She had untidy white hair, most of which she'd stuffed underneath a crocheted purple hat with a floppy brim. She was wearing a mauve pullover and a long blue skirt, thick black stockings and sensible shoes. She was carrying two glass tumblers and an ancient-looking china soup tureen.

"Mrs. Cummings...?" I said.

"Aye," the little woman replied, quickly arranging the items on the table. "I've got more in the back if nothing here takes your fancy."

"My name's Jason Figgis," I said. "I've been sent to collect a ticket."

The little woman smiled. "Ah, then. You'd better come along with me."

Leaving Tim to look after the dogs, Judy and I followed her around to the back of her cottage—and a shed, which was dug into an embankment of grass-covered earth.

"Did you know your house used to be a bakery?" Judy inquired, as Beatrix dragged open a creaky wooden door and disappeared inside.

"Oh aye, yes," she replied, coming out again with a small white envelope. "It were owned by friends of my parents—Mr. and Mrs. Hasfield. I remember the smell of the fresh-baked bread. After my parents passed on, and after the Hasfields were gone, and all their children had moved away, this house sat empty. My husband—Mr. Cummings—was gone as well, and I wanted to buy it. I had some savings set by, but not nearly enough. It were that Merritt lad who helped me out."

"Marcus Merritt?" I asked.

"Aye, yes."

"Will wonders never cease," Judy said, under her breath. "Where did he find that kind of money?"

"I can think of one obvious source," I replied. How often, I wondered, did Arthur Braskey check the balance of his bank accounts?

"Here you are," Mrs. Cummings said, putting the envelope into my hand. It was very thin and obviously contained nothing more than what had been promised—a ticket.

"If you don't mind my asking," I said, "how did you happen to know Marcus?"

"I knew the whole family," Mrs. Cummings replied. "My husband—Mr. Cummings—and I were very great friends with his parents. They lived in the next village over, Winster. That's where Marcus grew up, and his sister. I used to give piano lessons and Marcus was one of my pupils. His father taught in the school."

She took us around to the front again, where Tim was eyeing the soup tureen.

"You take this," Mrs. Cummings said, to me, choosing a beautiful little glass bottle that might have been a hundred years old. It was a very unusual pale blue. "No charge."

"Thank you," I said. "Are you sure?"

"Of course I'm sure," Mrs. Cummings replied, sounding annoyed.

I put it into my jacket pocket.

Judy bought the soup tureen, and a single cup and saucer. She gave Mrs. Cummings £5.

"I haven't got anything smaller," she said, apologetically.

I didn't think that was true, but I didn't say anything.

"Many thanks," Mrs. Cummings replied. "Do come again."

I looked inside the envelope as we walked back down the hill with Peter and Gordon. It was, indeed, the promised ticket for *Past Music Haunts of Soho*. And nothing else.

"No clues as to who I'm supposed to meet," I said. "Or what I'm meant to do."

"Perhaps it's the tour guide herself," Judy shrugged. "Lesley Wharton."

***

Tim and Judy and Peter and Gordon dropped me off at Matlock Station.

"We've got something for you," Judy said, through the open window of the Escort. She handed me an up-to-date, newly-printed *Geographers' A-Z Great Britain Road Atlas*. "Marcus wanted you to have it as a reminder of your visit."

"I'm not very likely to forget it," I said, accepting the spiral-bound book, nevertheless, and tucking it into my bag.

"Stay in touch," Judy said. "I mean it."

"I will," I promised. "And thank you."

I was the only person waiting for the little train that would take me down the branch line to Derby. And there was no sign of Braskey's Lunar Blue Mercedes in the station's parking lot, which, as far as I was concerned, was a very good thing. Matlock was the terminus station, so there was no possibility of him—or Matilda or anyone else he might have hired to keep an eye on me—boarding the train further up the line.

I watched the two-coach shuttle arrive from Matlock Bath and empty out. Nobody stayed around on the platform.

I watched the driver walk down to the other end of the train.

I was still the only passenger as we departed for Derby.

At each stop—Matlock Bath, Cromford, Whatstandwell, Ambergate, Belper and Duffield—I stood in an open doorway to see who else was getting on board. I took their pictures.

Half an hour later, I was in Derby. I studied all the photos on my phone and compared them to the passengers waiting with me on the platform for the fast Intercity to London. Nobody looked familiar. Still, if any of them turned up on that walking tour of Soho, I'd be able to spot them.

I boarded the train and claimed my spot in First Class.

There were only twenty-two seats, and all of them were occupied. My seat—14, facing forward, on the aisle—was in the middle of the carriage. Ahead of me were the galley and the driver's cab. Behind me, the toilet and vestibule and the door leading to the rest of the train. If I'd been allowed, I'd have got the last seat by the toilet, so that I'd have had a view of the entire carriage.

I stowed my bag under the table, acknowledged the gentleman in Seat 13 and the two ladies across from me in Seats 9 and 10, and settled in.

I had an hour and a half to kill. I got a slice of cake and two cups of coffee from the trolley, and then I plugged into YouTube on my phone, and listened to Elgar's Variation I. *L'istesso tempo*. Ascribed to Caroline Alice Elgar, the composer's wife. Famous for its repeating four-note melodic fragment, echoing what Elgar reportedly used to whistle, when arriving home, to Alice.

CHAPTER NINE

THERE WERE THREE MARQUEE Clubs. There had actually been five in total, but Lesley Wharton's *Past Music Haunts* tour was going to confine itself to the ones in and around Soho. There were two Ronnie Scott's. There were coffee bars and watering holes and recording studios and cafes and places where you could go late at night and listen to jazz, folk, blues, rock, and punk and rub shoulders with some Rolling Stones or David Bowie or even The Beatles, if you timed it right. Memorial benches. Iconic telephone kiosks.

In a previous life, the Montagu Pyke was better known as the location of the third Marquee Club, after it had relocated in 1988 from its second location, a few roads over.

I was the last to join the little group assembled on the pavement outside the pub. I'd deliberately hung back so I could watch everyone else arrive.

After the tranquil, uncluttered hush of Derbyshire, Central London was anarchic chaos.

I could very easily have spent another week...another month...roaming the solitary paths of Newlydale and its neighbouring villages. I'd felt at ease there. Protected. I'd been immersed in another world.

And now, here I was, unwillingly hurled back into the vehicular and pedestrian madness that was Charing Cross Road at eleven o'clock in the morning on Thursday, October 18.

"Your failure to locate my Elgar folio—and return it to me—would not be in your best personal interests, Mr. Figgis."

I hated Marcus Merritt for choosing me to fulfill his insane last wish.

But not as much as I hated Arthur Braskey, who was forcing me to complete it.

We were ten participants, in total, including me and our guide. There were two couples who were around my age; three women, probably in their thirties; and one older man, a loner, who looked the sort of guy who'd spend his days in a library searching for obscure references to a one-hit-wonder pop band that was active from 1962 to 1964 in Huddersfield.

None of them had been aboard yesterday's EMR train from Derby to London.

Our guide, Lesley Wharton, was about the same age as my son, Dom. She had short, messy blonde hair and a nose ring. She was dressed in a black winter coat and leggings, with neon orange trainers and a matching knapsack and a hand-knitted orange and black striped scarf.

"Jason Figgis," I said, handing over my ticket. "Or Davey. I have two names. One's on my birth certificate. The other's professional."

"Thanks," Lesley said, tucking the slip of paper into her knapsack. No hint of recognition? No "I've been expecting you…"?

"Figgis," she said. "As in Figgis Green…?"

"Tony was my dad."

"What on earth are you doing here? You must know this place inside out."

It was true. Soho's my playground. The Blue Devil, where my band and I had our residency, was just over on Wardour Street, not far from where the second Marquee Club had once been located.

"Just a casual re-acquaintance," I replied.

"Then you're in for a treat," she said. "Good morning, ladies and gents. My name's Lesley Wharton and I want to welcome you to *Past Music Haunts of Soho*. It's a long tour, but we'll stop about halfway through for some drinks and lunch. Is that all right with everyone?"

We conveyed our agreement. Mindful of the lengthy itinerary—and with no idea at which point I was meant to collect the Elgar folio—I'd brought along my own snacks: a little bottle of Tropicana orange juice, a bottle of sparkling water, three chocolate digestives, and a small packet of Maltesers. I'd crammed them all into a comfortable old brown leather buckle bag that I'd slung over my shoulder.

"A little about me, before we get started. My granddad was Clive Wharton, who some of you might have heard of." She paused, for effect. There were small sounds of murmured acknowledgement. "For those who haven't heard of him, my granddad Clive was an American Beat Poet who fell in love with an English lady—my grandmother. They pulled up stakes in San Francisco in the 1950s and came to London, where they opened one of Soho's best-known coffee bars, The Golden Gate, which was a haven for poets, writers and musicians. We'll walk past where it used to be located a little later on. My dad, Slade Wharton, was born during this period and he, of course, also went on to become a poet and lyricist in his own right."

There were further murmurs of recognition and appreciation.

"And I did just want to point out that the building next door to the Montagu Pyke—now occupied by the latest inhabitation of the prestigious Foyles booksellers—is the old Central Saint Martins Art School building. Which is where, you might want to make note, on November 6, 1975, four working class punk-rock teenagers performed in public for the first time. They would later become known as The Sex Pistols."

I knew that. There'd been about twenty people in the audience and they were the support band for Bazooka Joe, whose bass player was a guy who later became a solo act called Adam Ant.

But I wasn't going to say anything. There's nothing worse than a show-off trying to compete with an official bringer-of-knowledge. Everyone ends up hating you and nobody wants to sit beside you in the pub.

***

Leslie had trekked us across Charing Cross Road and paused us on the pavement beside a triangular red brick building that was standing sentry at the northwest corner of Denmark Street.

Back then, in October 2018, its ground floor was still occupied by one of Wunjo's instrument shops, with its screamingly-bright orange signage and huge white arrows on a black background directing those in search of keyboards down into the building's basement.

"So," Lesley said, "there's such a huge musical history attached to this street. It's only about a hundred yards long, but so much has happened here over the years..."

I stood on the corner and observed the road, which was in the midst of massive redevelopment, most of it concealed behind pipe-and-platform scaffolds and tied-down tarps and hammered-up wooden hoardings. The visible evidence of what was going on was over on the triangular red brick building's back side, where centuries of history were methodically being demolished to make way for dramatic re-imaginings of Tottenham Court Road tube station and St Giles Square.

Two of the three single ladies availed themselves of a photo op. The one who wasn't taking pictures decided instead to talk to me. She had a mass of very blonde hair that she'd pulled back into a pony tail behind her head. She had a fringe. And she was wearing a bright pink jacket and tight black leggings.

"I hate what they're doing here," she said. "I was in the middle of all the protests three years ago when they were closing down the old 12 Bar. The demonstrations and legal battles and occupations. So much for preserving London's musical legacy."

I didn't disagree. Poor old Denmark Street, on that morning, looked neglected, and empty.

"Isabel," she said.

"Jason," I replied.

"Yes, I've seen your show at The Blue Devil."

That did surprise me. I'd been on the road with the Figs, and hadn't actually played at the club in more than two months. "I hope we weren't too disappointing."

"Far from it. I like how you reinvent things. Not many musicians would have thought of doing the theme from Expo '67 as a jazz number."

I laughed. We'd added that to the set list just before the tour. Rudy's cousin Marielle lived in Montreal and had discovered the old 45 single in her attic. She'd hooked up her turntable to her computer and converted it and sent a digital copy to Rudy. We'd had a listen, and I was, of course, immediately inspired.

"I like how you retained that little musical phrase featuring the notes from 'O Canada' in the bridge after the third chorus," Isabel said.

"I like that you actually noticed that," I replied.

"I've got a pretty good ear. I teach music. Viola."

Was Isabel the person Marcus intended me to liaise with, regarding the Elgar folio?

I wasn't going first. She'd have to be the one to identify herself.

And, in the meantime, Lesley was walking us down the road.

My mum and dad had created their band, Figgis Green, in 1965. They'd landed a manager—Wrigley Beresford—who'd had an office on the top floor of the building at Number 19, next door to the red brick triangle.

We trudged along the pavement, skirting the scaffolds and the smell of old, exposed bricks and deconstruction wafting out from behind the giant shrouds and metal tube caging. We waited for a 24 bus to manoeuvre its way west past green bins and orange barricades and one or two construction workers in high-viz vests.

"Number 7," said Lesley, pointing out a grey-doored property mostly overshadowed by steel tubes, couplings and bracings. "The site of the Tin Pan Alley Club. Some of you might recognize the outside of it as the bar where Terry O'Neill photographed the Rolling Stones in 1964. And where Malcolm McLaren was photographed in 1979 by Barry Plumber for a story in *Melody Maker*."

"Notorious," Isabel added, quietly, "from the mid-1970s to the early 1990s, as a watering hole for criminals. It helped that it was owned by Ronnie Knight."

Who was, I recalled, famous for being married to the *Carry On* actress, Barbara Windsor, as well as being an East End bad guy with friendly connections to the Krays.

"Number 9," Lesley said, pointing out another nondescript property, with a white facade and glass-windowed doors at street level, and two more storeys of red brick above. "This is, of course, the fabled home of La Gioconda, the musicians' cafe, starting in 1960. In the mid-60s, David Bowie was a singer in a band called The Lower Third—which he formally joined inside that cafe. The Lower Third's tour bus was an old converted ambulance, which sometimes doubled as their hotel. Bowie would park the ambulance just over there, outside the cafe, and sleep in it after his gigs, as it was cheaper than paying rent on a flat. The proprietor used to wake him up in the morning with breakfast."

I recalled my mum telling me much the same thing, though it was from the perspective of someone who'd witnessed it firsthand, as she remembered popping into the Gioconda for a cup of tea in the summer of 1965 and spotting both the ambulance and its famous occupant. Said ambulance was apparently also handy for picking up girls and engaging in much improvised merriment in the neighbourhood of Piccadilly Circus. My mum's euphemism, not mine. I'd never actually asked her how she'd managed to come by that little nugget of information.

"As you can see, it's now called The Flat Iron—somewhat more upscale and trendier than its predecessor. And if you cast your eyes up, you'll see a round blue sign from the British Plaque Trust, identifying the road as 'Tin Pan Alley' and honouring the songwriters and publishers to whom this street was home between 1911 and 1992."

"Grade II listed building," Isabel said. "Dating from around 1686, along with Number 10, next door. I don't think our host will get around to mentioning that."

I had a fleeting memory of that building. On the first floor, above the cafe, there had once been a little studio—Central Sound—which was mostly used for demo's. In 1965, it was where Bowie and his new band had recorded a couple of covers and one of his original compositions. Two years later it was where the newly-arrived Bee Gees had demo'd parts of their album. That was all before I was born. But I'd always recalled being taken upstairs there when I was about three, and our destination *was* definitely a little recording studio and the building had always seemed to me to be exactly this one on Denmark Street.

Wrigley'd got the Figs to record their first demo at Regent Sounds' tiny downstairs studio along the way at Number 4. The studio was apparently a shithole, cheap, seedy, and dirty, with—as my mum recalls—egg boxes glued to the ceiling to help with the acoustics. But musicians had a soft spot in their hearts for the place.

That demo had led to their first record deal.

My parents were regular visitors to Denmark Street, because that was where you went if you wanted to buy sheet music or instruments or get your guitar mended or have meetups with people in the business who still had offices there. The guitar and drum shops moved around and changed names. The offices came and went. Frontages were repainted and re-signed. Mum and dad took me there a lot when I was a kid, and after I grew up and became a musician myself, Denmark Street was the first place I went when I was looking for a new guitar.

Lesley was moving us along, past the former site of another Wunjo's outlet on the north side, Number 20, where, upstairs, an American publishing company called Mills Music had hired a teenaged Elton John as a post boy in the early 1960s. Mills was also noteworthy for turning down Paul Simon, telling him "Homeward Bound" and "The Sounds of Silence" would never sell.

Number 20's butterscotch shopfront was empty and dark on that day, one of many on the road meekly awaiting their repurposed futures.

Beside it, at Number 21, a sign still touted the premises as London's biggest saxophone showroom. But the shop that had once been there was hidden behind graffiti-covered hoardings celebrating Chuck Berry. Its destiny would, in a few years' time, involve being completely gutted in order to create "an immersive LED tunnel for walk-through experiences and digital exhibitions."

Next door, at Number 22, was yet another abandoned instrument store, its plate glass windows—in common with the windows of all the empty properties along the road—protected by a security grille.

"This particular shop," Lesley said, "was once inhabited by Rhodes Music, purveyor of guitars to many, many well-known musicians, including Jeff Beck, Eric Clapton and Chuck Berry. A number of different retailers have occupied this address—and there was, at one point, a little recording studio in the basement, one of several in the street. But what I really wanted to point out is where my grandfather's coffee bar was once located. The buildings on the north side of Denmark Street all back onto a narrow laneway called Denmark Place. I can't, unfortunately, show you the site of my grandparents' coffee shop, The Golden Gate, as the alley's blocked off for demolition. But it was back there, very near to where we're standing now."

No one took pictures. There wasn't really a lot of point.

"I also wanted to tell you about something else that happened there, nearly forty years ago. In 1980, the top floors at Number 18 Denmark Place were home to two unlicensed bars. In the early hours of Saturday, August 16, 1980, a petty criminal believed that one of the barmen had overcharged him for a drink. He got into a fight and was ejected from the premises. In revenge, he filled a container with petrol and poured it through the letterbox of the front door, then lit a piece of paper and pushed it through. The resulting fire killed thirty-seven people and injured scores of others, some of whom tried to escape through one of the music shops here on Denmark Street. This one, Number 22, is the shop which backed onto the property at Number 18, but some reports have said that those who were rescued had found their way into Number 21, next door. Whichever the case, their escape was blocked by a security grille over the windows, and one account tells of a poor soul who was attacking that grille with an electric guitar, trying to break the glass to get to the fresh air."

"Did you know about that?" I asked Isabel.

"I did actually," she replied. "Didn't you?"

I shook my head. "I was twelve in 1980," I said. "I don't remember hearing anything about it at all."

"I'm not surprised," Isabel said. "It didn't get much coverage in the papers at the time. The fire involved two unlicensed and uninspected drinking clubs and all of the victims were assumed to have been in England illegally. Nobody wanted to talk to the press. Though a couple of years ago, there was an online effort to try and identify the victims and their families."

"What was the date of the fire?" I asked.

"It was Saturday, August 16," Lesley replied, overhearing my question. "At about half past three in the morning."

CHAPTER TEN

"I KNOW IT WAS August," Judy said, over the phone. "And I know it was 1980. But I can't be absolutely sure about the exact date."

I'd hung back from the group so I could call her, leaving Lesley and the others to trek on towards St Giles in the Fields, at the eastern end of the road.

"I just remember I smelled smoke on him as soon as he came in," Judy said.

"What time was that?"

"About half past eight in the morning. He'd been out all night."

"Did you have any idea where?"

"None. Though given his habits and the people he knew, I'm sure it was Soho."

"And he wouldn't talk about the smell of smoke on his clothes?"

"Not at all," Judy said.

"I'm surprised," I said, "because that night there was a fairly significant fire in Denmark Place. It was arson, and it killed three dozen people."

"I don't remember hearing anything about that. But I'd packed my bags and taken Julie to my mum's. And mum lived in Sturminster Newton. So I'm not surprised."

"And it wasn't widely reported," I said.

"Which probably explains why Marc wasn't bursting at the seams to claim his part in directing the fire brigade, rescuing victims, and probably even helping to apprehend whoever started it."

"Unless," I said, "in a rare moment of sanity, he had reason to believe it wouldn't have been a very good idea to admit to anything at all."

I ran to catch up with the rest of the group, passing a yellow-brick building midway down the block that I'd visited a year and a half earlier with Rudy, Ken and Dave. It was where we'd been offered a less-than-stellar touring gig as a support act for a duo who sang what Ken disparagingly referred to as "music for the middle of your mind."

The entire structure was now sitting abandoned and boarded up. I'd heard Knave Records had gone into administration that January. Music for the middle of your mind obviously wasn't the big draw their A&R guy had predicted.

Lesley led us all across to the south side of the road, and paused so that we were looking north again, this time at Number 26. Another location whose inhabitants were long gone, most of its frontage now obscured by scaffolding and, at street level, a black and white graffiti-scribbled hoarding that matched the one at Number 21, celebrating the legacy of Chuck Berry.

"And that, of course, is where the 12 Bar Club once stood."

"The very famous 12 Bar," Isabel added, standing beside me. "Late of the demonstrations, occupations and Bohemian squats. 'Without culture, society cannot exist'." She waggled her finger around. "Save our Tin Pan Alley!"

I smiled.

She didn't look old enough to have frequented the 12 Bar during its heyday in the 1990s.

I certainly had. The club was actually four rooms organized in an L shape, with a tiny live room at the back. It had been one of the smallest music venues in London, with one of the tiniest stages, backed by an old brick forge that dated from the 1600s, when that part of the building had been a stable and blacksmith's. The room could hold about 150 people, tops, with a handful accommodated upstairs on a very dodgy balcony that always seemed to me to be on the verge of collapse.

I remembered the place as being claustrophobic and sweaty.

And the toilets were grim.

Lesley was relating the club's history, reeling off a shopping list of performers, punctuated by the occasional A-lister. It hadn't really been known for its mainstream artists.

"Did you ever play there?" Isabel asked.

I laughed. "No. Audience only. But it's where I met my wife. She was with a couple of her mates. They were doing hair and makeup on a TV series filming over the way, in Covent Garden. The guys onstage that night were new to the scene and were calling themselves Coldplay."

"I'm impressed," Isabel said, meaning it.

"Monday, July 20, 1998," I added.

"I'm even more impressed."

"That it was gestational Chris Martin or that I remembered the exact date?"

"Both," she said.

"Emma and I got married two months later."

"Did it last?" she inquired. The next logical question.

"It did," I said. "Until she died. In a fire. Tuesday, October 27, 2009."

"I'm so sorry."

"It's OK. Nine years ago, now...and so much has changed in my life since then. She'd have been amazed."

"She is," Isabel said, with a smile.

Lesley was giving the black, paint-scrawled door next to the Chuck Berry hoardings a nod.

"Fans of J.K. Rowling—aka Robert Galbraith—might be interested to know that's the door to the office and attic flat of detective Cormoran Strike. Although in the TV episodes, the actual filming location was Number 6, down the road."

Lacking any moves on Isabel's part, I wondered if a workman in an orange safety vest was going to materialize from Cormoran Strike's doorway to hand me a nice fat envelope, courtesy of Marcus Merritt. Then I could discretely disappear and forget about the remaining three hours and twenty minutes of the tour.

Nope.

And there was no sign of Arthur Braskey's Lunar Blue Mercedes, either, though, given the restricted state of traffic along the road—and its one-way flow, east-to-west—I wasn't surprised. I knew he was having me watched. His spies were on foot. I'd already sussed one of them—a guy in a flat cap, a t-shirt, a black leather jacket, and jeans, who'd been following us since we left the Montagu Pyke. And I had my eye on a second guy, on the opposite side of the road, who'd been pretending to study guitars in shop windows, using the reflection in the glass to keep a close eye on me without being obvious.

Our allocated time in Denmark Street was over. Lesley led us back to Charing Cross Road, and then up Manette Street, where noisy construction on the site formerly occupied by Foyles (before it had moved over to the Central Saint Martins Art School building), funnelled us under the Pillars of Hercules pub and disgorged us out onto Greek Street.

And then, we trekked up to Soho Square.

I've been there plenty of times when it's been pelting down rain and miserable. But that day it was clear and, for the middle of October, quite warm. Soho Square's a beautiful little oasis in a neighbourhood that—churchyards excepted—is pretty much devoid of greenery. And at its centre is a mock Tudor gardener's hut, built in 1926 to hide what's actually an electricity substation.

Soho Square's also where there's a wooden seat commemorating Kirsty MacColl, who died in 2000, far too soon.

"Kirsty's bench," Lesley said, "was installed on August 12, 2001. You can see it's got a little brass plate on it, with a line from one of her songs, also called 'Soho Square', from her 1993 album, *Titanic Days*. And every year on the Sunday nearest to Kirsty's birthday—which is October 10—her fans come here and hold a gathering to pay tribute and sing her songs."

I debated whether it would be sacrilege to actually sit down on Kirsty's shrine while everyone else was respectfully standing in front of it, listening to Lesley and taking pictures.

I needn't have worried. Arthur Braskey had already decided it would be a good place to wait for me.

"Mr. Figgis," he said, patting the empty section of the bench beside him.

I wasn't keen about being captured on everyone's phones sitting next to one of Soho's top crime bosses.

But I thought the better of refusing.

I sat.

"Any sign of my folio?"

"If you'd been following me instead of relying on hired hands," I said, "you'd know the answer to that."

Arthur Braskey's face remained impassive. "I tend to avoid Denmark Street," he said. "It holds unpleasant memories."

Interesting.

"There was a fire," I said. "In 1980."

"Caused by an arsonist," Braskey replied. "A miscreant named John Thompson—not his real name—it was John Albert Andrews. He was subsequently arrested and one year later, convicted at the Old Bailey. He died in 2008, on the twenty-eighth anniversary of his crime."

"You seem to know a lot about it," I said, feeling courageous. "Could Marcus Merritt have possibly been there that night, carrying out a spot of work for you...?"

"I'd advise you not to pursue that line of questioning, Mr. Figgis, and to confine your inquisitiveness to the subject of Sir Edward Elgar."

"But why unpleasant memories?" I asked. "Something like that would have been business as usual on your part, surely?"

Arthur Braskey wasn't talking.

And I was treading increasingly dangerous ground.

"Why are you so keen to get the collection back?" I asked, deciding it would actually be wiser to change the subject. "Why not just write it off and move on?"

"That collection is worth half a million pounds, Mr. Figgis."

"So you said. But you can't sell it at auction. It's stolen goods—documented by the police. Nobody'll go near it, legit dealers or otherwise."

Braskey remained silent.

"Unless," I supposed, "you'd already made arrangements to sell it. Privately. And it's been promised to someone."

Braskey's expression didn't change.

"And that someone has given you his money. And now he wants his goods."

A slight twinge in the rubber-band lips. "You have an astute awareness of pecuniary enterprise, Mr. Figgis."

The realization that Arthur Braskey might have been on the receiving end of trouble, after a career of doling it out, was, I had to admit, rather satisfying.

"I'm guessing your finances are on shaky grounds," I said. "Why else would you be parting with things from your private collection? What else are you offering for sale?"

"Nothing that falls anywhere near your ability to pay, Mr. Figgis"

We were interrupted by Isabel.

"Sorry," she said, "but Lesley says we're off to Gerrard Street."

"Just coming," I said.

I stood up.

"The original Ronnie Scott's awaits," I said, to Braskey.

"Just like home," he replied, also getting to his feet. "Filthy and full of strangers."

CHAPTER ELEVEN

I HAD TO LAUGH. Arthur Braskey—who had just tossed me one of
Ronnie Scott's infamous quips—had probably been one of the local
heavyweights who'd ensured Ronnie's club had stayed open for business and free of harassment throughout Soho's more criminally-in-
clined days.

And now the great crime lord himself was in trouble.

Ronnie Scott's original address at 39 Gerrard Street was in the
heart of Chinatown. The tiny basement venue was reached via some
nondescript stairs that now belonged to a Taiwanese restaurant. These
days there's a blue plaque from English Heritage installed over the
entrance, though it wasn't there in 2018 when I was doing Lesley's
tour.

"Cellars were the location of choice," our guide provided, "because
they were discreet and the rent was cheap, and, being underground,
they were also a bit more soundproof than the venues at street level."

"I expect Ronnie Scott's your hero," Isabel said, to me.

"One of them," I replied.

"You'd have to be a disciple to know that in his younger years, he
worked as a musician on board Cunard ocean liners. Are you?"

"A disciple? Not really."

"But you do know about his early career at sea."

"I do," I said.

"A bit like you," Isabel ventured. "Eight till late in the TopDeck
Lounge?"

How did she know about my past life aboard the *Star Sapphire*? It
wasn't something I'd put on a website. And I rarely mentioned it on

social media, although back in my days aboard the *Sapphire*, I'd been very active on Twitter.

Lesley was telling us about the cellar, prior to its opening on Friday, October 30, 1959 as Ronnie Scott's first venue.

"It was best known as a room where taxi drivers could stop and have a rest break. It also operated as a tea-bar...but most importantly, it was already a familiar hangout for local musicians. Ronnie borrowed £1,000 from his stepfather, signed a lease for £12 a week rent, installed a mic, a bar, some lights, and furniture—and a piano. And that was the start of the legendary—and the first—jazz club of its kind in London."

"Apropos of nothing," Isabel said, to me, "but have you noticed that 'Go West' by The Pet Shop Boys not only sounds uncannily like the Russian national anthem—it's also got elements of Pachelbel's 'Canon' in the eight bar chord progression at the beginning of the song?"

I had no idea why she was asking me that.

Musicians.

"The Russian national anthem *is* Pachelbel's eight bar chord progression at the beginning of the song," I replied. "With the seventh bar slightly altered."

Isabel gave me a look of mischief. "Try all of 'Streets of London'," she said. "Ralph McTell."

"'Eyes of the World'," I said. "Fleetwood Mac."

"Now you're just showing off."

"So are you," I said. I offered her a chocolate digestive from my bag. "Biccie?"

"Thank you," she replied. "Bet you didn't know that in 2012, someone compiled a list of the most popular funeral music and Pachelbel's 'Canon in D' placed second on the Classical chart. Lost out to Sir Edward Elgar's Enigma Variation IX, 'Nimrod'."

She looked at me again, but this time, her eyes were not filled with mischief, but with a certain knowledge.

"I'll remember that," I replied.

"Yes," said Isabel. "Do."

She went back to her two friends as Lesley finished telling everyone about the issue with the British Musicians' Union, which, until the end of the 1950s, had prohibited American musicians from performing in

Britain because they would be taking work away from their British coun-terparts. And about the American Federation of Musicians responding by keeping British acts out of the US. And how Ronnie Scott and his partner Pete King had been instrumental in working out a reciprocal agreement that finally solved the impasse and allowed Zoot Sims to come over from America for a four-week residency at the club, in November 1961.

We were on the move again, walking to the lower end of Wardour Street and more basement clubs where jazz and R&B acts had flourished, where legendary names had gathered, Georgie Fame, Stevie Wonder, the Rolling Stones, the Moody Blues, the Animals....

Then we continued north, to Old Compton Street, where Lesley walked us 'round the corner and we stopped in front of Number 59, a fish and chips shop with a green plaque beside its front door, identifying it as the site of the old 2i's Coffee Bar.

"Some say, the birthplace of British rock and roll," she provided, reeling off another list of notable names like Tommy Steele and Cliff Richard and all of the musicians who eventually became his backing band, The Shadows.

There was a Four Eyes Coffee Shop in Stoneford, where we'd re-hearsed for our 50th Anniversary Tour. It had been there for as long as my mum could remember and most definitely dated back to the mid-1960s. Its signage had featured a pair of black-framed, Hank Mar-vin-style spectacles. The joke hadn't been lost on any of us.

***

I was starving by the time we finally got round to lunch.

Our planned stop was at The Sheep and Shears, a lovely little pub dating from the 1890s, near the corner of Wardour and Broadwick Streets and not too far from where I worked at The Blue Devil.

Lesley gave the club a little acknowledgement as we walked past, as the doors, which would normally have been shut until the evening, were open for a rare Thursday Lunch Show. A small but steady stream of jazz fans was making its way inside to hear my guys—Rudy, Ken and Dave—and their guest guitarist, Josh Baynard, a mate from New York who was in London to play some gigs of his own.

Outside, The Sheep and Shears is painted black—they all seem to be painted black in Soho, and they've all got gold lettering and, in the summer, huge baskets of flowers hanging from hooks over their windows.

Inside, The Sheep and Shears has red leather seats and polished wooden tables, a bar surrounded by beautifully-preserved dark wood, and a red-painted plaster ceiling that still boasts its original Victorian light fixtures. It has an amazing tile floor and huge mirrors on its walls, advertising old-fashioned mineral waters and long-extinguished cigarettes.

A year and a half earlier, this was where Rudy, Ken, Dave and I had convened following our disastrous meeting at Knave Records, and where we'd collectively decided to stick with our residency at The Blue Devil instead of going out on the road, twenty feet from stardom on the back of a tour where the audience couldn't tell the difference between Miles Davis and Thelonious Monk—and couldn't really have cared less anyway. The pub, on that day, had been packed.

Today, it was less busy, and all ten of us were easily able to appropriate three empty tables at the back.

"The Sheep and Shears," Lesley said, as we sat down, "was, of course, one of the favourite watering holes of London's rock elite in the 1960s and 1970s. Paul McCartney. Mick Jagger and Rod Stewart. Ronnie Wood. And actors too—Richard Harris and Oliver Reed. And in the Seventies—Malcolm McLaren and Johnny Rotten and the rest of the Sex Pistols."

I stowed my leather buckle bag under the table and sat with my back to the wall, so I could keep an eye on everyone else in the pub. Isabel chose the chair beside me, and her two friends sat down across from us. I looked at the lunch menu, decided on a Cheese and Chutney Toastie and a bottle of sparkling water, and relayed my request to Lesley, who collected all of our orders and took them up to the gentleman behind the bar.

Any professional working for Arthur Braskey was never going to allow themselves to become too familiar-looking. The guy who'd been wearing the flat cap and black leather jacket was doing his best to make me think he wasn't the same person I'd spotted in Denmark Street. He'd taken off the cap—he had a closely-shaved head—and switched out the black leather for a navy-blue windbreaker. He was sitting up near the entrance with a pint. His mate—the muso—was all in black—jeans, a fedora and a suit jacket—and he had the doorway covered from the outside, where he was repeating his favourite lingering act, pretending to be waiting for a mate who was never going to show up.

If this was where Isabel was going to hand me the Elgar folio, I couldn't think of anything riskier. An enclosed space. No easy exit. Everyone at the three back tables in full view of the two guys at the front. Whatever Isabel did...Arthur Braskey's beagles were going to clock us.

Lesley brought our drinks over from the bar and we sorted out the cash to pay for everything, including our food. Isabel had to dig around in her knapsack, under the table, to locate her change purse.

Ten minutes later, my Cheese and Chutney Toastie was delivered by one of the bar staff, along with Isabel's lunch—a Chicken and Avocado Sandwich with Skin-on Fries.

I topped up my glass with the sparkling water, and drank it. I made a start on my Cheese and Chutney Toastie.

The young lady from behind the bar carried two Chicken Burgers with Salad and plates of Fish and Chips with Mushy Peas over to Isabel's two friends.

"Perhaps," said Isabel, "you'd like to have a look through this."

She slid a printed booklet across to me.

It was a program from the recently concluded BBC Proms, an eight-week season of classical music concerts presented every year between July and September. The cover for 2018 was pink and gold, with purple and blue butterflies and brilliant beams of white light emanating from a stylized graphic of the Royal Albert Hall, the Proms' principal venue.

"Apropos our previous conversation," Isabel mused, as I peeked inside the front cover. "Have you heard the Trans-Siberian Orchestra's version of 'Nutrocker' played live with Greg Lake on bass?"

"I'm not sure," I said, vaguely, only giving her half of my attention. Was the Proms program important...?

"'Nutrocker' is, of course, the march from Tchaikovsky's 1892 ballet 'The Nutcracker'—Act 1 of which was featured on Thursday, August 2."

I looked at her.

She looked back, her eyebrows suggesting I investigate that date.

I flipped through to the listing for Prom 25, Thursday, August 2. A folded sheet of paper had been tucked in between the pages.

"Be careful with that," Isabel suggested, quietly, and then: "The Proms, of course, brings us right back to Sir Edward Elgar, whose 'Pomp & Circumstance March No. 1' is traditionally played each year on the Last Night..."

I didn't need to flip to the listing for Prom 75—The Last Night—to confirm what Isabel was saying. Anyone who's ever been to, or listened to, or watched the Last Night of the Proms can't help but be caught up in the hugely popular and slightly over-the-top patriotic revelry of the evening. But I did need to look at the pages in question because I could tell that something else had been lodged there.

And it wouldn't have been a very good thing if Arthur Braskey's beagles had caught me looking at it.

"I'll just go to the Gents," I decided.

I slid out from behind the table and, taking the Proms program with me, followed the sign directing me through the door on the left and up a steep flight of stairs to the first floor toilets.

I went in and locked myself in the single cubicle.

I read the folded-over piece of paper first.

Hello Jason. What you will shortly find in your possession is one-third of the whole. I hope you don't mind. It's more fun this way.

I had to stop myself from groaning.

And safer.

Safer for who? Certainly not me.

It was all very well for Marcus Merritt. He was already dead.

And I hated him for it.

There will be another two packages after this. And then, I promise—you'll have the entire collection. And your money.
  But I'm afraid you'll have to stay until the end of the tour in order to collect my next clue.

I actually did allow myself to swear out loud at that point.

If you put all my clues together, you might discover the congruence in the divergence. In the meantime, have one on me. Look at The Last Night.

I found the envelope that had been stuffed into the program near the end. Inside was a little wad of cash—enough for a couple of pints, if I'd happened to be a drinker, which I wasn't.
  I pocketed the money and tore up the envelope and Marcus's note and flushed them both down the toilet. And then I went back downstairs.
  I took my seat again and, without looking, casually reached under the table and felt for the shoulder strap of my leather bag. I gave it a little tug. My bag resisted. It was considerably heavier than I recalled.
  I bought everyone at our three tables a round of drinks.
  And then I gave Rudy a call to reconfirm our meet-up at Ardwick House on Friday.

CHAPTER TWELVE

The ten of us had started out as an enthusiastic huddle of Soho music historians, but now, after nearly four hours, we were strung out along the pavement, plodding through Walker's Court, a pedestrian alley connecting Peter Street to Brewer Street and which, like half of Soho in 2018, seemed to be undergoing major redevelopment. Shopfronts that had once purveyed the seedy promise of nonstop striptease, peep shows, porn, and fetish mags were buried behind shoring-up poles and scaffolding and hoardings featuring gigantic depictions of what used to be there. Although, at the end of Walker's Court—where it opened onto Brewer Street—there was still a big plate glass window in a book shop that extended a neon invitation to visit the Adult Licensed Dept Downstairs.

I'd stayed alert, watching out for Braskey's snoops. And for Braskey himself. Though if any of them had any inkling what sleight of hand Isabel had accomplished under the table at The Sheep and Shears, they certainly weren't in any hurry to do anything about it.

I was exhausted. My legs were aching and so were my feet. I'd purposely worn my best walking shoes—the same shoes I'd bought for touring—Mephisto Trevors, with excellent ankle support. They were already fabulous for standing onstage in, and when you factored in the weight of a solid body electric guitar hanging off your shoulder, they were phenomenal.

My well-worn Mephisto Trevors hadn't helped.

And the strap of my bag—which had been stuffed with one third of Elgar's stolen papers—was burning into my shoulder.

I really just wanted to sit down with a restorative cup of tea and a generous slice of cake.

We paused on Rupert Street to look back at what had once been the site of Madame Jojo's, and, above it, the giant white shrouds that I knew concealed an immense marquee that used to advertise RAYMOND REVUEBAR in huge, lit-up letters. Here, Lesley gave us a potted history of Paul Raymond, the venue's founder—"The absolute king of the soft-porn magazine trade and strip clubs!"—who had also bought up about fifty acres of Soho before his death in 2008, and whose company—Soho Estates—was now front and centre in redeveloping and rebuilding the entire area.

I'd been to Madame Jojo's. I'd been to the Raymond Revuebar, too—once—in 1989—to celebrate my twenty-first birthday with a couple of mates.

I recalled a fairly classy show featuring a bevy of not-unattractive young women stripping everything off and dancing with provocative props which were never actually inserted anywhere, in spite of a great deal of hinting and teasing. And the final act was a young lady who came out completely naked and proceeded to have a bath. She enjoyed herself immensely with the bubbles and soap, then climbed out of the little tub, towelled herself off, got dressed and closed the show.

Props to both Paul Raymond and the young lady for having a sense of humour.

We were standing beside a large window ad for an Easy to Make Clone-a-Willy (*the in-home penis molding kit!*), featuring a promise to make a vibrating silicone replica of any cock that, additionally, glowed in the dark.

"Not quite true," Isabel said, nudging me. "Only the Bright Blue, Dark Pink and Neon Green ones glow in the dark. The others are, sadly, un-illuminated."

Was this something to do with Marcus's next clue?

Evidently not. It was just Isabel, being funny.

"I'll remember that," I said. "Thanks."

The tour continued, to Archer Street and Great Windmill Street and Ham Yard, Beak Street, and then Carnaby Street and then Kingly Street, where the Bag O'Nails was, where Paul McCartney had first met Linda Eastman in 1967.

And then, finally, as my watch ticked up to three o'clock, we arrived at the last stop on our itinerary. Heddon Street. The same Heddon Street that featured on the cover of David Bowie's *Ziggy Stardust* album. And the outside of Number 23, where Ziggy was captured on camera, looking pensive, his elbow resting on his raised knee, guitar slung from his shoulder.

There's a plaque which identifies that specific doorway, although the furrier, K. West, is long gone. The street's been pedestrianized and the pavement where Ziggy and the jumble of cardboard boxes were forever immortalized is now an outdoor dining terrace for a trendy Italian restaurant.

Up the way a bit, if you turn left, you can see the iconic red phone box from the back cover of the album, nestled up against the end of a blind alley.

"Of course, it's not *the* red phone box," Lesley said. "*The* red phone box on the back cover of the Ziggy record was a K2 model, which was first introduced in 1927. Ziggy's K2 has six-times-three evenly spaced window panes. Whereas the phone box you see there now is a much newer K6 Jubilee model, and is distinguishable by its eight-times-three oddly spaced window panes."

I have absolutely no doubt there are Bowie fans in this world who consider the substitute box to be an outright desecration.

I'm not one of them.

"Would you like me to take your picture inside the phone kiosk?"

The person who was asking me this was the older guy, the loner, the one I thought looked like an anorak who spent his days at the library looking up obscure pop bands.

"Not really," I said.

"Oh, go on," he said, jovially. "Griff," he added, sticking out his hand, so I could, presumably, shake it.

"Jason," I replied.

"I know. You took your dad's place on the Figgis Green tour. I was at your opening night in Middlehurst."

Another one who had an inkling who I was. Interesting. I don't usually generate that much familiarity. My parents were the famous ones in the family, not me.

"You made one hell of an entrance."

"I did," I agreed.

In fact, I nearly hadn't got there at all. I'd been caught up in an investigation that had ended with me being kidnapped and held in a locked van. The Home Office had been involved. I'd been rescued somewhere near Basingstoke and given a lift to Middlehurst in the back of a police car. I'd arrived at the Cottage Theatre more than half an hour late, in the pouring rain, accompanied by lights and sirens.

Rather than delay, the Figs had started without me, completely rearranging our first set list on the fly to buy me a little more time to get there.

I'd run onstage to a round of cheers and appreciative applause.

"I remember," said Griff, "that you were caught in a thunderstorm."

A completely terrifying thunderstorm, in fact. Lightning is one of my most profound fears, something I've never been able to get over—perhaps because it was lightning that killed my dad. Lightning had struck the police car I was sitting in. With a hiss and a sizzle, I was simultaneously and momentarily blinded by 300 million volts of focused electricity.

There was no thunder. Just a deep and penetrating THUD, like a solid punch to my chest. The car's metal frame was what saved me.

I was probably still in shock when I took over the mic and launched into a detailed, two-minute explanation about my absence.

"I now know everything there is to know about Faraday cages," Griff said, humorously. "How about that photo?"

He had the same compelling look in his eyes as Isabel, when she'd told me all about the survey of favourite funeral songs that had included Elgar's "Nimrod".

"OK," I said.

I walked over to the red phone box as Lesley related the story behind the pictures on the album.

There was a puddle of something evil up against the dead-end wall, and inside the box it smelled like piss.

I kept the door open as I adopted my best Ziggy Stardust pose and Griff snapped the picture.

It took a moment before I spotted the small letter-sized envelope with my name written on it, tucked in between the handset and the metal face of the pay phone.

The envelope wasn't sealed.

Inside was a single sheet of paper, containing what appeared to be a photocopy of the first page of a printed orchestra score for another one of Elgar's Variations.

Number VII. Ascribed to "Troyte."

There was nothing else. Nothing scribbled on the back, no further instructions, nothing to decode or un-riddle.

What the hell was I supposed to do with that?

I folded the paper back into its envelope and put the envelope in my jacket pocket and turned around to give Griff my number so he could text me the photo.

He wasn't there.

And he wasn't with the rest of the group, either, although Isabel and her two friends had opted to stay and were straggling behind Lesley as she led us all back out onto Regent Street.

My phone vibrated with an incoming text. It was Rudy, checking to confirm everything was still on as per my previous message.

I sent him two thumbs-up emojis.

"A little bit of trivia for fans of Michelangelo Antonioni," Lesley said. "If you look behind you, you can see the part of Heddon Street that David Hemmings runs into when he's searching for Vanessa Redgrave in the 1966 film *Blowup*. What became Ziggy's iconic red telephone box six years later is quite prominent in the scene."

We all, obediently, turned around.

"You look like him," Isabel said, to me.

"David Bowie?" I said.

She laughed. "David Hemmings. In *Blowup*. It's the hair."

"As long as it's not the white trousers," I said.

"Griff wanted me to give this to you. He thought you might find it useful."

With the stealth of an Artful Dodger in reverse, she slipped another envelope into my jacket pocket.

Lesley was giving her wrap-up speech.

"But before I let you all go, I did want to give you these souvenirs. My brother works for a firm that makes replica packs for schools and tourists. Life during The Blitz. The 1950s. Victorian times. You'll find them in all the museum gift shops. This is a special one he's created for my Soho tours."

She handed out the little plastic pouches.

Looking quickly through mine, I found, amongst other things, a folded-up menu from La Gioconda; a handbill advertising a gig at the 12 Bar—weathered and suitably torn; an old Gibson paper packet for a single guitar string (no string inside, just the envelope—but it was absolutely vintage and actually had been imprinted with the impression a thick low E string would have made through the paper); and some lyrics from an unknown song, scribbled onto an egg-and-coffee-stained paper napkin, in peacock blue fountain pen ink.

It was completely brilliant. I couldn't have told the difference between the originals, and these imitations. They were completely authentic-looking, right down to the choice of paper and the dyes and inks.

"Keep an eye out for my brother's other work in the museums," Lesley said. "And thank you all for coming."

I pulled my bag off my aching shoulder and dropped it onto the pavement beside a pole identifying the location as the bus stop for Beak Street and Hamleys Toy Store.

And there, right on time, was Arthur Braskey, on foot, strolling past the Karl Lagerfeld shop, which was just behind the red and black bus shelter.

Moment of truth.

"Do you have something for me, Mr. Figgis?"

"Nothing escapes your eagle eye," I replied. I showed him the envelope I'd collected at the Heddon Street telephone kiosk and took out the piece of paper.

"What is it?" he asked.

"Variation Seven," I said. "Page 1. For a connoisseur of Elgar, I'm surprised you didn't recognize it."

"Not all of us share your ability to read music, Mr. Figgis. And I listen. I don't pretend to believe it necessary to understand the process of transcription from paper score to instrument in order to enjoy the results. You have nothing more for me?"

"Nothing," I said, intent on maintaining my bluff.

"Are you sure?"

His eyes drilled into me.

If he knew what Isabel had given me at The Sheep and Shears...why wasn't he demanding to see what was in my bag?

But then, two things happened.

The first was that a guy on a bike mounted the pavement behind me and cruised past, slowing just long enough to grab the strap of my bag and yank it on board before he pedalled away, furiously.

I took off after him, shouting, but he was well ahead of me. He veered across traffic to the other side of Regent Street, disappeared the wrong way down Beak Street, and evaporated into Soho.

The second thing that happened was a black four-door Audi screeching up to the curb and temporarily blocking the bus lane where Arthur Braskey was standing. Two men leaped out of the back and grabbed Braskey and bundled him inside. They were most decidedly not the same two men who'd been following me around Soho all afternoon.

The doors of the Audi slammed shut, and the car, with Braskey inside, was gone in a matter of seconds.

CHAPTER THIRTEEN

The red brick building that houses The Blue Devil was built around 1838, and a music venue's been on the premises, in one form or another, since 1930. The club occupies the basement, the ground and first floors of the building, and the floor at the top is leased out to offices.

It was nearly four o'clock in the afternoon. The Thursday Lunch Show had ended two hours earlier, and the doors had closed at three. I knew there was a security guard on duty all day. I also knew the kitchen and bars needed to be restocked, and those deliveries often arrived in the afternoon, when the place was empty, and before the doors officially opened again for the evening.

There were two skids blocking the pavement on Wardour Street, one loaded with a shrink-wrapped shipment of Moet and top-end drinkables, the other with bottles of mixers and boxes of craft beer. And there was a burly guy in a baseball cap and work boots wheeling a loaded dolly up a portable ramp and through the front door. I followed him inside.

A security guard I didn't know quickly stepped forward to intercept me. "Sorry, sir, I'll have to ask you to leave. We're closed until six."

"Understood," I said. "I work here. Upstairs. I'm due back next Wednesday with my band. Jason Figgis." I showed him my driving license. "And you are...?"

"Devinder," he replied, checking his roster.

"I might be down as Jason Davey," I added.

"Haven't got you on my list," Devinder said. "As it's Thursday, October 18 today. And not Wednesday, October 24."

"My guys were here earlier," I said. "The lunchtime gig. If you give one of them a call, they'll vouch for me."

Devinder consulted his clipboard again, flipping several pages back. "Which one?" he asked.

"Try Ken Moss," I said. "He lives in Camden. He'll be home by now."

Devinder dialed him up on his mobile.

"Good afternoon," he said. "It's Dev from The Blue Devil. Sorry to bother you, mate, but there's a bloke here called Jackson Davies—"

"Jason Davey," I said.

Dev gave me a blank look as my sax player, deciding to be funny, denied all knowledge of my existence.

"Open the pod bay doors, Ken," I said, loudly. "I'm tired and I've had a really long day. And my feet are killing me."

***

Before it was The Blue Devil, the club was called Diamonds. It was a rock and roll mecca in the mid-1960s—*the* place to mingle—if you could get in.

Fifty years later—when I'd showed up with Rudy, Ken and Dave to audition for a full-time gig—the club was struggling. The main lounge was tatty-looking and in dire need of renovations. Backstage—which the punters never saw—was even worse: narrow hallways littered with mic stands and lights and bundled electrical cords, broken chairs and three-legged tables, stuff from behind the bar, cardboard boxes, wooden crates.

The best thing that could have happened would have been for Diamonds to have been put out of its misery. But then, Harry Parfitt, the club's accountant and a true jazz fan, decided to give it one more shot. He made the place over and gave it a brand new name: The Blue Devil. And Rudy, Ken, Dave and I were hired to work upstairs as the late-night house band.

The dressing rooms are still tiny and old and windowless and shabby. But at least they have private toilets and showers, thoughtfully added sometime last century.

Our dressing room's walls are bare brick, painted white. We have large mirrors with good lights, a sofa and some chairs, a small fridge and a rack for hanging clothes, if required—though we usually just show up in what we're going to wear onstage. And we each have lockers.

The door to the room is kept locked, and we all have keys.

I let myself in, and went straight to my locker—which wasn't locked—and which was next to the empty space in the corner where my sax player usually parked his bike when he rode in to work from Camden.

My leather buckle bag was there, deposited as instructed, after Ken had completed his grab-and-run stunt on Regent Street and cycled madly back into Soho before anyone could clock him.

I carried the bag over to the sofa and sat down. I lifted out the folder and had a good and proper look at what was in it, taking care not to mix up the order of any of the papers.

There were about a dozen sheets of musical manuscript, all slightly yellowed and printed with staff lines.

Some of the lines were hand-drawn. All of the pages contained hand-written notes—musical notes—long pieces, small fragments, some identifying parts for particular musical instruments, some just bars of melody, perhaps composed for a piano, or perhaps just scraps of ideas that had escaped from the composer's imagination and found their way onto the page.

There were lines of music that were x'd through or scribbled over.

There were faded tea stains and purple and blue crayon marks and brown ink scratches and grey pencil jottings.

I was holding the very essence of something that had come directly from the creative mind of Sir Edward Elgar. His thoughts, the actual process of his acts of composing. The marks that were the results of the connection between his hand and his mind.

I sat there for what seemed like a very long time, in awed silence.

I'd arranged for Ken to steal my bag because I didn't want to take the chance that Braskey's bloodhounds had witnessed me receiving it. If my bag was gone, so was my involvement in retrieving it for Braskey. End of story.

Except Arthur Braskey was now gone as well.

And it didn't take a lot of brain work to guess who'd manhandled him into the back of the black Audi in the northbound bus lane on Regent Street. The guy he'd sold the folio to.

I'd managed to catch the Audi's registration number as it sped away. I'd keyed it into my phone, along with the colour and the make. I hadn't done anything with the information. I wasn't sure I wanted to.

This was Soho. The edge of it, anyway. All I could think of was that end-of-film advice Jake Gittes got from his associate..."Forget it, Jake. It's Chinatown."

I didn't want to end up with my nose slashed. Or worse.

I very carefully put the Elgar papers back into my bag. I returned the bag to my locker.

And then I went home, to Angel.

***

I made myself some dinner—prawns in a white wine sauce with garlic and butter, with a couple of slices of crusty bread and a Caesar salad made with a bottled dressing because I hadn't had time to do a proper shop. The prawns were in the freezer. I'd picked up the bread and the lettuce on my way home. The wine was in the cupboard, left over from the last time Katey'd been 'round for a meal.

I sat down on my sofa with my dinner and looked at Variation VII—the single sheet of music I'd picked up in the Ziggy Stardust telephone kiosk.

How was this meant to be a clue? Everything else I'd been given by Marcus had fallen neatly into place once I'd identified the right people, decoded the message or followed the trail of breadcrumbs.

This single sheet of paper didn't appear to be anything except what it was: the first page of the published score for Variation VII. It wasn't even a copy of the original handwritten composition. It was just an ordinary printout, 1:1 time in C major, *Presto*.

I knew that Elgar had composed each of his fourteen variations with a particular individual who'd meant something to him in mind. He'd accomplished that on two levels. The first was a general impression of that individual's personality. The second was a musical reference to a specific thing that characterized that person—a laugh, a speech habit, a memorable event or conversation.

Variation VII was ascribed to "Troyte."

And who was "Troyte"?

In 1927, Elgar had written some descriptive notes about his *Enigma Variations*. Portions of those notes were included in a little thirty-six-page booklet, *My Friends Pictured Within*, which had been published by Novello and Company in 1947. What made the booklet more intimate than anything I could find on the internet—to me, anyway—was that each page contained a copy of Elgar's handwritten score, a photo of the person the music had been dedicated to, and a concise explanation of the connection, many of the words having come from Elgar himself.

I knew I had that little book somewhere in my flat.

There. On a shelf. Wedged between *Who's Who in Pop Radio*, a fabulous paperback by Peter Alex which contained photos and bio's of every DJ who could be heard in the UK in 1966 (onshore, offshore, Luxembourg, AFN, pirate and otherwise); and a copy of *Alternative London* from 1974 that I'd picked up at a market stall when I was eighteen, and which had caused my Granny Vera to speculate, somewhat fearfully, that I was on the verge of becoming an anarchist, as it contained nine pages of helpful information on how to be a squatter; useful hints on how to avoid deportation if you happened to be caught working illegally; and a paragraph that suggested you could circumvent parking regulations by carrying an Out of Order bag around with you and popping it over a meter wherever you wanted to leave your car.

I hauled out Sir Edward's opus and paged through it to Variation VII.

There he was—"Troyte".

And there was his picture.

And underneath the picture, was a caption: "Troyte Griffith".

What was the name of the guy who'd wanted to take my picture in the phone kiosk?

Griff.

It could have been a coincidence.

But I didn't think it was.

I went online and consulted Wikipedia.

Arthur Troyte Griffith, a Malvern architect and one of Elgar's firmest friends. The variation good-naturedly mimics his enthusiastic incompetence on the piano. It may also refer to an occasion when Griffith and Elgar were out walking and got caught in a thunderstorm. The pair took refuge in the house of Winifred Norbury, to which the next variation refers.

Griff had gone to great lengths to remind me about my grand entrance in Middlehurst on the opening night of our tour. An entrance that had been delayed by a heart-stopping thunderstorm.

What was Marcus trying to do? Make the people who were delivering his clues the actual physical equivalents of the people who'd originally inspired Elgar's variations?

It seemed to me that was exactly what he was doing.

I cued up a full performance, and listened. There's an introductory theme, followed by fourteen small pieces. The last of these acts as a grand finale. It's scored for an orchestra, and consists of two flutes (one doubling piccolo), two oboes, two clarinets in B♭, two bassoons, a contrabassoon, four horns in F, three trumpets in F, three trombones, a tuba, a timpani, a side drum, a triangle, a bass drum, some cymbals, an ad lib organ, and strings. The complete performance lasts a little under seventy minutes.

The first movement—the theme—is a musical portrait of Elgar himself. My introduction to Marcus, at the top of The Shard.

Variation I had been dedicated to the composer's wife, Caroline Alice. Marcus's first message to me—the one tucked inside the program from the Figs' tour—had directed me to Judy Galpin, who'd once been married to him.

Variation II was dedicated to Elgar's friend, Hew David Steuart-Powell, a well-known amateur pianist. My instructions had been to go to Tissington, where I was to collect the next clue from a stone wall. I remembered the music I'd heard as I'd got out of the car...someone playing the piano along with Herbie Hancock on "Cantaloupe Island". Not brilliantly. But not all that badly, either.

Variation III belonged to Richard Baxter Townshend—an Oxford don, sometime author and amateur actor. Tricia, at The Bakewell Tart, had made a point of telling us she'd graduated from Oxford, and that she was an actor, about to tour the Peak District with an amateur theatrical production of *The Buddy Holly Story*.

Variation IV was dedicated to "W.M.B."—a "country squire, gentleman and scholar"—otherwise known as William Meath Baker, the brother-in-law of Richard Baxter Townshend and the step-uncle of Elgar's muse, Dora Penny.

I still had the decoded message from the *Lollygobble* wheel Tricia had given me.

PICK UP TICKET IN NEWLYDALE FROM BEATRIX THE BAKER

Beatrix wasn't a baker—but she lived in a cottage that had once been the village bakery.

Variation V was dedicated to Richard Penrose Arnold, the son of the poet Matthew Arnold. Lesley Wharton, who'd guided us around Soho, was the daughter of Slade Wharton, a poet and lyricist.

Variation VI was simply ascribed to "Ysobel". Isabel Fitton had been one of Sir Edward's music students. She played the viola. As did Isabel from the tour, who'd deftly delivered the first third of Elgar's stolen folio to me at The Sheep and Shears. Isabel with no last name, who'd gamely stuck with me all afternoon and then disappeared, silently, with her two friends, just as Arthur Braskey had been bundled into the back seat of the black Audi.

And Variation VII. The nerdy-looking chap who'd steered me into the Ziggy Stardust telephone kiosk on Heddon Street, the guy who'd introduced himself to me as Griff and then had also vanished.

Why? Was it just a whim on Marcus's part? A bit of fun, engaging me in a game of *Guess Who: The Elgar Boxed Set,* from beyond the grave?

What was it he'd written in that note he'd left in the Proms program at The Sheep and Shears?

At the time, it hadn't seemed to me to be important at all. Of course, now it was. And I was really beginning to regret tearing up that note and flushing it down the toilet.

If you put all the clues together...

I knew it was there, buried in my mental Recycling Bin.

I shut my eyes and leaned back on my sofa, letting my arms and legs and my brain relax. I let my imagination take me back to the pub, to the Gents toilet, to the cubicle and the slip of paper with Marcus's handwritten message.

If you put all the clues together...
...you might discover the congruence in the divergence.

I grabbed a pen and my notebook and scribbled the words down before they dissipated, like your dreams when you first wake up in the morning.

I read the two lines again.

And then I went back to my laptop and consulted a couple of online dictionaries.

Congruence. A state of agreeing or coinciding. Harmony. Compatibility.
Divergence. A situation in which two things become different.

That was no bloody help at all.

I rang Angie, my sister. Professionally known as Taylor Feldspar and the author of a hugely successful cozy mystery series featuring catering whiz and amateur sleuth Jemima Fielding.

"What's another word for 'divergence'?" I asked.

"I'm in the middle of dispatching a victim with a poisoned paella," she said. "Why do you want to know?"

"I'm in the middle of solving a riddle to do with Sir Edward Elgar," I replied. "My crime's patriotic. Yours is...Iberian."

"You'll have to do better than that," Angie said. "Have you looked in the thesaurus?"

"I've looked in the dictionary," I said.

"You're clearly not a writer. One moment."

She went silent. And then she reeled off a list of words which, I assumed, meant loosely the same thing as "divergence".

"Hang on," I said, interrupting her. "What was the last one?"

"Variety."

"Before that."

"Variation."

"Variation," I repeated. "Thank you. If I put all the clues together I'll discover the similarities in the variations."

"Sorry...?" said my sister.

"You're a life-saver. Put some mussels in your paella and give your victim a fatal shellfish allergy."

"Speak for yourself," said my sister. "Goodbye."

I disconnected.

What were the similarities in all of the people Marcus had arranged to deliver my clues?

Just like Elgar's variations, they all seemed to be individuals who'd actually played an important part in Marcus Merritt's life.

As I got up to make myself a fresh mug of coffee, I remembered the envelope from Griff that Isabel had slipped into my jacket pocket.

It was a greeting card. Gold, featuring a bunch of balloons tied with silver strings. The balloons were circles of varying sizes, cut from metallic paper—purple, scarlet, icy blue, bronze and indigo—and fastened to the cover with tiny pieces of double-sided tape, creating a 3D effect.

And scribbled inside, in Marcus's familiar hand, was a message:

You are invited for lunch
Saturday, October 20, 1.00 pm
Emil Wojeck
111 Banting Road
Sutton

No brain teasers. No codes or convoluted directions.

Just a simple instruction.

My mobile was ringing.

I didn't recognize the number and there was no name attached to it.

"Hello Jason. It's Matilda."

The driver from the middle of the night in Newlydale. Well well. "Not your real name," I said, humorously.

"I told you. It is." She paused. "Matilda Braskey."

That was...surprising. "Not his wife..." I guessed.

"Hardly," she said, with a small laugh. "I'm his granddaughter."

CHAPTER FOURTEEN

I knew Arthur Braskey had been married a couple of times. The last had been to a stripper named Tatiana Melnic, who'd also gone by the name Holly Medford. She was the dancer who'd had £10,000 stolen from her locker at Cha-Cha's. But Matilda was, quite obviously, the result of a much earlier relationship.

"So, he's got you working as his driver."

"After what Marc Merritt did, he didn't trust anyone else," Matilda replied.

"I don't blame him," I said. I didn't particularly trust Matilda—I'd learned, after my dealings with Holly Medford, that anyone who had anything to do with Arthur Braskey was best kept at arm's length. And Matilda was no exception.

"I saw what happened this afternoon on Regent Street," she said. "I saw my grandfather talking to you, and then that man on the bike stole your bag. Did it have the Elgar collection in it?"

"It didn't," I said. "Just a bottle of orange juice, a bottle of water, a mostly-eaten bag of Maltesers...and a souvenir pack from the tour. The bag had sentimental value. But...no loss, really."

Matilda didn't say anything for a moment. And then:

"You saw the two men who manhandled my grandfather into the black car."

"I did. And I got the registration number and the make, if that helps. I haven't done anything with it. I'm assuming they're connected to whoever your grandfather sold the folio to?"

Again, a pause.

And then: "He told you about that?"

"When we met up in Soho Square. It wasn't difficult to work out. He's got money problems. He's selling off bits and pieces from his private collections to try and make those problems go away. Marcus threw a huge spanner into the works."

"The collector my grandfather sold the folio to is Igor Plaksin. A Russian. I've met him. And he's not someone you'd want to cross. He thinks my grandfather's reneged on his promise. He's not a happy man."

"I can imagine," I said. "Actually, I'd rather not imagine."

"Plaksin called me half an hour ago. Using my grandfather's phone. He let me speak to Granddad. He let me see him. He's alive. He's all right. But he's very frightened."

I found that difficult to believe. Nothing fazed Arthur Braskey. Still, I'd never witnessed him in a situation like this—someone with more control than he had, running the whole show.

"Granddad told Plaksin the truth. Marc stole the collection from him, and that he—my Granddad—had absolutely nothing to do with it, no advance knowledge, nothing. Marc acted on his own. And Granddad has no idea where the folio is now, but he was doing his best to try and locate it—by following you."

"Oh great," I said. "Well, I don't have it. Would you mind calling Plaksin back and letting him know that?"

"I will," Matilda said. "But that won't stop him. My grandfather told him you're the person Marc chose to retrieve the folio. So when you do eventually find it...you will, of course, hand it over to Plaksin. My grandfather's life depends on it."

"If I do give it to him," I said, "can you count on Plaksin letting your grandfather go?"

"I don't really have any choice, do I?" Matilda said.

I actually felt sorry for her. Not for Arthur Braskey, who'd subjected me to a beating and abandoned me in a disused warehouse where I'd come very close to dying. I'm not a hateful person. But Arthur Braskey could override that in me. Matilda seemed decent—as far as someone who shared his genetic imprint could be.

"Can I ask you about something else?" I said, before she could disconnect. "There was a fire in Soho, in Denmark Place, in 1980. Talking about it makes your grandfather uncomfortable. I think he might have had something to do with it. And Marcus, too. Did either of them ever mention anything about it to you?"

"No," Matilda said, thinking. "No, nothing at all."

"OK," I said. "Do you mind if I ask about your parents? Who they are?"

"Are you just being nosy?" she replied, "or does it have something to do with the Elgar collection?"

"I'm just being nosy," I said.

"I'm sure, given that you're a private investigator—well-schooled, if not entirely sanctioned—you have the resources to look that up."

***

Generations is a family-tree research site I pay for with a yearly subscription. Part of that's because I'm obsessed with discovering my own ancestry, as there are any number of ongoing mysteries attached to my DNA that I'm rather keen to resolve. It's also because Generations is my favourite go-to destination for tracking down the details of other peoples' lives.

The website very kindly supplied me with a plethora of hints, clues and documents related to Arthur Braskey, his marriages and his offspring. Braskey's first wife was Doreen Dyball, whom he'd married in 1955, when they were both twenty. Three children had emerged from that union. A daughter, Cassandra Rose, who'd been born five months after Doreen and Arthur had made their relationship official. A son, Stuart Edward, who'd come along two years after that. And another son, Leslie Francis, in 1959.

Given that Matilda's last name was Braskey, it seemed a good starting point to assume that her father was either Stuart or Leslie. I did a search of the England & Wales Civil Registration Birth Index for Matilda Braskey, and located her in the calendar quarter for April-June 1980.

The birth indexes from that era are also very handy in that they helpfully list the child's mother's maiden name. In Matilda's case, it was Braskey.

Had either Stuart or Leslie married a cousin or some other person whose last name was, coincidentally, Braskey?

They had not.

Stuart had married Sophie Hill. And Leslie's wife was Debra Dinsdale.

There could have been an error when the clerk had entered the information in the system. But what was more likely was that Matilda's mother—whose last name was Braskey—wasn't married to Matilda's father. And that could only have been Cassandra. Following the prescribed process, Matilda's father had not given his permission to be listed on his daughter's birth record. And so Matilda's mother's surname was entered instead.

I thought about ordering a copy of Matilda's birth certificate. I had all of the pertinent information and it would have been a simple thing to enter it all into the online General Register Office form, pay my fee and have it dispatched on the next working day from receipt of order. Which, given the time—I checked my watch; it was now nearly midnight—would be Friday for the receipt of the order, and Monday for Next Working Day delivery. There was an option for a Royal Mail Saturday 9 am delivery, but I needed to have put in my order before four that afternoon.

I rang Matilda Marie Braskey back.

"When's your birthday?" I asked. I was feeling brash.

Matilda laughed. "Couldn't you find me?"

"April-June Quarter," I said. "1980." And I provided the District Name, and the Volume and Page numbers.

"April 3, 1980," she confirmed. "Anything else?"

"Send me a copy of your birth certificate...?"

"You really are being nosy."

"I'll get it anyway," I said. "Anyone can order a copy of someone's birth certificate in the UK, as long as you know the correct details—which are a matter of public record. I'm just impatient. Don't want to wait 'til Monday."

Moments later a screen shot of Matilda's birth certificate arrived as an attachment to a text on my phone.

"As you can see," Matilda said, "my mum's name is Cassandra. She wasn't married to my father. I have no idea who my father is. I actually have no idea where Cassandra is, either. She abandoned me when I was a baby and she's never bothered to get back in touch. I was raised by my uncle and aunt—Stuart and Sophie. Happy now?"

"Very," I said. "Thank you."

It was interesting—to me, anyway—that Arthur Braskey's eldest offspring had disappeared when Matilda was an infant.

I emailed Matilda's birth certificate to myself so that I could look at it properly on my laptop and not have to squint at it on my phone. The details confirmed what Matilda had just told me, but there was one fact she hadn't mentioned: where she'd been born. That line usually has the name of a hospital and its location. In Matilda's case, it was just an address. Further down the page, there was a space for the mother's usual address, but only if it was different from the place where the child had been born. That line was blank. Cassandra Braskey had given birth at home.

And where Cassandra had been living on April 3, 1980, was Number 27, Denmark Street.

CHAPTER FIFTEEN

I WAS PRETTY SURE the upstairs accommodations in Denmark Street forty years earlier weren't all that suitable for living in, although when they'd originally been built in the 17th and 18th centuries, they were exactly that—regular houses with front doors, stairs, reception rooms, and bedrooms. By the time Matilda Braskey had been born in April 1980, they'd largely been converted into offices and workshops. And some of those were in pretty rough shape.

Over the years, I knew there had been some notable and not-so-notable people who'd called Tin Pan Alley home, at least temporarily. Aside from David Bowie and his ambulance parked outside La Gioconda, and a well-documented Sex Pistols tenancy down the road, Sara and Keren from Bananarama had lived in the room above the Sex Pistols' rehearsal space at Number 6 for nearly a year. And there was a hopeful poet named Lizzie who'd used the rickety balcony above the old forge at the back of Number 26 as a bedroom, until a guy named Andy Preston came along and turfed her out and turned the old workshop into the club that eventually became the 12 Bar.

Number 27 was Grade II Listed, and was next door to the 12 Bar. It was built in the late 17th century as a three-storey terraced house. In the 1950s, Number 27 had been the home of the Suffolk Dairy, a cafe where you could regularly run into the musicians, comedians, publishers, songwriters, agents, and managers who populated the road. By 1975, it was derelict. Then, in 1978, Andy Preston arrived, and turned the basement—once home to a minicab company—into a guitar workshop. He eventually expanded up to the main floor and then the three floors above that, until his firm had taken over the entire building. It's now where Hanks Guitars is located, if you're looking for a familiar cue.

I had no idea how long Cassandra had been living there before Matilda was born, and for how long afterwards, but one thing was pretty clear to me. If that's where she was staying on August 16, 1980, she'd have been just down the road from the Denmark Place fire that her dad, Arthur Braskey, didn't want to talk about.

***

I still hadn't slept well.

I'd assumed, after Thursday's exhaustive walk around Soho, that I would fall into bed and stay there until morning, dead to the world. I'd assumed that all of the anxiety and the bad dreams that had haunted me since Marcus's death had been left behind in Derbyshire.

I was wrong.

I did fall asleep quickly. But then, three hours later, I was jerked awake by whatever mechanism controls your subconscious when you have bad dreams. It was 2009 and I was back at my house in Hampstead Garden Suburb. The house was on fire and I was running in through the front door, trying to find Em, my wife. There was so much black smoke, and there were flames in the front room. I got partway up the stairs, but I couldn't breathe and I couldn't see and I had to turn around before I passed out. I stumbled back outside where I was rescued by a fireman. But they couldn't save Em. Her body was found by the bedroom window upstairs, covered in soot.

All of it was true, and the over-and-over-again dreams I'd had about it, back when it had actually happened, had gradually stopped. Once in a while, I'd go there again, in my sleep, but instead of the desperation, the terror and the choking, I'd see the house from the outside, in daylight, the door wide open, downstairs windows smashed out, red bricks stained black from the smoke. And, in those dreams, I'd reach a sort-of understanding. I was calm. And sad. The grief was still there—it always is, it doesn't ever go away. But you get better at dealing with it. And those dreams were how my unconscious self-checked in with my waking self, to remind me how far I'd come in accepting what had happened.

Why, then, had I woken up at 2 am, choking and coughing and stumbling through the imagined smoke on the stairs in the front hall of my house? Why was my dreamstate taking me back there now?

I got up, went to the toilet, got myself a glass of cold sparkling water from the fridge and sat on the sofa to try and make sense of it all.

It had to be the other fire. The one in Denmark Place, August 16, 1980. Something about that was obviously triggering for me.

I've been involved with other fires since Em died. The worst was aboard the *Star Sapphire*, the cruise ship where I'd been working as an entertainer in 2012. That one really had nearly killed me when the *Sapphire* herself had ended up rolling over and sinking. And I'd not be telling the truth if I didn't admit I had nightmares about that for about two years afterwards as well. But that fire hadn't resulted in any deaths. In fact, I'd actually saved a couple of lives—one of them being Katey. In a way, it had given me closure for the fire that had killed Em. It had shown me how to forgive myself for the things I had no power to change.

I needed to find out what had happened to Cassandra Braskey. And I needed to learn more about that fire in Denmark Place. But I also needed to be at Ardwick House, to rehearse our second set list with my band.

***

We were planning to start up our regular gig at The Blue Devil on the following Wednesday, at our usual time, 11 pm until 3 am.

I knew I wasn't on top form. And so did Ken, Rudy and Dave.

"Sorry," I said, as I fucked up for the third time.

"You all right, mate?" Rudy asked.

"Not really," I said.

They didn't know much about what had happened to me since our last rehearsal. I'd been economical with the details. And when I'd asked Ken to grab my bag at the end of the Soho walking tour, he'd done it, no questions asked.

It was time to tell them. I started with my meeting with Marcus at The Shard. And ended with Arthur Braskey being manhandled into the back seat of the black Audi at the bus stop on Regent Street.

"Jesus," Dave said, when I'd finished.

"Poor Marcus," said Rudy. "Poor you."

"If I'd known your bag was filled with priceless bits of Elgar," Ken said, "I'd have added an extra touch of spit and polish to my okibiki smash-and-grab."

I smiled. "Did you look inside?"

"I did, yeah. But all I saw was loose pages of handwritten music. I thought you'd had a clear-out."

"I owe you one, Ken. Thank you."

"Not a problem, mate."

"You don't look good at all," Rudy said.

"I'm not good," I said.

"There's only one thing for it," Dave said. "'Robbin' the Cradle'."

We have a lexicon of tunes that we often fall back on when we need a break. They're good for dissipating tension or, at the very least, cracking a smile. And they're outside our usual realm—nothing to do with jazz. Mostly they're songs that nobody else has ever heard of. "Robbin' the Cradle" was one of those—a North American one-hit wonder from 1959, written and sung by Tony Bellus, who was then a twenty-two-year-old accordion-player from Chicago.

It's rockabilly and it's two minutes and thirty seconds long, and it's a lament about an older guy with a younger girlfriend and all the grief he gets from his mates about their relationship. The other stars of this really catchy, contagious number are the backing band—pianist Ray Stevens (you know him from "Ahab the Arab" and other novelty hits), a drummer (Nelson Rogers) and a bass player (Jimmy Estes), and two guys on guitar who ended up with fairly major careers in the business: Jerry Reed and Joe South.

We'd retooled the tune to fit our sax, drums, guitar and keyboards. I usually sang lead and Rudy and Dave provided the background vocals.

It was a good distraction that afternoon, and it did make me feel marginally better, especially as we extended it by an additional three minutes because I didn't want it to stop.

When we finally finished, there was a timid knock on the heavy wooden door at the far end of the studio.

"Annoying the neighbours again," Rudy said, getting up to see who it was.

It was a woman who looked to be in her mid-seventies...perhaps a little older. She had very fine features and white hair drawn straight back into a tidy bun, and she was wearing a full skirt and a loose top and what my mum would call "sensible" shoes.

"I'm so sorry to interrupt," she said, with a beautiful smile, "but I overheard you playing, and you brought back such a lovely memory. I haven't actually heard that song since I was a child."

"Number 25 on the *Billboard* Hot 100 in August 1959," Dave provided, helpfully.

"Which was exactly when my sister and I were on a summer holiday with our parents in Canada. And we heard that song on the radio. We were so excited, my sister immediately went to Woolworths and bought the record, and we listened—and danced—to it, incessantly." She smiled again, and extended her hand to me. "Florence."

"Jason," I said.

"Do you dance?" she inquired.

"You'll regret asking him that," Rudy said.

Florence's eyes were filled with mischief. "I'd love a little dance with you, Jason, if you could play it again."

"Oh dear," said Dave.

I do, as a matter of fact, dance. And I am quite good and I know all the moves. Rockabilly, swing, boogie-woogie...and whatever you want to call that energetic rhythmic thing that teenagers launched themselves into after popular music changed forever in the late-1950s.

I took off my guitar. Dave improvised what I would have played, on his piano. Ken coaxed his sax into a reasonable facsimile of Dave's original keyboard contribution. Rudy, on the drums, took over my vocals. And Florence and I did a two-minute rockabilly mash-up that left Florence laughing, and me completely winded.

"You are amazing," I said, collapsing onto my chair.

"I belong to a dancing club," Florence said. "All seniors. All exceedingly fit."

"Far more than me," I said, trying not to cough.

"I'm out of breath just watching you," Dave said.

Florence gave us a little gesture that was a cross between a curtsy and a bow.

"And now," she said, "I shall leave you. Thank you for a most entertaining interlude."

She had a pocket in her skirt, and from it she withdrew an envelope and something small—about four inches long—wrapped up in white tissue paper.

"For you, Jason," she said, placing both in my hands. "Ta-ra."

She left.

Was this my next clue? Next up in the sequence was Variation VIII. Winifred Norbury, one of the secretaries of the Worcester Philharmonic Society, in whose house Sir Edward Elgar and his friend Troyte Griffith had sought shelter from that thunderstorm.

This lady's name wasn't Winifred.

I unwrapped the object in the white tissue paper first. It was a single, very unusual earring, the kind that goes through a pierced lobe: a golden snake, semi-coiled and ready to pounce, with a ruby red jewelled droplet dripping from its mouth.

Rudy, Ken and Dave expressed their admiration. I wondered if the gold was paint, and if the ruby was glass. I had no idea what it was supposed to mean.

I wrapped it up again, and put it in my pocket, and then opened the envelope.

Inside was a sheet of paper that contained a logic problem, the kind you get on IQ tests.

A train leaves London at 5.30 am and is travelling at 80 km/hr. Aboard the train is a family of six: Peter, Susan, Robert, Ellen, Toby, and Mary Ann.

Their occupations are: singer, landscape painter, personal manager, shop assistant, farmer and train engineer. The engineer is driving the train.

The farmer is the grandfather of Mary Ann, who is a singer.

The landscape painter, Ellen, is married to Peter.

Robert, the personal manager, is married to the shopkeeper.
Susan is the mother of Toby and Mary Ann.
There are two married couples in the family.
What are everyone's professions and relationships?
Who is driving the train?
Who knows the answer to Elgar's enigma?
Ask the singer.

Who knew the answer to Elgar's enigma? How in God's name was I supposed to work that one out? Mary Ann was the bloody singer—but who the hell was she?

I bolted out of the room. Where had Florence gone?

I pulled open the front door and raced down the path to the road. I looked left and right, frantically, but there was no sign of the fine-featured lady with the white hair.

I buzzed Ardwick House's office and was re-admitted. I went across the entry hall, to the small room where a young man with long hair, an earring and an earnest face was typing something into a computer.

"There was an elderly woman here," I said. "White hair, wearing a flowered skirt."

The young man disengaged himself from his screen. "Yes, she was upstairs in the Blue Room. With her accompanist. You've just missed them, actually."

I knew the Blue Room. It was tiny. It had a baby grand piano squeezed into one corner, with just about enough space for two more performers and their music stands.

"I don't suppose you could give me their names...and details."

It was a long shot. I knew Ardwick's rules. They traded on discretion. It was one of the reasons why their expensive rehearsal rooms were in such high demand in my industry.

"Sorry," said the young man, with an apologetic shrug.

"Understood. Thanks."

I wasn't sure what I'd hoped to accomplish, even if I had caught up to Florence. She was only the messenger.

I went back to the main rehearsal hall and Rudy, Ken and Dave's questioning faces.

"This," I said, showing them the piece of paper.

"I hate those train problems," said Rudy. "I could have joined Mensa if they hadn't put that on the membership test."

"Jason once tried to join Mensa," Ken said. "He gave up when he realized he couldn't fret his way in with six strings and a dream."

I looked at him.

"So," said Dave, expertly changing the subject, "what does the last question mean—who knows the answer to Elgar's enigma?"

"All fourteen variations," I said, "plus the theme, are widely believed to involve a hidden melody. A lot of musicians have tried to figure out what that is. I don't think anybody's actually come up with a definitive answer that everyone can agree on."

"There is no secret melody," said Rudy. "It's Elgar's last laugh. A joke he played on the world."

Given Elgar's penchant for games and riddles, Rudy might have had a point. What better way to leave your mark in the world and guarantee notoriety than to compel scholars to run around in circles, trying to solve a problem that had no answer, in perpetuity?

"More to the point," said Ken. "Is there a woman named Florence who's associated with Variation VIII?"

"Not as far as I know," I said, getting out my phone. "Variation VIII's dedicated to Winifred Norbury."

I looked it up, nevertheless.

"Variation VIII," I said, reading aloud, "is less a portrait of Winifred Norbury than of Sherridge, the 18th-century house where Winifred lived with her sister."

"Her sister's name being...?"

"Florence," I said, putting down my phone.

***

I was exhausted. And my guys needed some rest time and dinner before they were off to the club for their regular Friday night gig.

I loaded my guitars into my car and drove back towards Angel. It was the middle of rush hour and there'd been an accident somewhere and it took me about an hour to go six miles, skirting Hampstead Heath and then heading south along Holloway Road.

But the stop-start crawl through the traffic gave me time to reflect on what had happened that afternoon, and what was bothering me about it.

If Florence had been dispatched by Marcus, how could he possibly have known I'd be there, at Ardwick House, on that day, and at that time?

Everything up until that point had been planned in advance, and had been more or less predictable. My train journey to Derbyshire—Marcus had supplied me with the ticket. Newlydale—Marcus had sent Judy the instructions and Judy merely had to wait for me to turn up. Tissington—Marcus had put the clue into the stone wall and again, I just had to turn up to collect it. The Bakewell Tart—Marcus had hand-delivered the envelope, and Tricia simply had to wait for me to appear.

Likewise, Beatrix Cummings. And then, the four-hour trek around Soho, where Isabel just needed to transfer the folio into my bag at The Sheep and Shears, while we were having lunch. And Marcus had left me that note instructing me to stay 'til the end of the tour...which I had...and that had guaranteed I'd be on hand when Griff had delivered his single sheet of paper and Isabel had given me the invitation to tea in Sutton on Sunday.

How could Marcus possibly have known when I would be at Ardwick House rehearsing? We'd originally been booked into the studio for Wednesday, but I'd got Rudy to change that to Friday while I was in Newlydale.

I'd told no one. The only people who knew my schedule were my band, and the guy in the office who looked after bookings.

I took advantage of a red traffic light and a line of cars going nowhere to make three calls.

Dave was still living on his own after his divorce from Helen, and he assured me he hadn't discussed our revised rehearsal day with anyone.

Ken's partner, Patrick, knew about Ken's schedule, but neither one of them could recall mentioning it to anyone, either.

It was the same with Rudy and his wife.

I made a fourth call.

"Good afternoon, Ardwick House, this is Joseph."

I guessed it was the young man with the earring I'd spoken to earlier.

"Just checking," I said, after telling him who I was. "If someone were to ring you up and ask if I had a booking there, would you give out that information?"

"Absolutely not," Joseph replied. "As I assured you earlier, all booking details are strictly confidential."

"OK," I said. "What about if I were to ask you exactly when the elderly woman in the flowered skirt had made arrangements to use the Blue Room?"

There was a moment of silence while Joseph weighed up whether or not he was allowed to reveal that tidbit of information.

"You told me she'd been upstairs with her accompanist," I reminded him.

"But they'd already finished their session," he replied, "and they'd left."

"I'll make it easy for you," I said. "Last minute booking?"

Joseph paused. "Yes."

"Made after I'd arrived?"

"Yes."

"Over the phone?"

"Yes," Joseph confirmed.

"Thank you," I said, disconnecting.

The line of cars was creeping forward again. Florence had only needed to be in the same place as me to deliver her envelope. I could have been anywhere in London—or out of London, for that matter. Someone would have just needed to keep tabs on me to make the appropriate arrangements. If the Blue Room at Ardwick House hadn't been available, Florence could have come up with some other excuse to visit. Worst case scenario, she could have just waited outside until we were finished rehearsing, and approached me then.

I waited until there was another red light, and then double-checked the weather for Derbyshire in October on my phone. It had been raining in Tissington, on and off, for three days before I got there. But when I'd pulled the paper bag and the envelope out of the chink in the wall, they weren't even damp. And neither were the papers inside the envelope.

They couldn't have been there for much more than a few hours.

Someone other than Arthur Braskey was obviously keeping an eye on me.

CHAPTER SIXTEEN

THE FIRST THING I needed to do when I got home was sleep. Which I did, for about six hours, after I'd finished some leftover dinner from the fridge.

It was midnight when I woke up again. I was caught in that weird twilight when everyone else who's sane has gone to bed, and you've got the world to yourself. I love being wide awake when everyone else is tucked up in bed. I've often wondered if it has something to do with the time I was born. A few minutes past 10 pm, according to my mother. All that work, pushing my way out, and there I was, eyes wide open, wondering what was going to happen next. I'm a normally night person, well-equipped to handle our late hours at The Blue Devil. But this past week had thrown everything into chaos. And now I was just trying to get some normality back into my life.

I decided to try and solve Marcus's logic problem.

I'm all right with logic, as long as I can create a grid and colour in the squares.

I hunted down a packet of highlighters, and started drawing.

A train leaves London at 5.30 am and is travelling at 80 km/hr. Aboard the train is a family of six: Peter, Susan, Robert, Ellen, Toby, and Mary Ann.

Their occupations are: singer, landscape painter, personal manager, shop assistant, farmer and train engineer. The engineer is driving the train.

The farmer is the grandfather of Mary Ann, who is a singer.

The landscape painter, Ellen, is married to Peter.

Robert, the personal manager, is married to the shopkeeper.
Susan is the mother of Toby and Mary Ann.
There are two married couples in the family.
What are everyone's professions and relationships?
Who is driving the train?
Who knows the answer to Elgar's enigma?
Ask the singer.

An hour later, I'd worked out everything except the last question, *Who knows the answer to Elgar's enigma?*

Peter, the farmer, was Mary Ann and Toby's grandfather.

Ellen, the landscape painter, was married to Peter—which made her Mary Ann and Toby's grandmother.

Susan, the shop assistant, was married to Robert, the personal manager, which made them Mary Ann and Toby's parents. Robert was Peter and Ellen's son.

Mary Ann was the singer—that clue had been supplied.

And Toby was driving the train.

So what did it all mean? How was I supposed to ask the singer, when I had no idea who she actually was? And what the hell did it have to do with where I was going to locate the second part of Arthur Braskey's stolen folio?

***

I still couldn't sleep.

It was that fire in Denmark Place.

I've got a subscription to the British Newspaper Archive, which is incredibly useful if you're investigating people—and events—that go back into recent history.

I started looking for all of the stories about the fire in all of the papers for August 16, 1980, and the days that followed.

Isabel had been right. There was virtually nothing at the time.

There was, however, quite a lot that had been written and published since.

In 1980, Denmark Place was a rundown alleyway backing onto the buildings on the north side of the slightly more respectable Denmark Street. It was home to a variety of different establishments, including a couple of unlicensed bars occupying the top two floors at Number 18.

Because the bars were unlicensed, there weren't many safety measures in place. Windows had been boarded over, the staircases were dodgy at best, and apparently the only way you could get access was to stand in the alley outside and shout up to someone at an open window, who would then toss you down the key to the door. There was, apparently, another door on Denmark Street that led through to a tiny courtyard and a second set of stairs, but that door was bolted shut.

The club on the top floor of Number 18 was called The Spanish Rooms, or El Hueco. It had a jukebox and a bar and was filled with a mix of British, Irish, Jamaicans, and South Americans who all knew one another. Underneath El Hueco, on the first floor, was Rodo's, or El Dandy, a salsa club which was particularly popular among Colombians who worked in the hospitality industry, came off-shift late and wanted somewhere to socialize after everywhere else was closed. An empty space on the ground floor was used as overnight storage for trolleys belonging to street vendors selling hot dogs.

According to the sparse reports at the time, there were more than 150 people crammed into the two clubs at around three o'clock in the morning on August 16. That was when a small-time criminal named John Thompson, who had a drinking problem as well as a temper, decided that he'd been shortchanged by a bartender in The Spanish Rooms. He got into a fight and was kicked out of the club. Angry and drunk, Thompson had located a two-gallon container in the alley outside. Then, not being the brightest light in the string, he'd got a taxi to take him to a petrol station in Camden that was open all night. There, he'd bought a gallon of petrol and put it into the container, and then he'd taken a taxi back to Denmark Place. He'd poured the petrol through the mail slot in the door of Number 18, followed by a lit piece of paper, and then he'd scarpered.

I found a report written by a former London firefighter who described what had happened next. The petrol had exploded and rapidly ignited the wooden staircase. Flames and super-heated gases flew up in a fireball to the top of the building, destroying the main entrance and the exits. A few of the 150 people trapped in the two clubs found a way out, smashing windows and leaping into the alley below. Others managed to get down into the little enclosed courtyard and broke into the back of the music shop on Denmark Street, where they were trapped behind the security shutters.

Crews from the nearby Soho Fire Station on Shaftesbury Avenue were alerted at about half-past three, as well as firefighters from Euston, which was a little further away to the north and, finally, the station at Manchester Square, in Marylebone. The Soho crew, entering Denmark Place, immediately encountered a distressed and injured man, who told them there were a lot of people trapped in the burning building. The firemen had trouble breaking through the bolted door in the alley but once they got it open, they encountered smoke and flames that were growing exponentially. They also witnessed survivors, who, despite being injured, scattered anonymously into the night.

Over on Denmark Street, the crews from Euston had broken in through the music shop and out, through its back door, into the enclosed courtyard. They met the Soho firemen on the stairs going up to the two clubs. Together, they fought the fire, which was put out in about two hours. The death count was initially reported as eight—including one body found on the outside staircase, another on the landing, and a third just before the entrance to the clubs. The toll climbed to thirteen as the firemen entered The Spanish Rooms on the second floor.

In the end, it proved to be incredibly difficult to determine the exact number of fatalities, as the fireball had spread so rapidly that it had caught people where they were standing or sitting. Others had tried to escape but had been unable to open windows or doors. The bodies were so badly burned it was impossible to tell whether they were men or women. Some were reduced to ash. Some were fused together. The final count was thirty-seven, but it took four pathologists and three dentists two months to identify all of the victims.

The estimate of 150 patrons was a guess by a local policeman who was familiar with both clubs. The true count of people who were actually there at the time of the fire was never determined. Officially, fifty people were recorded as having escaped, and of those, thirty were treated at hospitals for injuries, including serious burns.

There was a reluctance on the part of those who'd survived to come forward with information. Speculation in the papers was that many were living and working in the country illegally, or were known to police, but this was never proved. It was determined almost immediately that the fire had been deliberately set, and *The Times* reported that police might look at the possibility of rivalry between international drug dealers, a grudge attack between businesses, or even the possibility of "the intricate web of South American politics."

Police appealed for survivors to come forward to help with their inquiries, and less than two weeks later, John Thompson was arrested. Among those providing statements to the police were the attendant who'd sold the petrol to Thompson at the all-night station, and the taxi driver who'd taken him back to Denmark Place. In early 1981, he was found guilty at the Old Bailey, and sentenced to life.

After the initial flurry of coverage in the press, the fire seemed to have been largely forgotten. The feeling at the time was that the thirty-seven victims were somehow unworthy of attention. They just weren't important. There was never a formal inquiry. Even the court case didn't attract much attention, mostly because, next door at the Old Bailey, the Yorkshire Ripper was on trial.

I found a 2012 blog from Matt Brown at *Londonist*, recalling the fire at Denmark Place and referencing it as a Forgotten Disaster. The piece attracted an avalanche of comments, from people who were regulars at the clubs, who'd made plans to be there that night but had either left early, or changed their minds about going; others from friends and relatives of the victims who'd died, many of whom were still struggling to find out details about what had happened.

The comments led to connections and connections to actions, and three years later—and thirty-five years after the tragedy—all thirty-seven victims were at last given names, published in the *Independent* by reporter Simon Usborne. To go along with it, Simon told their stories—and, in doing so, gave them back their humanity. And, finally, the momentum was begun for a memorial plaque which, in 2018, was still only being discussed, but which, I can tell you, came to fruition in 2022.

I emerged from the research feeling like I'd just run some kind of marathon. I was drained. I'd known nothing about the fire. I didn't recall my parents ever mentioning it, though, of course, they must have known about it, because Denmark Street was so much a part of their lives. I also knew that Marcus Merritt most probably had nothing to do with the actual fire, although he had to have been nearby in order to have arrived home smelling of smoke.

Perhaps he'd actually been in one of the clubs, and was one of the lucky few to escape.

Perhaps he'd been there with Cassandra Braskey, and that was why Arthur Braskey was so reluctant to talk about it.

It was, by then, about 6 am. I was exhausted. I needed to sleep.

I logged off my laptop, and went to bed.

Before I dropped off to sleep, I reconfirmed, in my mind, the one thing that had become abundantly clear. In all of the reports, and in all of the followup narratives and discussions and remembrances, neither Marcus Merritt, nor Cassandra Braskey, had ever been mentioned.

CHAPTER SEVENTEEN

I woke up in a panic.

What day was it?

What time?

My mind muzzled by sleep, I reached for my phone.

It was Saturday.

It was 11.30 am.

And I'd nearly forgotten about the card Isabel had slipped into my jacket pocket at the end of the walking tour.

It was there, lying open on the little table beside my bed.

You are invited for lunch
Saturday, October 20, 1.00 pm
Emil Wojeck
111 Banting Road
Sutton

I leaped out of bed, brewed myself a mug of very strong French press coffee, and headed for the shower.

Following Marcus's pattern, Florence—who was representing Variation VIII in Elgar's collection of compositions—ought to have delivered a clue that pointed me towards Variation IX. Except, she hadn't. Florence's clue seemed to have nothing whatsoever to do with Elgar at all. It was all about a family aboard a train, and identifying how they were related. Only the last line had anything to do with Elgar.

Who knows the answer to Elgar's enigma?

And I had no idea at all where I was going to find the solution to that—other than being told to ask someone named Mary Ann.

As for Griff's invitation...my educated guess was that Emil Wojeck was going to turn out to be the clue Florence should have delivered, but hadn't.

Elgar's Variation IX is exceptionally well-known. Ascribed to "Nimrod", it's often played at funerals—including Princess Diana's and, more recently, that of Prince Philip. And, always, every year, on Remembrance Sunday, it's performed by the massed bands at the Cenotaph in London's Whitehall. "Nimrod" opened our 2012 Olympic games, and composer Hans Zimmer threaded his own adaptation of it throughout the 2017 film, *Dunkirk*.

The reason it's called "Nimrod" is because of Augustus J. Jaeger, who was the music editor at Novello & Co, the London publisher of my little Elgar bible, *My Friends Pictured Within*. In the Old Testament, Nimrod is described as "a mighty hunter before the Lord." The German word for "hunter" is Jäger.

Augustus Jaeger was one of Elgar's closest friends and confidants, providing advice and criticism throughout his career. Elgar was prone to bouts of depression, and at one point in his life was contemplating giving up composing altogether. Augustus Jaeger paid him a visit and convinced him to keep going.

I hadn't been given a phone number for Emil Wojeck, just his address in Sutton: 111 Banting Road.

I had looked online for more information about him, but I hadn't been able to find out much. Other than the fact that "Wojeck" might have been a variation of one of the oldest and the fourth most common surnames in Poland—and that it was derived from the word *wojak*, or "warrior".

And to my way of thinking, a warrior was as good as a hunter.

***

Sutton's in South London, close to the major centre of Croydon, which is a few miles away to the northeast. And Banting Road runs alongside one of the borough's many green spaces, with dogwoods, privet and hawthorn growing on one side of the little street, and rows of Victorian cottages on the other.

I'd kept an eye out for any cars that looked like they might have been following me, but in London traffic, that's a tricky thing to try and accomplish. Once I'd got off the main roads and motored into the quiet suburbs, it got a little easier. I didn't see anyone suspicious. But then, if I was dealing with Russians, they were probably professionals, and that meant they could easily evade my rearview-mirror surveillance.

I parked my car around a corner and waited for a few minutes to see if anyone drove past or turned down—or up—the same road. Or if anyone trudged past on foot.

Nothing.

I walked back to the end house in a 19th-century terrace of four. It was painted bottle-green and had a lovely little bay window overlooking a front garden overrun with wildflowers. There was a paved path leading up to the front door, which was sheltered by a tiny porch with open sides and a sloping roof. The door had a knocker, which I used.

I was greeted by an elderly woman wearing a pale blue cardigan and a blue pleated skirt and tiny earrings which matched the string of pearls around her neck. She couldn't have been more than five feet tall, and she was smiling up at me.

"Hello," she said, pleasantly. "You must be Jason." She called out over her shoulder: "Emil!"

She was joined a few moments later by an elderly man who was taller than me, and heavy-set. He had a neatly-trimmed white goatee, and an equally-neat grey moustache, and silver aviator-style spectacles. His hair was grey and combed neatly back from his broad forehead. He was wearing a black cardigan with a knitted collar and very old jeans, which didn't fit him particularly well.

"Hello," he said, warmly, clasping my right hand with both of his. "We've been expecting you. Come inside."

He had a way about him that made me feel immediately at ease. I followed him into the front room, which was crammed with all sorts of furniture—chairs and a sofa, several tables, a glass-fronted cabinet filled with plates and cups, a TV on top of a second cabinet that held a radio and a record player, and a third cabinet with a mirror, drawers and doors, and elaborately-carved legs.

"Please, sit down. Polly will bring us some tea."

Polly disappeared into what I could see was a long, narrow kitchen that had probably been added to the back of the house a century after its original construction.

I sat in an armchair that was a deep, dark red colour, with high arms and a thick cushion and so much soft padding underneath that I sank down and ended up with my knees up around my chest.

Emil settled into a similar armchair that had been arranged at an angle, so that our knees were almost touching.

"I imagine you have some questions," he said.

"I have a lot of questions," I replied. "I'm not sure where to begin."

"Perhaps I should go first, then. Let me tell you a little bit about Marc Merritt, since—as you've undoubtedly worked out—he's the reason you're here."

Polly brought a tray through from the kitchen, with a jaunty blue and white striped teapot and matching cups and saucers, and a plateful of Jammie Dodger biscuits. She cleared a spot on a very cluttered side table and deposited the tray, then went back to the kitchen, where I assumed she was going to see to our lunch.

"I first met Marc when he was fifteen," Emil said. "He'd just left school, and he'd come down to London—as many youngsters did in those days—to try and make a name for himself."

"As a musician?" I guessed.

"You've been doing your research," Emil said. "Yes. But Swinging London was all a bit less swinging and much tougher than Marc had anticipated, and he ended up at the drop-in centre I'd organized in the cellar of our parish church. I was a priest in those days. RC. The sixties provided the perfect opportunity for me to try and make a difference. Marc was in need of a job. We gave him a sandwich and a cup of tea, and a list of places we knew were hiring. And the name of a lady with a little room to let. He had his guitar with him, so I offered him an opportunity to play at our weekly coffee house. It was just the boost he needed."

"I knew he'd worked as a session musician," I said. "I've met his ex-wife."

"Judy," said Emil. "The jingle-singer. She's a lovely person. As is Tim."

"I'm guessing then, that you must have stayed in touch with Marcus over the years," I said.

"I did," Emil replied. "I was always very forward-looking and a bit unorthodox—which tended to put me at odds with the bishop and some of the other priests in the diocese. But it situated me perfectly for people like Marc, who would continue to seek advice from me throughout their lives."

"And the last time you saw him was...?"

"Two weeks ago," Emil said. He reached over to the table and picked up a large cardboard box and leaned forward to hand it to me. "From Marc," he said. "For you."

Yet another gift...? I unfolded its top flaps. Inside was something carefully wrapped in bright yellow tissue paper. I lifted it out and parted the paper. It was an airplane. A model of one, anyway. And beside it was the original Airfix box all of the pieces and decals had come in.

"Marc put that together," Emil said. "He was apparently quite keen on model planes when he was a boy—his bedroom in Winster was filled with them, hanging from the ceiling. This one's a bit more recent. He bought the kit a couple of years ago...off eBay, I believe, as it wasn't available from the original maker anymore. He had some time on his hands, and needed a diversion. He's included a list of the paints he used...in case you need to touch it up."

"It's very good," I said. The level of detail was astounding, right down to the little pilots sitting in the cockpit. "A Nimrod."

"Nimrod the warrior," Emil replied. "Marc was very much a warrior when he assembled that. I believe it sustained him through all the chemotherapy."

I looked up. "He had cancer...?"

"Twice. We were never sure whether the first bout was actually in remission or just taking cover until a better opportunity came along. He put up a good battle the first time around. But when he was given the second diagnosis, which was, unfortunately, terminal, he felt he didn't have it in him to fight anymore. He couldn't see the point in suffering through the sickness and the pain when it was only going to delay the inevitable."

I held the plastic airplane in my lap. I ran my finger over all of its surfaces, touching the places where I could see—and feel—some very subtle brush strokes left by the Humbrol Acrylic 168 Hemp paint Marcus had applied to the fuselage. Arthur Braskey hadn't said anything to me about Marcus being ill.

"When did he discover the cancer had come back?"

"Four months ago. I don't believe he told his employer. He was able to keep working for a little while, but then, the symptoms got worse and he felt it best to leave before he became too debilitated."

"Was that why he jumped?" I asked, quietly.

"He told me he was going to end his life," Emil said, "but not how or when. He didn't want anyone to interfere. I might have guessed that he'd choose to go out with a bang."

"I wish," I said, "that he hadn't chosen to do it in front of me."

"I understand your anger."

Was I angry? I hadn't thought I was. Shocked, yes, followed quickly by sadness, which had lingered alongside my sense of helplessness and frustration at being unable to stop him.

"I believe," said Emil, "that Marc may also have seen it as an act of atonement."

I looked at him. "For what?"

"For causing you harm. Think back to the time you two first met, when he was working as a driver for Arthur Braskey."

"I've done my best to forget that."

"And you had a very good reason for doing so. But Marc regretted a great many things in the final months of his life, and the pain he caused you was one of them. He was acutely aware of the issues with his mental health. And in his last weeks, in spite of his refusal to take the medications that would manage his cancer, he was bound and determined to maintain the regimen of drugs that kept his overly creative mind in check."

"You could have fooled me," I said. "All the brain-teasers and logic problems..."

"Marcus may have been medicated," said Emil, "but his sense of humour remained untouched. Sorry about that."

I watched Polly carry plates of sandwiches and a huge bowl of salad greens from the kitchen to a table which had been set for lunch in the corner of the little living room, next to the stairs.

"I told you that I'd once been a priest," Emil said. "After I met Polly—who was, at the time, a nun—I didn't want to abandon my vocation and so, after some persistent inquiries on my part, I was able to get a papal dispensation, which basically allowed me to stay a priest, but I was no longer allowed to administer the sacraments."

"Not officially, anyway," Polly volunteered, from the table.

"Two weeks ago, when I last saw him, Marc made a confession to me. There were others he'd caused harm to in his lifetime, and he wanted me to know that he'd made amends to them. We agreed that he would employ you to retrieve and restore the Elgar collection to its rightful owners. That was his act of contrition, to you."

"The irony being that in trying to atone for harming me, his last act caused me pain."

"It was never within your power to stop him," Emil said. "I hope you can understand that."

I wrapped the yellow tissue paper around the Nimrod again, and gently placed it back in the big cardboard box, and closed the lid.

"He left me with a logic problem," I said. "And a question: Who knows the answer to Elgar's enigma? And a clue: Ask the singer. The singer's name is Mary Ann. Do you know who Mary Ann is?"

***

When I left the little bottle-green cottage in Sutton some two hours later, I was much the wiser about Marcus's life. But not much wiser about Mary Ann.

I paused in the doorway, holding the box containing my model Nimrod, as Emil produced the inevitable brown envelope. The flap wasn't sealed.

Inside was a postcard of my old ship, the *Star Sapphire*.

"Vintage," said Emil. "It apparently dates from the time she was regularly crossing the Atlantic."

I studied the picture, which I guessed was from around 1968. She'd been called the *Royal Sapphire* back then. Her original livery was a smart white, with a navy stripe running around her hull, and a blue two-toned funnel bearing the logo of her parent company, British Canadian Steamship lines.

I flipped the card over. In tiny letters, there was a little potted history: Launched at Newcastle-upon-Tyne on May 9, 1960. 27,984 Gross Tons, 650 feet long, Eighty-six and a half feet wide. Two sets of geared turbines, twin screws, a published service speed of twenty-one knots. Fitted with stabilizers and a bulbous bow to reduce the negative effects of pitching and rolling in heavy seas. Hull rated Winter North Atlantic.

It had been six years since I'd last seen her, foundering on her side, slipping, silently, under the surface of the dark Alaskan waters. It seemed like a lifetime ago.

Underneath the potted history was space to write a short message. And a vertical line separating that from a space where you could write the name and address of the person you were sending it to. Along with a rectangle where you could affix a stamp.

In the address section, someone—presumably Marcus—had simply drawn three stars.

There was one other thing in the envelope: a photo, printed on UK standard A4 paper—laser or Inkjet, I wasn't sure. The picture showed two women. One had blonde hair teased into a carefully curated mess, her fringe falling over her smokily-made-up eyes. She wore fuchsia lipstick and dangling chain earrings with a cluster of gold balls at the bottom. The picture was from about mid-chest up, but I could see she was also wearing a black leather jacket over a low cut hot pink top.

The other woman in the picture had black hair and very blue eyes, the hair in even more of a mess than the first woman's, the earrings even more unusual—a pair of golden snakes, semi-coiled and ready to pounce, each with a ruby red jewelled droplet dripping from its mouth.

I put the postcard and the picture back in their envelope.

"God bless you, Jason," Emil said, wrapping his arms around me in an unexpected hug that made me feel at once both warm, and comforted. "Peace be with you."

"And with you," I said, as his strong arms let me go.

CHAPTER EIGHTEEN

THERE WERE ONLY FIVE variations left in Marcus's collection of clues. And, logically, the next in line after "Nimrod" should have been a clue pointing to Variation X, "Dorabella".

Except, it wasn't. And that was twice, now, that Marcus had broken the sequence.

The postcard of the *Royal Sapphire*, with its three asterisks, was all about Variation XIII, which Elgar had ascribed to "* * *".

According to the composer, "* * *" referred to a lady who was, at the time he was writing the piece, away on a sea voyage. This lady wasn't named, but the publisher had included a picture of a woman—Lady Mary Lygon, the sponsor of a local music festival. And there was a suggestion that the drums played in the piece might represent the distant throb of the engines of an ocean liner, over which a clarinet quoted a phrase borrowed from *Calm Sea and Prosperous Voyage,* an overture by Mendelssohn.

Other scholars, however, in other sources, believed that Elgar was being deliberately obtuse, and that "* * *" was another woman altogether—Helen Weaver, who'd once been engaged to him, and who'd sailed out of his life forever in 1884 aboard a ship bound for New Zealand. As evidence, they pointed to the atmosphere of brooding melancholy in the piece, and its subtitle, *Romanza*.

I unwrapped Marcus's Nimrod and placed it on my coffee table. It was an MR1, according to its original Airfix box. Originally developed in 1964 to replace the RAF's aging Avro Shackleton maritime patrol, and based on the design of the civilian Comet 4, which had reached the end of its commercial life.

I propped the postcard of the ship up in front of it.

And beside that, I placed the picture Emil had given me of the two women—one of whom was wearing the earrings that matched the singular earring that Florence had handed me at Ardwick House.

I took a picture of the picture with my phone, and loaded it into a reverse image search online. That quickly identified its original source: a 2013 piece in *The Guardian*, a retrospective celebrating London's post-punk, pre-New Romantic club scene in 1978, and the regular inhabitants of Mahony, a new venue in a cellar underneath a former brothel in Soho. The accompanying photos showed men and women with bleached or blackened hair gelled into unruly spikes and impossible Flock of Seagull fringes, sunset pink and coal dust shadowing their eyes, bright red lips and clothing statements put together by art students, with accessories featuring chains and military medals and cadet caps.

The blonde in the picture Emil had given me was identified as Cassandra Braskey.

Close-up, I could see that the eyes of the second woman—the one wearing the snake earrings—betrayed a druggy blankness. She was apparently Cassandra Braskey's best friend, and her name was Mary Ann Brett.

***

The logical place to start looking for Mary Ann Brett was the same place I'd discovered Cassandra: online. I keyed her name into Google—in quotation marks—along with Mahony, and up came the clues. Mary Ann Brett had been one of the bright young things who'd frequented the Tuesday club nights at the Blitz in Covent Garden roundabout 1979 and 1980—the same group that was credited with launching the New Romantic movement a couple of years earlier.

She'd apparently had a career as a singer after that, with a couple of tunes on the radio that I might have remembered if I'd put my mind to it. That took her up to 1986, after which she seemed to have vanished from the public eye. She hadn't been important enough to merit a page on

Wikipedia. And, interestingly, she didn't appear on any of the Electoral Rolls.

I checked the socials—Facebook, Instagram, Twitter, TikTok (which, in 2018, was only just starting to make some splashy noises in the western world). Nothing.

She could have been dead. She could have moved to another country. She could have married and changed her name. I didn't even know if Brett was something she'd made up, or if she'd been born with it.

I made myself a cup of tea and when I came back, I looked up Cassandra Braskey's two brothers, lied about who I was (a newspaper reporter doing yet another story on the disappearing musical legacy of Denmark Street), and asked them about their sister.

The younger of Arthur Braskey's two sons, Leslie, wasn't helpful at all. "She was four years older than me," he said. "She had her own friends. We were never that close."

It turned out that around the time his sister had disappeared, Leslie was doing a stretch in a young offenders' institution for theft and assault.

Stuart—the man who'd raised Matilda as his own daughter—was more helpful, but only to a degree. "She was living with dad when that picture was taken," he said, after I'd texted it to him. "I was off married to Soph by then and getting a start on my own family."

"Do you know anything at all about Mary Ann Brett?" I asked.

"Not a lot. I met her a few times. Quite a lot older than her, so it was a bit of a mismatch in terms of mates. Still, it takes all sorts."

"What do you remember about Cassandra's disappearance?" I asked.

"I remember about six months before that, she and dad had words. She stormed out. Went to live with Mary Ann, I think. Or Mary Ann fixed her up with digs. One or the other."

"Words about what?" I asked.

"Amongst other things, the bloke who knocked her up. Refused to have anything more to do with her when she told him she was pregnant. Dad wanted him seen to. She wouldn't have it."

"So she ended up in a squat in Denmark Street."

"She liked it. I think she thought it was dangerous and romantic."

"How about the night she disappeared? Do you remember anything about that?"

"It was her birthday. August 15. She'd left Matilda with another friend—not Mary Ann. She said she was going out to celebrate and she'd be back later—but she never turned up. Dad had all his feelers out but—nothing."

"Did your dad ever mention the Denmark Place fire?"

"He did. I think that's where he thought she'd gone. It's what we all assumed, anyway. Never any proof, but there you are. One line of inquiry out of many."

"Do you know who Cassandra's boyfriend was? The one who made her pregnant?"

"She wouldn't say. Probably married. You know how it is." Stuart paused. "You're asking a lot of personal questions for a journo doing a piece about a street. What paper did you say you worked for?"

"Freelance," I said. "Thanks for your help. I'll be in touch when the story's up."

I slid the logic problem that Florence had given me at Ardwick House out of the way to make room for my tea.

The farmer is the grandfather of Mary Ann, who is a singer.
Who knows the answer to Elgar's enigma?
Ask the singer.

The rainbow-highlighted lines leaped off the page at me.
Mary Ann.
She was the sister of Toby, the train driver.
Mary Ann and Toby's parents were Susan, the shopkeeper, and Robert, the personal manager.
Robert's parents were Peter, the farmer, and Ellen, the landscape painter.
I searched for "Toby Brett" and came up with the producer of a film about a musician named John Otway offering a lesson on how to survive in showbiz. Much as I was intrigued by the subject matter, I doubted that was who I was supposed to be looking for.

And there were no personal managers named Robert Brett who had family members that matched the names I'd been given.

Taking a wild stab, I typed all of their first names into Google, with quotation marks: "Peter", "Susan", "Robert", "Ellen", "Toby", and "Mary Ann". The quotation marks told Google that all of the names were mandatory in the search. And then they'd be grouped together when the search engine went looking for websites that mentioned them.

Sometimes it worked. Sometimes, when I'd tried it in the past, I'd get a useful obituary or a mention of a celebration somewhere.

But not this time.

Nothing.

The engineer is driving the train.

The engineer was Toby, Mary Ann's brother. He was the guy making sure the train pulled away from the station on time.

Maybe Toby was a pseudonym.

I should have done it days ago, right after Marcus died. I should have looked him up, discovered who he was, asked all the right questions and worked up a dossier. But I hadn't been thinking. I was in shock. I was busy tumbling down a rabbit hole.

But I wasn't in shock anymore. And I'd clambered out of that hole.

I keyed "Marcus Merritt" into all of my search tools.

By the time I was done, I knew that Marcus's middle name was Tobias. And that his grandfather, Peter Merritt, had been a farmer in Derbyshire, near Winster. His grandmother's first name was Ellen, and she'd been well-known in Winster for her watercolour landscapes. Marcus's parents were Robert and Susan Merritt. Robert had been a school teacher who'd dreamed of bigger things. He'd moved to London in the early 1960s, lured by the music and effectively abandoning his family, leaving Susan to find work as a shop assistant in order to stay solvent.

Once he'd arrived in London, Marcus's father, Robert, had set about reinventing himself. He picked up a new name—Bob Winster, after the village where he'd once lived. Starting in the mid-1960s, he'd begun to manage solo singers and music groups, hopefuls who were inspired by the Beatles, the Dave Clark Five, the Rolling Stones, the Animals.

His stable of acts kept up with the changing times. He'd survived in the business until he retired, at the age of eighty-six, in 2012. He was, according to Wikipedia, still alive.

And for the entire time Bob Winster had worked in the music business, he'd maintained an office in Denmark Street.

Marcus was Robert and Susan's middle child.

He had a younger sister named Catherine, who'd moved to Manchester and got married there and had a family.

And he had an older sister named Mary Ann who'd married a guitar player named Murray Brett. She'd become a singer, using Brett as her professional name.

She'd been born in 1948, which made her about seven years older than her best friend Cassandra.

Mary Ann's relationship with Murray Brett must have ended at some point, because she'd got married a second time in 1986, at the age of thirty-eight, to a guy named Corin Hastings, who'd made a career out of producing and directing music videos, concert footage and TV specials. He'd died in 2015. Mary Ann now lived alone in a flat in North London.

Something I'd read earlier snagged my memory, and I looked again at the birth certificate Matilda Braskey had texted me. Usually, it's the mother or father who register a child's birth. But anyone can do it, as long as they provide their details to the registrar. In Matilda's case, it wasn't Cassandra Braskey's name that appeared under the box labelled "Informant".

The name written there was Mary Ann Brett.

CHAPTER NINETEEN

I DIDN'T NOTICE ANYONE following me on the short walk from my flat to Angel tube station. But that didn't mean anything.

Before I went through the ticket gate, I stopped and pretended to read the messages on my phone. Two other people also stopped—a tallish fellow with fair hair, wearing a black overcoat, and a bald guy in a navy-blue puffer jacket. Both were apparently just as curious about what was on their own phones.

I tapped my Oyster card and went through. I raced down the two escalators, not pausing and not looking back until I got to the northbound platform.

And there they both were, the timing of their arrival indicating that they'd also had to run in order not to lose sight of me.

I waited at the western end of the platform, next to the mouth of the running tunnel, so I could keep an eye on them. When my train arrived, I got into the first carriage. The two guys split up, the one with the fair hair boarding towards the back of the train, the one in the puffer jacket getting on in the middle.

I purposely stayed standing, so, at each stop, I could look outside through the open door to see if either of them disembarked.

The fair-haired guy got off at Euston but, after checking the platform—and his watch—he got back on board.

At Camden Town, I remembered a trick from an old film where the good guy—being pursued by a baddie—steps off and on a tube train, causing the baddie to do the same, until—just as the doors are closing—the good guy slips off a final time, and waves goodbye to the baddie as the train leaves the station.

I got off the train.

So did the fair-haired guy.

And the guy in the puffer jacket.

I changed my mind and got back on board.

They both did the same.

I waited until the doors were closing, and then I slipped through. The doors rumbled shut behind me.

The platform was empty.

The train started to move.

I purposely walked towards the Way Out—in case they were watching through the windows—and then I doubled back to the platform to wait for the next train.

***

Mary Ann Brett's flat was one of three six-storied brown brick buildings that were constructed in the late 1930s, just up the hill from Chalk Farm Underground, which was the next stop north of Camden Town.

Chalk Farm's one of those amazing original Leslie Green stations faced in glazed terracotta, officially referred to as "ox blood red" in all the official London Underground documents. I've used that particular station many times. It's got two lifts, though the trains are only about twenty feet below street level, so it's a short trip and almost quicker to climb the fifty-three spiral steps instead—which is what I did, exiting onto Adelaide Road.

I'd seen flats in Mary Ann's building advertised for sale in the £675,000 range, and the building itself described as a "portered mansion block", though it had a bit of a way to go before it could compete with the grand edifices built for wealthy Victorians in the more fashionable districts of central London.

A private, paved drive led to a front door with an intercom entry. It was half past ten in the morning—time enough, I guessed, for Mary Ann to be up and about. I pressed the button.

"Who is it, please?"

"My name's Jason Figgis," I said. "I'm looking for Mary Ann."

"For what purpose?"

"I'm a private investigator," I said. "I'm looking into the disappearance of Cassandra Braskey."

There was a slight delay. And then I was admitted.

The foyer was all original 1930s decor—bold geometrics and inlaid black and white marble—with a very modern pair of stainless steel lifts beside a little desk where a uniformed concierge gave me the once-over. He was an older gentleman with thinning white hair, and lips that seemed to take up most of the lower half of his face in an impish smile. He looked a bit like a gnome, and reminded me of an Oxford gate porter at one of the colleges in the old *Inspector Morse* television series. I fleetingly mused it might be Colin Dexter himself, in one of his customary cameos. Except, alas, he'd passed away the year before.

"Flat 100," I said.

"Third floor, sir. Turn left when you leave the lift."

I found Mary Ann's door at the end of a long, blue-carpeted hallway.

She still had the black hair and the very blue eyes that I'd seen in the *Guardian* photo, although now they were clear and bright, and not dulled by the amphetamine cocktail she'd ingested in 1978. Her hair was cut into a neat, short bob, and her makeup was minimal—a little liner and mascara, and carefully-tended brows. Some powder, and no attempt to try and hide the lines around her mouth and chin. Blue earrings to match her eyes. Clip-ons, not pierced. A blue cardigan that matched the earrings.

"As I told the authorities at the time of Cassandra's disappearance," she said, leading me into an immaculate white entrance hall filled with gold-framed mirrors, antique furniture and pictures of children, "I'm afraid I cannot be of much help."

Mary Ann's voice was deep and informed, I guessed, by years of inhaled nicotine. She spoke carefully and with an artificial precision that made her sound exotic. If I hadn't known about her childhood in Derbyshire, I'd have guessed she'd grown up in Monaco.

She took my coat, and hung it in a cupboard, then took me into the reception room.

"Please, do sit," she said, and then she disappeared into the kitchen.

I sat. The reception room was also painted white, and dominated by a black leather sofa that seemed slightly too large for the space it was in. The window was a series of panes separated by white cross-bars, covered with a black fabric blind that you could raise and lower with a drawstring. There were more family pictures in here, and a large, flat-screened television.

"I'm very sorry about your brother," I said, when Mary Ann came back from the kitchen with a tray set with tea things and, of course, biscuits—chocolate Bourbons. "I was there when he jumped."

"Is that what happened," Mary Ann replied, pouring out the tea. "I hadn't actually spoken to him in nearly forty years, so you'll have to forgive me for my absence of grief. We had a falling out which was never resolved."

I helped myself to milk and sugar and two of the biscuits. "And the reason you fell out...?"

"A minor argument which was permitted to escalate," Mary Ann replied, using a tone of voice to indicate she really wasn't prepared to discuss it further. "What is it you wished to discuss about Cassandra?"

"You were good friends with her," I said, showing her the picture from *The Guardian.*

She studied it with interest.

"I recall that photograph," she said. "The earrings were a birthday gift from a very dear friend. Designed and hand-made by a bespoke jeweller. One of a kind. The most-refined gold—twenty-four karat. And the rubies—exquisite specimens, mined in Madagascar."

She gazed at the picture for a little bit longer, and then gave me back the printout.

"Do you still have the earrings?" I asked.

"I do not, alas."

"I wonder if this is one of them...?" I said, taking it out of my pocket, and unwrapping the white tissue paper, and offering it to her in the palm of my hand.

I saw the look of surprise on her face as she picked it up and examined it.

And then: "How did you come by this?"

"It was sent to me," I said. "Anonymously."

Florence hadn't quite been anonymous, but I had no idea who she really was, and I felt I could probably get away with substituting the word "sent" for "given".

"Is it one of the earrings from the photo?" I asked.

Mary Ann tried to keep her face impassive, but there are things you can't hide—microexpressions—that ultimately betray you. Tiny muscles twitch and contract. Your eyebrows give you away—as do your eyes and your mouth.

"I think not," she said. "It must be an imitation."

"But you said it was one of a kind. How would you know?"

Mary Ann removed one of her blue clip-ons and showed me a little vertical scar that ran from the middle to the bottom of her earlobe.

"One earring was stolen from me by an opportunistic thief—at a club. Torn from my ear."

"Ouch," I said.

"It was...traumatic. To say the least. My ear was repaired by an eminent plastic surgeon. An acquaintance of my father. But I was left with a sensitivity which has always prevented a subsequent piercing."

She replaced the blue clip-on.

"I was advised, by those who made it their business to know such things, that the earring had been melted down for its gold, and the ruby removed from its setting and sold on the black market."

"And you no longer have the other one?"

"I do not. It held unpleasant memories for me."

"Fair enough," I said, offering the white tissue paper so that Mary Ann could return it. I didn't believe a word of what she was saying. I put the earring back in my jacket pocket.

"I was much older than Cassandra, of course," Mary Ann said, changing the subject. "You might think it strange, given who her father was, but she was vulnerable and quite waif-like. She had an innate trust in everyone, which, of course, was to her detriment. She needed someone to look after her."

"And her father couldn't provide that kind of protection?"

"There was, shall we say, a disconnection in that regard," said Mary Ann.

"How did you meet?"

"Through my brother. It was 1976 and Cassandra was barely twenty-one. She was still living under Braskey's roof, of course, but she was a frequent patron of London's many clubs. Marcus was employed by Braskey, and Braskey tasked him with the job of keeping an eye on his daughter. My brother had multitudinous other duties to perform at the time, and so he asked me if I would assist."

"Marcus asked you to spy on Cassandra?" I said.

"In not so many words," said Mary Ann, "yes. That is what defined the basis of the beginnings of our friendship. Although by the time she disappeared, it was, I can confidently say, a genuine affection. I considered her one of my closest friends."

"But you continued to report back to your brother on her activities."

"I did. But I did not consider it any sort of betrayal. I was looking after her best interests."

"Did she know?"

"What do you think?" Mary Ann asked, impaling me with her clear blue eyes.

"And then she had the falling out with her father," I said. "Do you know why?"

"A complexity of issues, as these situations sometimes are. The treatment of her mother in the matrimonial relationship, the subsequent divorce, finances, a father's wishes for his daughter, the daughter's simmering resentment, the eruption of outright anger."

"An argument over the paternity of her child?" I suggested.

"Who told you that?"

"Her brother, actually. Stuart." I consulted my notes, which were on my phone. " 'She stormed out. Went to live with Mary Ann...or Mary Ann fixed her up with digs. The bloke who knocked her up refused to have anything to do with her when she told him she was pregnant. Dad wanted him seen to. She wouldn't have it.'"

I put down my phone, and waited for Mary Ann's response.

"She did not reveal the paternity of her child to her father. She did not reveal him to me. And she most certainly did not reveal him to Marcus."

"You know that for a fact," I said.

"I do."

"So you were still on speaking terms with your brother at that point."

"I was," said Mary Ann.

"Strange that you wouldn't know who your closest friend was sleeping with."

"Not strange at all," said Mary Ann. "She consorted with many."

I wasn't sure whether to believe that. Stuart Braskey had given me the impression that Arthur Braskey, at least, had a very good idea who was responsible for impregnating his daughter.

"How did she end up living in Denmark Street?"

"I had heard about somewhere she might stay. Temporarily, at least. There were rooms above a music shop. So that was where she went. They were completely inappropriate accommodations, of course. But she was intoxicated with the idea of, shall we say, slumming it."

I understood. My sister, Angie, had done something very similar at around the same age. She'd declared her opposition to everything our parents stood for, cut off all communication with us and disappeared. She'd surfaced a few months later somewhere in Mexico, where—she'd informed me, by way of a postcard—she was living in a shack on the beach with an artist named Emilio. A year and a half later, she was back. She had a nice tan and offered nothing by way of explanation, other than a rather dark hint that Emilio had run into a spot of trouble with a local drug gang. We made no more mention of him. Angie went round for a meal with mum and dad. And that was that.

"And she was not without access to funds," Mary Ann added. "She was provided with an allowance. But she was loathe to accept it. Whatever money she did agree to was largely spent on the child."

"So, Matilda was born on April 3, 1980," I said.

"She was not expected for another month. I was present when Cassandra's waters broke. There was no time to go to the hospital. The labour was premature and quick. Cassandra had no telephone in her flat, so I convinced the owner of the music shop downstairs to allow me to use his to ring for the ambulance. By the time I returned, the child was partially born. I assisted as best I could. She was small but healthy. The ambulance personnel arrived, and mother and daughter were duly transported to the hospital—where Cassandra ended up staying for an extended period, due to unexpected complications.”

“Is that why you registered Matilda’s birth, and not her mother?”

“It is precisely why,” Mary Ann replied.

“And what do you know,” I said, “about the circumstances surrounding Cassandra’s disappearance?”

Mary Ann poured herself another cup of tea. Then she got up and rummaged around in a sideboard which was decorated with pictures of a man I assumed was her late videographer husband. She returned to the table with a little book.

“I’ve kept journals all of my life,” she said. “Unfortunately, during that period, they’re enlightening only insofar as they illustrate a creative mind impaired by pharmaceuticals. Thankfully it was not a lengthy abstraction and I recovered, in time, without lasting residual effects.”

She sat down, licked her finger, and paged through the little book.

“I can only tell you,” she said, “what I told Cassandra’s father and the police. My memory was, understandably, somewhat diminished at the time, due to the circumstances I’ve already related. And my journal-keeping was, regrettably, also impacted by those same...deficiencies.”

She showed me the relevant pages. They contained almost unintelligible scribbles, random words, several doodles and three stains of an indeterminate nature.

“I can tell you that on the night of August 15, 1980, Cassandra had made arrangements to celebrate her twenty-fifth birthday. And that she was fond of going to a club across the road from her flat.”

“One of the illegal ones?” I said. “In Denmark Place.”

“One of those, yes.”

“What about Matilda?”

“Cassandra had befriended one of the women who worked in a little cafe which was also in Denmark Place. The Golden Gate. Once upon a time, an establishment of some renown.”

I recognized the name of the coffee bar where Lesley Wharton’s grandfather had hosted beat poets, writers and musicians.

“It was, by then, much diminished in reputation,” said Mary Ann. “The waitress had entered into an agreement whereby she would look after Matilda when Cassandra went out. That night, I was meant to meet

Cassandra at her flat and we were going to go to El Hueco together. But I became indisposed, and it was necessary to take to my bed. I placed a telephone call to my brother, who had business in Soho that evening, and he was able to visit Cassandra to pass along my regrets. Whereupon I went to sleep."

"So you were still asleep when El Hueco caught fire..."

"I was dead to the world," Mary Ann replied. "If I had not been, there is a very good chance I would have been dead in reality. I was awakened by my brother telephoning me to say that he had accompanied Cassandra to El Hueco and that there had been a fire, and that he had managed to escape but, in the chaos, he had lost sight of Cassandra, and he'd not been able to locate her. He assured me he would keep looking. But, in the end, the conclusion was that she had quite tragically met her death in the inferno. Of course, Cassandra's father was notified. As were the police."

"And her body was never recovered," I said.

"It was not," Mary Ann replied. "Given the fact that she could not be found, she had not turned up in a hospital and she had not gone back to her flat or collected Matilda, the assumption had to be made that her body was incinerated. There was simply no other feasible explanation."

"But she was never listed among the victims."

"Precisely. Because her body was never recovered. She remains officially missing to this day. However, when it became apparent Cassandra would not be coming back, custody of the infant was handed to Arthur Braskey's son, Stuart and his wife. It was all very simple and required no legal change of name. But I expect you know that already."

"I do," I confirmed. "Thank you."

"Is there anything else?"

"Would you tell me what caused the falling out between you and your brother?" I asked, again.

"Nothing would be gained if I did," she replied. "Please now do me the courtesy of leaving."

***

On my way out of Mary Ann's building, I was stopped by the porter.

"Mr. Figgis?"

"Yes?" I said. I hadn't given him my name. And I was pretty certain he hadn't overheard me introduce myself when I'd buzzed Mary Ann's intercom.

"This was left for you, sir."

It was a small white cardboard box, about the size of a bar of soap, with my name printed on its lid.

"When?" I asked.

"Just after you took the lift upstairs."

So, Marcus's watchdog *had* been following me.

And was evidently better at it than the two guys working for Igor Plaksin.

"Was it a man or a woman who dropped it off?"

"It was a young gentleman who arrived by motorbike," the concierge replied, "and if I didn't know better, I would say he was employed as a courier."

"No idea which firm, I suppose."

"None at all, sir."

"Thanks," I said.

I walked down the steps and opened the box while I was still inside the building's entrance hall.

Inside was a toy—a black London taxi—exquisitely fabricated, with working wheels and a detailed undercarriage, windscreen wipers, head-lights and front grill work.

Underneath the toy were two sheets of paper.

The first contained a single sentence in Marcus's familiar messy hand:

Mr. Sinclair will be walking his dog at the summit of Primrose Hill today at half past one.

The second sheet of paper was another one of Marcus's favourite Mensa tests—but this one was a time and distance problem. The kind I've never been able to solve.

Train A leaves London at 5.30 am. Its speed is 80 km/hr
Train B leaves London at 7.30 am. Its speed is 105 km/hr
The trains are travelling in opposite directions
How far will the two trains be from each other at 11.30 am?

I stared at the problem, which was the equivalent of a massive brick wall in my brain.

I hated Marcus Merritt.

CHAPTER TWENTY

THERE WERE ONLY FOUR variations left. And Number XI was ascribed to "G.R.S."—George Robertson Sinclair, an organist at Hereford Cathedral, who'd owned a bulldog named Dan. Dan was apparently a well-known character who'd once tumbled down a steep bank into the River Wye, had paddled upstream and barked excitedly as he'd found a place to land on shore. "Set that to music," George Robertson Sinclair had apparently said to Sir Edward Elgar—and he had.

I checked the time. It was only half past eleven, and Primrose Hill was only a ten-minute walk to the south of where I was.

Mr. Sinclair wasn't due to be there for another two and a half hours.

In another life, I'd have had a handy lighter in my jeans pocket and I'd have been able to burn the instructions that had come in the box with the toy taxi and the logic problem. But I'd given up smoking.

The message had been printed in the middle of the page. I tore off the paper on either side, and gave the blank pieces to the porter to dispose of.

Then I shredded the remaining strip into tiny pieces, chewed them up, and swallowed them.

Eating paper's something I hadn't done since I was about two. I don't recommend it. It's revolting and paper doesn't disintegrate between your teeth the way food does.

It also gives you indigestion.

I walked around to Haverstock Hill and then up to Steele's Road, where I knew there would be a collection of shops and eating places where I could sit and stay visible and keep a watchful eye out while I waited for my appointment with Mr. Sinclair and his bulldog.

I found a very welcoming pub, and went in, got myself a sparkling water to wash down the remnants of the shredded paper, and a burger with chips for lunch. I found a quiet table in a dark corner that allowed me to watch everyone who came and went.

I'm a musician. Music has a lot to do with mathematics. I have an excellent mathematical brain. I just can't get that brain around those bloody train problems.

I rang my son.

"Why are you concerning yourself with these things?" Dom asked.

"I've got a bet with my sax player," I lied.

"Foolishness," said my son.

"You don't know how to solve it, do you?" I said.

"Why don't you look online?" Dom suggested. "I'm sure if you did some hunting, you'd find the magic formula."

He didn't know how to solve it.

"Thank you very much," I said.

I gave my sister, Angie—the author of all those cozy mysteries—a call.

"Didn't you learn it in school?" she asked.

"I don't recall," I said. "Did you?"

"I did. And if I did, you must have. We had the same teachers."

I was pretty certain I'd been at home, sick, on the day they'd taught us how to solve the train problem. I felt like I'd missed some fundamental part of my education. Like the time I'd come down with tonsillitis on the day they'd taught us the meaning of *pi*.

"In any case," said my sister, "it's a linear equation. Give me a moment."

She put her phone down, went to fetch some paper and a pen, then came back on the line.

"First," said my sister, "you need to determine if the trains are travelling in the same direction, or opposite directions."

"They're travelling in opposite directions," I said.

"And what is the question you're being asked?"

"How far apart the two trains will be at 11.30 am," I said.

"So...total distance travelled, yes?"

"I think so. Yes."

"So, you need to assign variables. DTotal equals the total distance travelled by both trains. D1 is the total distance travelled by the first train. What's the variable for the total distance travelled by the second train?"

"D2?" I guessed.

"Very good. Now we'll construct the equation. It's very simple. Since the two trains are travelling in opposite directions, their total distance apart is the sum of the distances they've travelled. DTotal equals D1 plus D2. It helps if you draw a picture."

I dug out my black Sharpie and drew a sketchy cartoon on my paper napkin of a train haring off in the direction of the bar. In the middle of the napkin, I constructed a station that looked more like an outdoor privy. And on the right side of the napkin, I scribbled in another train, heading off towards the toilets. I joined them all with lengths of railway track.

"D1," I said, labelling it. "And D2."

"Can you see how adding the two together equals DTotal?"

"I can," I confirmed.

"It's the next bit that everyone slips up on. You need to know the equation that the problem is built around."

"And there you have it," I said. "One of the many examples of obscure, practically useless information that nobody can be arsed to remember from school."

"Some of us," said my sister, "were obliged to memorize it. And you know I have a mind like a steel trap. The equation is Distance Equals Rate—or Speed—Multiplied by Time. Write it down. Fix it in your mind for next time. D equals RT."

I wrote it down. $d=rt$. There wasn't going to be a bloody next time.

"Now you need to break down the equations for both parts of the question."

I wanted to scream. Why do they even bother with these things? I imagined some train-math-nut sitting in an attic somewhere, chuckling insanely while he invented convoluted distance-rate-and-time problems, the sole purpose of which was to confound people who needed the answers to pass intelligence tests. Or retrieve stolen Elgar scores.

Two well-dressed women sat down at a table across from me. Could they be working for Igor Plaksin...?

Or Marcus?

"The distance for train one," said my sister, "is r1 times t1. The distance for train two is r2 times t2. Because they're travelling in opposite directions, we must add the two bits of the total equation together. Therefore Dtotal equals r1t1 plus r2t2. Write it down."

I wrote it down. *dtotal = r1t1 + r2t2*

A young guy with a beard and a young lady with blonde dreadlocks sat down at the table beside the two well-dressed women.

How could Plaksin have found me?

Perhaps he'd followed Marcus's courier.

"And now we substitute. The rate—or speed—for train 1 is 80 km/hr. The rate for train 2 is 105 km/hr. Write it down."

I wrote it down. *dtotal = (80)t1 + (105)t2*

"You then need to know the times involved. So for train 1, 11.30 am minus 5.30 am is six hours. For train 2, 11.30 am minus 7.30 am is four hours. Write it down."

I wrote it down. *dtotal = (80)(6) + (105)(4)*

"Now do the math."

One of the well-dressed women was looking at me while her friend described a skirt she'd bought online.

"Which math?"

My sister sighed. "Multiply 80 x 6. Multiply 105 x 4. Add the two answers together."

I used the calculator on my phone. I wrote it down.

The friend who'd bought the skirt was complaining it didn't fit.

dtotal = 480 + 420

dtotal = 900 km

"The two trains are 900 km apart," I said.

"Very good," said my sister. "By the way, I'm putting you in my next book."

"I wish you wouldn't," I said.

"I've already put you in three others," she said, "and you didn't recognize yourself, so I feel I'm on safe ground. This time I'll make a point of highlighting your character's deficiencies in mathematical formulas and problem solving. How would you like to be killed?"

"Who was I in your other books?"

"Not telling," my sister replied, pleasantly. "Goodbye."

***

Primrose Hill, which is a Grade II listed Royal Park, sits just to the south of Chalk Farm tube station. It's the second highest natural point in Camden (the first is Hampstead Heath) and it's named after the steep hill at its heart. It's 210 feet high—and it's a good hike up.

Once you're there, though, the view is spectacular and very familiar—you've seen it in countless films and TV programs, actors sitting on a bench making life-changing decisions while they overlook the panorama of Central London's skyline.

I remember a time in the 1970s when, if you happened to find yourself at the top of Primrose Hill, the only three landmarks that really stood out were the BT Tower to the west, the vacant vertical slab of windowed concrete that was Centre Point at Tottenham Court Road, and then, off to the east, St Paul's Cathedral. And in between, a handful of church spires and low-rise flats. The Tower's still there, as are the spires, but they're jumbled in with the London Eye and a juggle of high-rise office blocks, Canary Wharf, the Gherkin and the Walkie-Talkie building. And you have to look hard to locate the placid dome of St Paul's, dwarfed by the piercing spike of The Shard.

I checked to see if anyone from the pub was following me up the hill. Nope.

I spotted a couple of people flying a bright, colourful kite as I began my trudge up. That surprised me, as I've always thought of kite-flying as a summer activity, and here it was, a Sunday in the middle of October. I thought it might have been a bit of a good auspice, as Elgar himself was a keen flyer of kites. (Apparently he'd once tried to invent one that was self-adjusting, but had succeeded only in knocking down the chimneys on the roofs of his neighbour's houses.)

At the top of Primrose Hill there's a sign that tells you what you're looking at, identifying all the landmarks, and there's a bench, and on this day there was a guy with three brilliantly-coloured macaws, two of them yellow and blue, and the third predominantly scarlet, with blue and yellow on its wings. They were soaring overhead, their immense wings and long tails mimicking the kites.

"How do you make sure they won't fly away and never come back?" I asked, out of curiosity.

"They know who's got their dinner," their owner replied, easily, as all three landed on the sign, turning their backs on the view.

I checked the time as I sat on the bench. Half past one, precisely.

I looked around for anyone who might possibly be representing George Robertson Sinclair and his bulldog Dan.

There was a woman, wearing jeans and a short blue puffy jacket. She was standing at the perimeter, taking pictures of the panoramic view with her phone. No dog.

There were four individual men, two of them in their twenties, wool caps pulled down over their hair, having a conversation in what sounded like Swedish. The other two were on their own—an older fellow, in his forties, with a buzz cut. And a long-haired, heavily-bearded bloke who looked like he needed a bath and a change of underwear. No dogs.

Three helmeted cyclists, who'd paused at the summit to take in the view and have a drink from their water bottles. One woman and two men. No dogs.

The guy with his macaws.

There he was—a bald man, squatting on the raised circular perimeter of the hilltop, hanging onto his bulldog's harness for dear life as it strained to go chasing after the three birds.

Suddenly, there was chaos. The little bulldog managed to slip its harness and make a barking bee-line for the macaws. Its owner scrambled to his feet, but he was elderly and rotund, and not very fast. The macaws, freaking out, launched themselves off the panorama sign and swooped and squawked and dive-bombed the woman in the puffy jacket, the two Swedes, the guy with the buzz cut, the hermit who needed a bath, the dog, its owner, and the three bikers—who, screaming obscenities, pedalled furiously towards the bird guy.

"Get down!" somebody yelled at me—it might have been the bird guy...or, it might have been one of the kite-flyers who'd earlier been at the base of the hill but who now seemed to have materialized at the summit.

I ducked. I actually fell onto the ground, because all three birds had just soared perilously close to the top of my head. And it was while I was on the ground, with my arms protecting my scalp, that one of the Swedish guys quickly tucked a package of something underneath me, then raced away.

"Dan!" I heard the dog-owner shout. "Heel! Now!"

The dog stopped barking and returned, obediently, to its owner.

The macaws continued to circle, squawking in annoyance.

I pulled the package inside my jacket and zipped it up.

I got to my feet, slowly.

One of the men I'd seen over by the perimeter—the one with the buzz cut—was lying on the ground, bleeding from his face. Another—one of the kite-flyers—seemed to have been injured by one of the cyclists, who was now apologizing profusely while another of the kite-flyers tended to the guy with the buzz cut.

The owner of the macaws was quietly trying to get my attention. He gave me a small nod, then gestured in the direction of the park's main gate on Primrose Hill Road.

I walked briskly down the hill, not looking back.

I left the park and turned onto Regent's Park Road and continued on through the village, not stopping, not slowing down, not even checking to see if anyone was following along after me.

I crossed the pedestrianized bridge over the railway tracks and carried on to Chalk Farm tube station. I ran down the short flight of circular steps and waited, nervously, my heart still pounding, on the southbound platform, until a Bank-bound train arrived from Belsize Park and I got on board.

It wasn't until I was safely back at Angel, and inside my flat, with the door locked, that I relaxed enough to see what the Swedish guy had tucked underneath me.

It was a collection much like the other, contained in a large brown envelope. Again, there were day, dozens of slightly-yellowed sheets of musical manuscript. Hand-drawn lines, hand-written notes...scribbled bars of melody, tea stains and ink scratches and pencil jottings.

Part Two of the missing folio.

Once again, I was in awe.

And, once again, there was a hand-printed brain-teaser.

What used to be, but now is new
Twixt Charing Cross and Waterloo
Kinks, Aerosmith and Leonard Cohen
'Tis mostly gone now, no mo moanin'
Nina and Mark, Charles, David and Carrie
Sunset today, linger and tarry
Soon enough you will be dazzled
Wait for him, his name is Basil

Well. At least it wasn't another bloody time and distance train problem.

CHAPTER TWENTY-ONE

Marcus Merritt was a terrible poet.

But it was obvious he wanted me to be somewhere at sunset.

I checked the time. Just coming up to three o'clock. And sunset? I looked online. 5.56 pm.

Where? Central London? Between Charing Cross and Waterloo? I called up Google Maps on my laptop. The Thames, obviously, was the one thing that separated the two rail stations. Well, that narrowed it down.

Something that had once existed...was new again, recreated, reinvented...

My brain was still rattled by the chaotic anarchy that had overtaken the summit at Primrose Hill. I couldn't focus. I called my sister back.

"Not another train problem," Angie said.

"What used to be, but now is new," I said. "Twixt Charing Cross and Waterloo."

"You've composed a new song and you want the next line. Don't sample my stem files or I shall sue."

I laughed. "Sorry," I said. "It's another brain teaser. I need to solve it a bit urgently. I'm thinking the river, and something that used to be there, but has since been replaced."

"Boat wharves," said my sister. "Or tunnels. Any number of those, when you look at all the building and rebuilding and renaming involving Trafalgar Square, Charing Cross, Strand and Embankment. Is it to do with the Underground?"

"God knows," I said, looking at the tube map on my computer. "What's under the Thames?"

"The old Charing Cross Loop. It juts out under the river beside Hungerford Bridge. But that was shut down and sealed off in 1925. Parts of it, anyway. They kept other parts when the line went south. Look it up. It's why the Northern Line's northbound platform at Embankment has such an atrocious curve, and the southbound doesn't."

"Over the river," I said, discarding the tunnels.

"Hungerford Bridge," said my sister.

I switched back to Google Maps. Hungerford Bridge carried the above-ground trains over the Thames between the two mainline stations, Charing Cross and Waterloo.

"It's very old," said my sister. "And it hasn't been replaced."

"Except for the pedestrian walkway," I said.

I remembered the creaky old footpath that ran adjacent to the railway tracks on the eastern side of the bridge. Scene of a nasty murder in 1999, when a gang of youths, for fun, attacked and threw two men over the side into the river at four o'clock in the morning. One survived, the other didn't. The path had once been an adventure—I remembered the thrill, as a kid, of walking alongside the trains as they rumbled north and south, shaking the wire fencing that separated me from the tracks, shaking the lattice girders that comprised the bridgework, shaking the pathway itself. Over the years, the walkway had deteriorated, and it was never a good choice late at night. They'd finally demolished it in 2002 and replaced it with the two Golden Jubilee footbridges, one on either side of the train bridge.

What used to be, but now is new
Twixt Charing Cross and Waterloo

"I think that must be it," I said. "Thanks for your help."

"Are you sure?" my sister asked. She sounded doubtful.

"Not at all," I replied, but I didn't have time to debate. I disconnected.

What was the next line?

Kinks, Aerosmith, and Leonard Cohen

What did they have in common?

Other than being highly successful musicians, bloody nothing.

I forced myself to focus. Band members? Song lyrics? Song titles. Kinks. "Waterloo Sunset". That made sense.

Sunset today, linger and tarry

I checked the time again. 3.24 pm. I still had a couple of hours.

But, as far as I knew, neither Aerosmith nor Leonard Cohen had ever recorded anything remotely to do with Waterloo or Charing Cross.

I got a list of Aerosmith's songs up on my screen and scrolled through it.

"Crazy"…"I Don't Want to Miss a Thing"…"Livin' on the Edge"… "Rats in the Cellar".

That wouldn't have surprised me.

"Walk This Way".

Walk this way…?

OK. Was Marcus was directing me to walk over the Golden Jubilee Footbridge, from Charing Cross to Waterloo, at sunset…?

I had the Kinks. I had Aerosmith. As for Leonard Cohen…

He'd written nearly 300 songs.

I looked at the rest of the clues. They seemed to have to do with something lost. The old Hungerford footpath on the eastern side of the railway bridge. Or the neighbourhood around Waterloo. Or the South Bank itself.

That had been the downside of crossing Hungerford Bridge when I was a kid: the labyrinth of misdirection surrounding the iconic, bleak permanence of the performance venues and galleries surrounding the iconic Royal Festival Hall. A continuing development of permanently raised walkways and buildings showcasing the "International Modernist" style—but which always resonated with me as "Brutalist"—naked concrete, sunbaked on hot summer days, depressingly soaked in wet grey in winter, all straight lines, no greenery, nothing to delight the eye.

But at least the South Bank was still evolving. Bright minds had recognized the need to bring people back down to the riverfront, to make it friendly, and were investing money in designing walkways along the Thames that were an inviting place to visit.

Marcus was really assuming a lot with these clues.

I ran through the long, long list of Leonard Cohen's songs.

Could it be "Suzanne", who had a place by the river?

Or was it "Closing Time"?

What had recently closed along the South Bank?

'Tis mostly gone now, no mo moanin'
Nina and Mark, Charles, David and Carrie

Why *no mo*? Why not write out the entire word "more"?

I needed Dom's wildly-agile student brain once again.

"What's something that used to be on the South Bank that has 'mo' in it," I said, "and some people named Nina, Mark, Charles, David and Carrie might have been regulars there."

"More foolishness from your sax guy?" my son inquired.

"Yes. Another brain teaser."

"No mo. MOMI."

"What's that?"

"Museum of the Moving Image. Opened in 1988, underneath Waterloo Bridge. Shut down eleven years later. I'd have loved to have seen it but...born too late. Alas. They had life-sized Daleks. The building's still there, part of the BFI complex."

"OK," I said. "Any idea who Nina, Mark, Charles, David and Carrie are?"

"Characters in a film?" Dom guessed. He paused while he thought. "Nina and Mark, *Truly Madly Deeply*. They've got scenes on the South Bank just outside that building. And Charles, David and Carrie...*Four Weddings and a Funeral*. They have a conversation outside one of the doorways. It's red."

"Thank you," I said.

I disconnected just in time to take a second call. It was Emil Wojeck.

"I've been thinking about your question concerning Mary Ann," he said. "I told you that two weeks before he died, Marc had come to see me. In the Roman Catholic church, there's an obligation of secrecy known as the Seal of Confession, or the Sacramental Seal. It's the absolute duty of a priest hearing a confession not to disclose anything that they're told by the penitent during the course of the administration of that Sacrament. It's the Code of Canon Law. The seal remains even after a penitent's death. The penalty for breaking the seal is instant excommunication."

"I understand," I said.

"But...I feel very strongly that you should be warned about something. And I don't think you're likely to be texting Rome anytime soon to report me for what I'm about to tell you."

***

I still had a couple of hours, but I wasn't going to take any chances. If Marcus wanted me to be outside MOMI on the South Bank at sunset, I was going to make damned sure I was there on time.

I let myself out through the big black front door that services all four of the flats in my Georgian townhouse. I intended to get down to Charing Cross by tube.

I suppose I was unduly distracted by what Emil had just told me. I was debating whether I ought to be calling the police. I was also distracted by I was meant to do once I'd reached MOMI on the South Bank at sunset. I suppose I had confidence that whoever Marcus had recruited to follow me around was still on the job, and that the instruction to cross the Thames by way of the Golden Jubilee footbridge was the signal that I was on my way and on time. I suppose I was still rattled by the chaotic convergence of the bulldog, the bike riders, the kite flyers and the macaws at the summit of Primrose Hill. In any case, I wasn't paying attention. And that was precisely why, as I left my front garden and turned right onto Pentonville Road, I was stopped by three men.

Two of them looked familiar. The first had followed me into the Underground when I'd gone to see Mary Ann Brett and got into the middle carriage of my train. The other guy had a buzz cut and a couple of white plasters stuck to his face, and quite a few scratches that might have been caused by the claws and beaks of some thoroughly-spooked tropical birds.

"Привет," he said—which I've since discovered translates loosely as "Howdy." "We have not met. Igor Plaksin."

I didn't say anything.

"You have something for me."

Had he seen what the Swedish guy had tucked into my jacket as I'd huddled on the ground, protecting my very vulnerable scalp from the marauding macaws?

"I don't think I do," I said.

Plaksin said something in Russian to his two colleagues, and they laughed. The first guy produced a large knife from inside his coat and sprang it open.

"Let me take fingers," he said. "Left hand. What he need for music play."

He illustrated with some air-fingering on a fretboard on a pretend-guitar and an air-swipe with the knife. And then he grinned. He had a gold incisor.

Plaksin said something else in Russian to the guy. With a disappointed look, he put the knife away.

"You cooperate," Plaksin said, to me. "Keep fingers."

I made an executive decision. In spite of my unspoken promise to Marcus Merritt, Braskey's stolen *Variations* were not worth sacrificing my livelihood.

"I'll cooperate," I said.

"Where is Elgar?"

"In my flat," I said.

"We go."

I took them back inside and up the stairs. All three crowded into my reception room and waited while I retrieved a single fat brown envelope from a shelf in my bookcase.

I handed it to Plaksin, who pulled the papers out and spread them across my coffee table.

"Be careful," I said. "They're valuable. Don't damage the pages."

"Am well aware, Figgis."

He finished his inspection.

"Is not complete."

"It's all I have," I said, thinking I might still be able to salvage the first part of the collection, which was still in my locker at the club.

"Where is rest?"

"I don't know," I said. "Everything's in pieces. I'm given clues. I follow the clues. I collect the pieces."

"Look, please."

He showed me his phone. There was a live stream of someone tied to a chair in an otherwise empty room. I recognized that someone as Arthur Braskey. He seemed to be sleeping—or perhaps he was unconscious. His head was slumped forward, in any case, and there were bloodstains on his shirt.

"You got something in Soho."

So, had Braskey's watchdogs actually clocked Isabel's sleight of hand under the table...?

"A clue," I said, gambling they had not. "That's all. A single sheet of paper. Variation VII." I dug it out and showed it to Plaksin. "It was in the Bowie telephone box in Heddon Street."

Plaksin studied the sheet of music, then shrugged. He exchanged some texts on his phone.

"Look again, please."

He turned the screen to me.

It was a different room this time, with no furniture. Sitting cross-legged on the floor, with her back to the wall, her hands tied behind her, was Matilda.

"Please give them what they want, Jason," she said, her face looking—and her voice sounding—desperate. "They know Isabel gave you the first part of the collection in the pub. I had to tell them. I'm so sorry."

A rough-looking man walked into the frame, wearing a leather jacket and carrying a steaming kettle. He pulled at Matilda's shirt, popping the top button, yanking the collar away from her neck. As she struggled, he made a move to pour a stream of boiling water from the kettle down inside her shirt. Then, he chuckled, and let her go, and tipped the water out on the floor beside her leg, instead.

My heart stopped pounding. I let myself breathe.

How could Matilda have known about Isabel and the pub, and not Braskey?

And how could she have known it was only the first part of the collection, and not the whole thing?

And then, it was suddenly clear to me.

Of course.

"It's in my dressing room at The Blue Devil," I said.

"We take taxi," said Plaksin. "Avoid London Congestion Charge. Highway robbery."

***

Dev, still working security at the club's front door, let me through with Plaksin. His two friends remained in the lobby as we went upstairs. I checked the time. Five o'clock. I had a little under an hour 'til sunset.

I took my buckle bag out of my locker and handed it over. Plaksin removed the papers.

"Still not complete," he said, after he'd studied them. Did this guy have a photographic memory or what? "Where is rest?"

"I told you," I said. "Everything's in pieces. I'm given clues. I follow the clues. I collect the pieces."

"Stupid English," said Plaksin. "Nothing straight. Always crooked, this way, that. Like stupid London roads."

"This is all down to Marcus Merritt," I said. "It's his convoluted mind, his brain-challenging games. Not mine."

"So, what is next clue?"

I showed him the badly-written poem.

"This means what?"

"As far as I can work out," I said, "I need to cross the Thames using one of the Golden Jubilee footbridges, and then walk along the South Bank to BFI, and then wait there until sunset."

Plaksin digested this. "And then you collect last piece?"

"I think if Marcus is staying true to form," I said, "there will be three more clues before that happens."

"Perhaps my friends take son for safekeeping," Plaksin decided. "Make sure no funny business."

My heart sank even further. Of course, Plaksin knew I had a son, and where he lived. Why wouldn't he?

"It could be days," I said.

"Days," Plaksin shrugged. "Weeks. Years."

He dialed up someone on his phone, speaking Russian to them. I heard Dom's name mentioned, and his address, in English.

***

The taxi dropped us in front of what had once been the Charing Cross Hotel. Nowadays it's London's Clermont. In 2018, it was an Amba. The two Russian thugs and Igor Plaksin—with my leather buckle bag slung over his shoulder—stuck close to me as I walked under the forecourt's glass canopy, through one of the main doors, and along into the station concourse.

Of course, it was Matilda who'd been keeping an eye on me for Marcus.

Of course, it was Matilda who'd been making sure all the clues fell into place—Matilda who'd arranged for Florence to dance with me at Ardwick House, Matilda who'd got the courier to deliver the little white box to the porter at Mary Ann's flat in Hampstead, and Matilda who'd choreographed the chaos on top of Primrose Hill.

Matilda, who was obviously at odds with her grandfather when it came to the fate of his precious Elgar collection.

It was Matilda who should have been watching me as I walked across the river, conveying my location to whoever I was supposed to meet on the other side. Except, Matilda wasn't watching. She was sitting with her hands tied behind her back on a floor in a room somewhere, and I had no idea whether Plaksin planned to let her go, or would simply dispose of her—and Braskey—and me—as soon as he got hold of the last part of the folio.

There's a shortcut onto the Golden Jubilee Bridge's eastern side if you know where to go. The route through the station concourse takes you past cameras—a lot of them. They're hanging from the ceiling, capturing every passenger and pedestrian who passes that way. At least if I disappeared, my last moments could be tracked. And they'd see who I was with.

I led Plaksin and his two colleagues off towards Platform One, and then onto the walkway that skirted the Villiers Street side of Embankment Place. As the road below dropped down to the river, we carried on into a Victorian brick passage that had been constructed at the same time as the original walkway on the eastern side of Hungerford Bridge. It was narrow and claustrophobic and painted a glossy white.

That passageway took us onto the Golden Jubilee Bridge.

I checked the time. Nearly six. Twilight. Usually, my most favourite part of the day. The lights were coming on all over the city. The panorama from the bridge was breathtaking: the Thames, Waterloo Bridge, the floodlit dome of St Paul's Cathedral, the towers at Canary Wharf. The Shard.

Something to remember.

Quite possibly, my last view of London.

I hurried us the rest of the way across the bridge to the Royal Festival Hall, and then down and along the Queen's Walk, past all the bare-branched and pollarded plane trees, the eating places, and the graffiti-strewn skateboard park in the undercroft of the Southbank Centre. We reached Waterloo Bridge, and the South Bank Book Market in front of the remains of MOMI.

I stopped in front of a handy bench by one of the dolphin lamp standards, facing the theatre.

"If you want to make sure I make the connection," I said, to Plaksin, "you'd probably be better off not sitting with me."

"Agree," Plaksin said, with a shrug. He and his friends skulked off to the next seat along and sat there, looking for all the world as if they'd escaped from a Neil Jordan neo-noir crime drama.

I was only a little bit late. The sun had set. But "sunset" could be interpreted in so many ways. I sat down on my bench, thankful, at least, that it wasn't raining.

Wait for him, Marcus had written, *his name is Basil*

Variation XII had been ascribed to "B.G.N." Basil George Nevinson, an accomplished amateur cellist who'd played chamber music with Elgar.

I looked around.

Nobody was turning up.

Had I guessed wrong? Did the clues actually mean something else entirely, and I was waiting in completely the wrong place?

Or had Matilda's sudden absence thrown the entire process into disarray, and this exercise was effectively over before it could begin?

I glanced across at Plaksin, who stood up, and walked over to me, and showed me his phone.

I could see a live feed of my son, sitting cross-legged on the floor beside Matilda, the two of them looking extremely frightened. But at least they hadn't been harmed—as far as I could tell.

Plaksin returned to his bench.

CHAPTER TWENTY-TWO

"Jason?"

I'd been looking in the direction of Waterloo Bridge, to my right. The voice had come from my left. I swivelled around. It was a very elderly man in a flat cap, not unlike the one Trisha had given me at The Bakewell Tart. He was carrying two hot coffees in cardboard cups.

"Yes," I said. "Basil?"

"Indeed," he replied, handing me one of the cups. "I guessed cream and sugar, two of each?"

"Perfect," I said, prying the lid off.

Basil sat down beside me on the bench.

"I'm Marc's uncle, by the way. Brother of his mother."

"Hello," I said. At the next seat along, Plaksin was talking on his mobile in Russian, and laughing, while his two friends were heads down over their own phones, checking their messages.

"I was once a musician on board the ships," Basil said, conversationally.

"So was I," I replied.

"I know," he said, his eyes twinkling. "Marc told me all about you. My employment was much earlier than yours, of course. I worked on transatlantic passenger liners after the war. You did Alaska cruises what, about...six years ago?"

Why was I not surprised that he knew so much about me?

"Six years ago," I confirmed. "Aboard the *Star Sapphire*."

"Lovely ship," Basil mused. "I knew her when she was the *Royal Sapphire*. Used to see her a lot in port. Shame about how she finished up, but..." He looked wistful. "Better than the knacker's yard."

I didn't disagree.

"Marc inherited his musical talents from my side," Basil continued. "God knows his father was absolutely tone deaf and if you heard him sing anything it was in the pub and it was enough to put you off your drink."

I smiled. "You played the cello," I guessed.

"I did. The highlight of my career was the *Queen Mary*. 1947 to 1950. Booked by Geraldo of London—have you heard of them? The Agency for Good Entertainment. Bands and Cabaret for permanent and occasional engagements. 73 New Bond Street. W1."

"I have," I said. "Gerald Walcan Bright. And you were aboard the *Queen Mary* at the same time as Ronnie Scott."

"I was indeed. And Johnny Dankworth. I was very young—just turned eighteen. And they were with the dance bands. Whereas I was in a very traditional orchestra. But there we all were. History!" His eyes twinkled again. "I loved that ship as I'd love a lass."

That was how I'd felt about the *Sapphire*. And I knew he wanted to talk more about his time on the *Queen Mary*. I felt bad. In another place, at another time, I'd have indulged him. But those live feeds of Dom, Matilda, and Braskey were preying on my mind.

"Do you have something for me?" I asked, trying not to sound rude and impatient.

"I do," Basil replied. He took a folded piece of paper out of his pocket, and handed it to me. "It's a passenger quiz. Distributed every day, mid-morning. Deviously designed by the Purser's Bureau to keep the punters from expiring of transatlantic boredom."

This time I did laugh. "Where did Marcus get this?" I asked.

"Marc's talents for digging things up knew no bounds," Basil replied.

I read over the quiz. There were thirty-six questions, and, at the bottom, space to write your name, your cabin number, and the time you'd deposited your answers in the slotted box outside the Purser's Bureau. A prize would be given for the first correct, or nearly correct, solution.

All of the answers to the questions required a word that ended in "IUM". The first letter of the word was supplied, as were the number of actual letters in that word. Each answer was a different word—there were no repeats.

An example had been provided at the top of the page.

Name of the Goddess Freya
Answer: "VANADIUM" (V)..... 8 letters

"Lacking a convenient Purser's Bureau," I said, "what am I meant to do with this once I have it solved?"

"Ah," Basil replied, his eyes twinkling again. "There's this."

He handed me a second piece of paper from a second pocket.

Written down the left side of the page were the numbers 1 to 36. Beside each of the numbers was a clue referring to a specific letter from each of the answers to the "IUM" quiz.

An example had helpfully been provided for this part of the brain-teaser as well.

Letter - 7
The solution: Find letter 7 in the word "Vanadium". The answer is "u". Write it in the blank space beside the number that corresponds to the number of the clue's answer.

I glanced down the page. There was a space after #6, and a free clue (the letter F) after #8, a space after #9, another one after #17, two free clues after #19 (the letter K and the letter F), a space after #21, another one after #27 followed by a free clue (the letter G) and another space after #32.

And at the very bottom of the page was a series of fill-in-the-blanks:

Shop: _ _ _ _ _ _ _ / _ _ F _ / _ _ _ _ _ _ _ _
Person: _ _ K / F _ _ / _ _ _ _ _ _
Item: G _ _ _ _ _ _ / _ _ _ _

"You'll need to refer to your answers, in order, and then put your letters into those blank spaces," Basil said, helpfully.

"I'll be here all night."

"I do hope not," he chuckled. "The shop shuts at seven. Good luck." He stood up.

"Lovely to meet you."

"I would like to see you again," I said, meaning it. "To talk about your time on board the *Queen Mary*."

"I would very much enjoy that," Basil replied, with a warm and very generous smile. He took my empty coffee cup, and his own, and dispatched them into a nearby rubbish bin. "You'll be getting an invitation to Marc's celebration of life. See you there."

I checked my watch. It was ten past six. I was sitting in darkness, with the two sheets of paper readable only by the illumination given off by the streetlamp beside me, and the light in my phone. And I was cold, in spite of my winter jacket and scarf and gloves.

I beckoned to Plaksin, who came over with his two friends.

"I've got two quizzes to solve," I said, "and I've got a little under an hour."

I nodded at a cafe that was still open beside the National Theatre.

"I'm going in there where it's warm and there's some decent light."

***

The black Sharpie that I'd used to sign Marcus's program was still in my jacket pocket.

I sat down at a table beside a window, flanked by Plaksin's two colleagues. Plaksin himself sauntered off to buy something to eat. While he was at the counter, I got the answers to the first nine questions.

Sanatorium. Harmonium. Honorarium. Equilibrium.

A metal named after an asteroid: palladium. I knew that one because I'd once looked up why the London Palladium was called that, and I'd discovered that the name came from Greek mythology and an ancient wooden image of the goddess Athena which was kept in the city of Troy. The image was said to have fallen from heaven, and was the great protector of the city. A palladium was therefore any image believed to protect or ward off evil. It had nothing at all to do with asteroids or metals, but, by extension, I'd ended up reading about how the metal palladium was discovered in 1802, and was named after the asteroid Pallas, which had been identified two years earlier. Sometimes my mind is a hoarder's nightmare. All sorts of bits and pieces of random information lying about, just waiting for the opportunity to be used.

Any irregular quadrilateral...trapezium. I didn't have to ask my sister about that one. I was actually at school on the day they'd taught it.

Belgium. Opium. Auditorium.

Plaksin came back with coffee and sandwiches.

"Two cream, two sugar," he said, sitting down in the empty chair across from me. "Hope you like chicken salad."

"Thanks," I said.

A three-year period, nine letters, starting with T. I used logic. Trio something. I typed my best guess into Google along with "three years" and got my answer: triennium.

"You should know this next one," I said, to Plaksin. "An administrative governing committee in the USSR."

"You mean Russia."

"No, I mean the USSR. As it was when this quiz was devised. Ten letters, starting with P."

"Presidium," said the guy with the knife.

I wrote it down. "That's only nine letters," I said.

"Presidium is correct answer," said the guy with the knife.

I really didn't want to risk an argument with him.

The English language has weird and archaic roots and spellings. I typed it into Google with an extra "a" before the "e". Praesidium. My hunch paid off. Done.

Emporium. Pandemonium. Delirium.

A thousand years. I knew that one. Starting with M, ten letters. I wrote it down but only came up with nine.

"You spell wrong," said Plaksin. "Two 'n's. You have low blood sugar. Eat your sandwich."

He was right. Millennium. I ignored the sandwich.

An aromatic gum resin, eight letters starting with B. I've no idea how anybody could have got that right aboard an ocean liner in the middle of the Atlantic, unless they were exceptionally clever or they'd located the ship's library and had literally spent the entire day paging through a dictionary. The answer was bdellium, anyway. Google provided the solution, though I had to give it a few successive prompts.

Alluvium.

A glass container for raising plankton or animals indoors. It wasn't an aquarium. It started with a "V" and it had eight letters. I googled it. Nothing. I swore at my phone and finally, completely exasperated, typed "What is a glass fish box called?" into the search engine. The answer came back almost immediately: vivarium.

Proscenium.

A condensed summary. My mind went back to my childhood, and a collection of board games I'd once had, all supplied in one box. Compendium. Ten letters. It fit. I wrote it down.

A supreme power. My first guess was dominion, but even though it had eight letters, it needed to start with an "I", not a "D". I consulted Google. Nope. Building on my previous success with utterly stupid questions, I asked for a list of words ending in "ium"—and was rewarded with a website containing 2,000 words in no particular order that all ended in "IUM". I quickly scanned the list. Imperium? I clicked on the word. It was indeed another term for a supreme power.

An orrery. Google was my friend again. Otherwise known as a planetarium.

The capital of Roman Britain. That was easy. Londinium.

The disgrace that follows evil or wrong conduct. Ten letters, starting with "O". I searched the "IUM" site with the keyword "disgrace". One word came back that matched the definition. Opprobrium.

Warm or high praise. Encomium. There was a word I'd never, in my entire life, had occasion to use. It sounded like something unpleasant associated with childbirth.

Symposium. Condominium.

A dwelling place of happy souls after death. Seven letters, and I knew it started with an "e" and it had a "y" in it—I just couldn't remember the word. I scanned the "IUM" site. There it was. Elysium.

The name for the four liberal arts in medieval times. Quadrivium.

I was down to the last seven clues, and it was 6.40 pm.

Moratorium. Aquarium. Solarium.

Fellowship, partnership, or union. Nine letters, starting with "C". Scrolling down the "IUM" page, I discovered I could actually search the site with specific terms: starting with, ending with, definition... I wished I'd found that to begin with, but better late than never. I keyed it all in. Convivium.

Down to the last three.

Compensation for injury, or wounded feelings. Eight letters, starting with "S". I really had to hunt for that one. What was the resource my sister had referred to when I'd asked her about other words for "divergence"? A thesaurus. I checked to see if there was one online. There was. I went there and put "compensation" into the search box. It gave me a list of words. I picked "reimbursement", which suggested "recompense", and when I clicked on that, I got a list of other words, and right at the end was "solatium". Eight letters. Done.

The heaviest metal—osmium. I knew that. I don't know how the hell I knew it, but I did. Perhaps I'd recently done a crossword and that had been one of the answers.

Last question. A middle or intervening quality, state, or body. Six letters. I went back to the "IUM" site and typed in what I wanted: words starting with "M" and ending in "IUM" and I got an immense list back...but they were sorted by how many letters each word contained. And amongst the six-word choices were three that could fit. Milium, minium and medium. Google was my friend yet again. Minium turned out to be a pigment. A milium was a keratin-filled cyst—a word I felt accurately described Igor Plaksin. Medium it was, then.

Done.

I drained my coffee cup. It was 6.40 pm. I had twenty minutes to finish the second test, then identify and get to a shop that I really hoped was located somewhere very close to the National Theatre.

I'd written all of my one-word answers down in the same order as the clues on the paper. And I'd numbered them, just to be on the safe side.

I tackled the second quiz, which involved identifying a specific letter within each one-word answer and fitting it into its allocated space in three sets of words.

Shop: _ _ _ _ _ _ / _ _ F _ / _ _ _ _ _ _ _ _

Person: _ _ K / F _ _ / _ _ _ _ _ _
Item: G _ _ _ _ _ / _ _ _ _

It took me three minutes. And when I'd finished, I had the complete answer:

Shop: UNIQUE GIFT EMPORIUM
Person: ASK FOR ALBION
Item: GUITAR CASE

I searched Google. There was a shop called Unique Gift Emporium at ground level in the OXO Tower, along the river to the east. I could just about make it, if I ran.

"Let's go," I said, to Plaksin.

We got there with three minutes to spare, me legging it, flat out, and Plaksin—with my bag—and his two friends jogging along behind me.

"I'm looking for someone named Albion," I said, out of breath, to the young lady who, reluctantly, had let me and Plaksin in through the door she'd been about to lock up for the night.

"Over there," she said, pointing to a young man with pink hair who was on the point of abandoning the counter with the cash register.

"Don't leave!" I said. "My name's Jason Figgis. I've been instructed to ask for a guitar case."

The young man grinned. "Ah," he said, "hello." He popped down behind the counter. "Here you are."

He handed me a black tin thing in the shape of an acoustic guitar travelling case. It was about a foot high and six inches across and covered in stickers, and it had a carry handle and latches.

"Our ever-popular rock star lunchbox," he said. "Party on, dude."

There was something inside. It was rattling.

"We're closing now," said the girl at the door.

"Just going," I said, pleasantly. "Good night."

Outside, the four of us stood underneath the sheltered overhang of the brick structure that had been built around the old, original OXO Tower. I unlatched the lid of the guitar-case lunchbox.

Inside were two keys on a keychain, with a miniature red London phone kiosk on the end of it. Both keys looked like they probably belonged to padlocks. And there was, of course, the ubiquitous piece of folded paper, which revealed a pencil sketch, along with a series of directions involving street names and buildings. And there was an address, which I immediately recognized.

It was the derelict, boarded-up building halfway down the block on Denmark Street. The building where, a year and a half earlier, Rudy, Ken, Dave and I had been offered that less-than-stellar touring gig by the A&R guy at the now defunct Knave Records.

CHAPTER TWENTY-THREE

"So," said Plaksin, removing the paper directions from my hand, along with the telephone box keychain and its two padlock keys. "How many clues?"

"This is the third-last," I said. "We're still missing Variation X—'Dorabella'. And XIV, Elgar himself."

I took back the paper directions and the keychain.

"Sorry," I said. "You still need me."

***

The address might have belonged to the derelict building in the middle of Denmark Street. But the hand-drawn map, and the accompanying note, directed me somewhere else.

Flitcroft Street, to be specific. More a narrow alley than a road, it begins at the eastern end of Denmark Street, next to St. Giles' Church, and then carries on south and then dog-legs west, past old brick turn-of-the-century studios and the backside of the Phoenix Theatre and the redeveloped site of a Victorian-era Crosse & Blackwell factory. The western end finishes at Charing Cross Road, quite near to The Montagu Pyke, where I'd met up with Lesley Wharton for my four-hour walking tour. And that western end was where Marcus instructed me to go.

It was, by then, 8.30 pm, and Plaksin and his two colleagues and I had got there by taxi. Sitting in the back of the cab, Plaksin had shown me another live stream of Matilda, Dom and Braskey. Braskey was, this time, lying on the floor, his eyes closed and his mouth open. It wasn't my imagination that there seemed to be even more blood on his clothing. Matilda and Dom were now in the same room as him, and Dom was looking at Braskey, the expression on his face one of immense concern. Matilda's hands were untied, and she was huddled in the corner, her head resting on her arms, which were crossed over her raised knees, her face hidden.

"Tell your friends," I said, "that I want some kind of indication that both Matilda and my son are unharmed."

Plaksin shrugged, and said something into his phone.

He waited for a few moments, then turned the phone around so I could see it. "I'm OK, Dad," Dom said.

"Good to hear," I said. "And Matilda?"

"She's fine. Just do what they want."

"I will," I promised.

I still had no reason to believe Plaksin would let us all go, once I'd provided him with his folio.

"Soon be over," I said. "We're nearly there."

The Charing Cross Road end of Flitcroft Street wasn't particularly inviting. It was only about six feet wide, and it was dark and it wasn't very well-lit. I imagined Marcus had chosen it so that Matilda could continue to track me—had she not been extricated from the process by Plaksin. Basil had shown up late for our meeting on the South Bank. He'd no doubt been waiting for Matilda's confirmation, which had never come. Still...he *had* eventually appeared. So, I still had a faint hope that whoever I was supposed to meet on this final leg of the Marcus's clue-hunt was going to come through.

I spotted a couple of CCTV cameras as we made our way down the alley. Useful for tracking crimes after the fact. Not so much for preventing it in progress. Although I had every confidence that if anybody lurking in the shadows was entertaining thoughts of a mugging, my Russian companions would be able to dispatch them without a lot of effort. Especially the guy with the knife.

Halfway along the alley, the little road formed a "T" junction with Stacey Street. There, Marcus's drawing indicated an opening in a brick wall. I spotted an old, abandoned doorway, covered with a corrugated metal sheet, just beside a utility entrance guarded by a steel-grilled gate.

The instructions were to go through the doorway and into an enclosed courtyard.

The corrugated metal sheet could be pulled aside—just—and squeezed through—just.

Inside the courtyard there was a single light. It felt like we'd stepped back centuries, to the era of the Crosse & Blackwell factory. We were surrounded by cobblestones and high brick walls and dirty windows. I imagined street urchins crouching in the shadows, but in reality, there were only an assortment of bins overflowing with 21st-century rubbish, wheeled there for later collection.

There were no cameras. None that were obvious, anyway.

Marcus's hand-drawn diagram pointed to another doorway in the wall opposite the gate. That, in turn, led to a short, unlit passage, and that took us into to a tiny enclosed courtyard, this one filled with all kinds of debris—broken bits of furniture, old mirrors, planks of wood, discarded cups and chipped saucers, wire coils, and lengths of pipe. The back wall of this little yard was yellow brick, and it was overlooked by a series of dark, empty windows, and there was a door. It was made of weathered wood, and whatever paint it had once had, had worn completely off. But it was also substantial. The door was secured with two heavy-duty padlocks and a pair of equally heavy-duty latches. I got out the keychain with the red telephone kiosk attached, and tried one of the keys in the first padlock. It opened. As did the second lock, with the second key.

Plaksin took the padlocks—and the keys—off me, and put them in his pocket.

We went inside.

I recognized the entrance hall of the derelict building, fronting Denmark Street, that my band and I had attended for our interview at Knave Records eighteen months earlier.

Plaksin and I had come in the back way and we were now looking at the staircase that Rudy, Ken, Dave and I had climbed for our interview with the A&R guy. Most of its balustrades and all of its handrails were missing—the result, I suspected, of some speculative pre-demolition.

I shone my phone on Marcus's acutely printed directions.

Go upstairs to the second floor.

All four of us stayed close to the wall as we climbed the steps. The sound of unstable wood rubbing against untrustworthy nails did not inspire confidence. I didn't recall the stairs being in such bad shape when I was last there—but a lot could have gone on in eighteen months, and many things seemed to have been ripped down and stripped away. And the building itself had already been in pretty rough shape.

At the first landing, the situation improved a bit. There was a carpet. The remnants of one, anyway, with a faded Turkish design, threadbare, that carried on up to the second floor. And there was now at least a balustrade—wooden spindles, elaborately carved and very worn, like the wide flat handrail they supported. But at least they gave a semblance of security.

At the second-floor landing, I recognized the record company's door with its frosted glass window and painted sign:

KNAVE RECORDS
PLEASE COME IN

It was eerie, looking at it by the light of our phones.

Marcus's diagram and instructions told me, this was where he wanted me to go.

I tried the handle. It wasn't locked. I pushed the door open.

I remembered that door had led to a main reception area. There it was, in front of us, an empty room, no furniture. There were old-fashioned round light switches on the wood-panelled walls, but nothing was working. There were shelves. A blocked-up fireplace, left over from the days when the building had been a 17th-century terraced house. Two windows with shattered glass and splintered frames, and they were boarded over.

It was as cold inside as it was outside. And the room had a smell. Ancient bricks, damp, mould, old toilets.

I had no idea why it smelled of old toilets until I saw what was behind the reception area. Knave Records' conference room. I remembered that from a year and a half earlier, too, a small space largely taken up by a big table and half a dozen chairs, with a couple of whiteboards fastened to the walls.

Those had all been removed, but I could see that the room had recently been occupied.

It had a single window, in a better state of repair than the two at the front, this one overlooking the back courtyard—and not boarded up. And there was furniture, all of it the sort of stuff you could buy at outdoor stores if you planned on going camping. An inflatable bed, covered with a down-filled sleeping bag. Two pillows. A folding table and a folding chair. The table had a couple of battery-operated flashlights on it, and plates, cutlery—including a large butcher knife—and a mug, which was turned upside down. A battery-powered travel alarm clock. Which was still running and telling me the correct time: 8.50 pm.

There was another table in the corner by the window, and it had a lightweight gas cooking stove on it. And another lamp. And a microwave. Both of which were plugged into a portable mains kit, which was, in turn, attached to an electrical cable which I saw led out through a pur-pose-drilled hole in the window frame and presumably down into the courtyard where it was plugged into something providing pirated power.

I tested the microwave.

It worked.

As did the lamp.

There was a large container for fresh water. And there was a portable camping toilet in yet another corner, which was where the smell was coming from. It hadn't been emptied.

I guessed this was where Marcus had been living for the last month of his life. No wonder Braskey hadn't been able to find him.

It's an odd thing to say, but I sensed his presence. I felt as if he was behind me, watching everything. *I've got your back.* I looked around. Nothing. Of course. Just Plaksin and his two colleagues, waiting for me to figure out what I was supposed to do next.

A note had been left on top of one of the pillows on the camp bed. Beside it was a little ornament, about 12 cm tall—a perfectly cast metal replica of The Shard that I remembered seeing for sale in the gift shop as I'd lined up to go through Security.

I picked up the note and read it.

Go to Bob Winster's office and collect your money.
The Shard is for you.

One more gift. I put the ornament in my pocket.

Bob Winster was Marcus's father. He was the talent agent. His office had been on the third floor.

"Upstairs," I said, to Plaksin, taking one of the flashlights from the table.

The stairs were less rickety than the ones lower down. Less traffic over the years, I supposed. The carpeting here was intact, and there was actually still paper on the walls. an odd repeating pattern of bunches of fruit on a cream-coloured background, featuring whole pineapples and plums and pears and strawberries.

We reached the third-floor landing. There were two doors. One faced the back of the building. It was shut and missing its handle. I gave it a push, but it wouldn't budge.

The other door faced the front of the building, and it was open. On the other side was an office, well-kept, as if its occupants had only just moved out. I guessed this was where Bob Winster had run his talent agency, though he'd retired years earlier. I swept the flashlight around the room and spotted a reusable Sainsbury's shopping bag nestled against a wall.

The bag contained rather a lot of cash.

"It's my fee," I said, to Plaksin. "The balance of it, anyway. For collecting and re-assembling the folio." I didn't say, "and delivering it to the Elgar Foundation." No need to cause aggravation. And it obviously wasn't going to happen, anyway.

"Where is last part?" Plaksin replied.

"God knows," I said. It certainly wasn't in the Sainsbury's bag.

There was, however, a note. There was always a note, with Marcus. He must have excelled at it in school. Note-writing, and note-passing. Penmanship, however, could have done with some improvement.

How far apart were Train A and Train B?
And how was the distance recorded?

What the hell.

At least I could still remember the answer to that problem—the one my sister had solved when I was sitting in the pub on Haverstock Hill, waiting for my rendezvous with the kite-flyers, the bike riders, the macaws and Dan the Bulldog.

900 km.

But now there was a new question. How was I supposed to work out how the distance was recorded?

I stood in the middle of the floor, shining the light from the torch on the piece of paper, staring at it, as if that was going to trigger some kind of intelligent strategy in my brain.

What was Denmark Street known for?

Music.

Musical instruments.

Musical people.

Agents, managers, publishers, magazines, books, recording studios...

Distance recorded...recording studios?

Regent Sound, at Number 4. Where the Rolling Stones had laid down their first album in 1964. Southern Music at Number 8, a little studio on the ground floor, where Donovan had done "Catch the Wind". Central Sound, a small demo room on the first floor above the shops at Number 9, next door to La Gioconda. The place in the basement at Number 22, first called Tin Pan Alley Studio, then Acid Jazz Records, then finally Denmark Street Studios. And here, in this building. Down in the cellar. Knave Music. Affiliated originally with Knave Records, upstairs, but long since abandoned.

Knave Music.

Their record labels were, I recalled, black and red, with stylized lettering spelling out the word K N A V E and a little "900" floating above that word—a nod to founder Gareth Payne, who'd borrowed £900 from his uncle to launch his new venture in 1964.

900 KM

Of course.

"Downstairs," I said, to Plaksin. "The basement."

We made our way back down the three flights to the ground floor landing. The stairs leading to the basement were around the other side, but they were barricaded with a sheet of chipboard, and a sign had been posted which warned:

DANGER
UNSAFE STAIRS
DO NOT USE

Shining the light from the torch down, I could see why. The steps were sloping and dodgy, the wood splintered and, in several places, completely broken off. Entire boards were missing. There was no handrail along the wall, and the banister on the open side was in pieces, uprights fallen over, nothing to prevent you from tumbling into the abyss if you took a wrong step or the wood gave way under your feet.

Plaksin and his friends made quick work of the sheet of chipboard, tossing it onto the floor.

"You go," Plaksin said.

I decided the steps would probably be most stable where they were attached to the wall, so I tested each tread and riser with my foot before I transferred my whole body weight onto it. The wood squeaked and groaned and I could hear—and feel—centuries-old nails complaining, giving up, letting go.

I'd thought Plaksin would be right behind me, but he'd evidently decided common sense should prevail over greed, and he—and his friends—had elected to stay behind on the landing.

I got to the bottom, and shone my light around. This had, decades ago, been the site of Knave Music's little basement studio. It would have been as wide and as long as the building itself, and buried under its footprint.

The staircase was in the middle of the building, so I had to walk around a wall to locate where the office and reception area had been. It was empty except for a broken chair and a cracked mug. But there was a door that opened into the studio itself. I went through.

There was a lot of rubbish lying around, left over, I guessed, from the removal of anything that was worth salvaging—control boards and speakers, monitors and mics and mic stands and amps, things torn out of their mounts. They'd left the acoustic tiles on the walls and ceiling, although they were stained with water and God knows what else. And a number of them had fallen onto the floor.

It was a horrible place in which to find myself, on my own, and in the dark. It smelled like a cave. It was damp. And I could hear things that didn't inspire confidence. Noises overhead, creaking floor joists. Cracking and snapping, like tenuous connections, ready to let go at any moment. What had we disturbed, going up and down the stairs and creeping along landings and into long-unoccupied rooms? Seventeenth century houses were built to last in England, but if they weren't maintained, and if bricks came loose or turned to powder, and wood was left to rot...

I followed my torch beam through another doorway into a tiny, narrow mixing room, where the sound engineer and producer would have sat, with a view through a big glass window to the main part of the studio and the musicians they were recording.

There was very little left in here, either. Another chair, several pieces of discarded metal that looked like they had made up a frame, some cables and leads.

And there, against the wall, was an old-fashioned school satchel, the kind of thing kids carried in the sixties, leather, with straps and buckles.

I sat on the discarded chair—which had a broken leg, but the other three were strong enough to support me, as long as I leaned in the right direction. I opened the satchel. I could see it contained papers that were similar to the other two parts of the collection I'd retrieved. I could see that this was, indeed, the third and last section of Elgar's missing folio.

I felt sad. Plaksin was going to abscond into the night with this. I'd failed Marcus. And Elgar.

I'd failed myself.

There was, of course, a note. And it contained only four words.

Look under the stairs.

"Figgis!" It was Plaksin, calling from the landing. "Do you care for your son? Time is wasting!"

I carried the satchel back to the staircase, where Plaksin and his two colleagues were waiting, standing about a third of the way down, one behind the other, like three of the Beatles in their white suits in the 1967 video for "Your Mother Should Know".

I tossed the bag up to him.

Plaksin looked inside and was evidently satisfied.

"So," he said. "Here we leave you."

"What about Dom?" I said. "And Matilda? And Arthur Braskey?"

"Give me your phone," Plaksin replied.

"Why?"

"You think I'm stupid? We leave, you call police."

"Not while you've got my son," I said. "I promise."

"This way is certain," said Plaksin, holding out his hand and snapping his fingers.

Reluctantly, I handed over my mobile. "Do I have your word you'll let them go?"

Plaksin shrugged. "Why not?" he said.

He dialed up a number on his own phone, and spoke to someone, in Russian. He was joking with them. He waited, and then turned the face of the phone to me. I could see Dom and Matilda walking out through the doorway of a terraced house, and down a path to a dark road lit by suburban streetlights. The garden of the house had a waist-high brick wall in front of it. Matilda and Dom looked behind them. Braskey was being half-carried through the same doorway by two men. They escorted him down the path and lowered him to the pavement, where he slumped with his back against the wall, looking bewildered.

The two men walked away, along with the guy who was filming them. The screen went black.

"They serve their purpose," said Plaksin. "My instructions are followed. They are released."

It couldn't have been that simple. Could it?

"What about me? I've served my purpose."

"You stay here," said Plaksin. He took the padlocks out of his pocket, and the keys, still attached to their little London callbox chain. He yanked them off the chain—it wasn't really very substantial—and tossed me the little red callbox. "You keep as souvenir of fun time on South

Bank with new friend Igor Plaksin. Is nice guy. You keep bag of money. Success. Someone finds you. Sooner. Or later."

The guy with the knife laughed. He'd been denied the pleasure of cutting off my fingers. Perhaps the thought of me locked in a derelict building until I expired of hunger and thirst appealed to his less-violent side.

As a parting gift, he kicked the tin guitar case lunch box—which he'd had with him the entire time—down the stairs. It landed at my feet.

"Take on tour," said Plaksin. "Good for dressing room snack."

He laughed, and all three men then turned and carefully made their way back up to the main floor. As Plaksin's foot landed on one of the steps near the top, the tread gave way and the riser disintegrated, both pulling completely out of the wall and collapsing. It was only the guy with the knife whipping around to grab Plaksin's arm that prevented him from plunging, feet first, through the resulting gap.

Once Plaksin was safely on the landing, the other two guys made quick work of what was left of the step, as well as the two above it, kicking the rotten wood away and finishing the job with a couple of improvised clubs made out of the broken spindles.

I heard their footsteps on the floorboards overhead. And I actually heard them shoving the outside door closed, and the loud metal clinks of the two padlocks being secured.

If Plaksin had really wanted to make sure I didn't tell anyone, he could have killed me and left my body there, in the basement, where it wouldn't have been found until workmen arrived to undertake the inevitable rebuild for the newly re-imagined Denmark Street.

I was grateful for his generosity. For what it was worth.

CHAPTER TWENTY-FOUR

I walked back around to the side of the staircase, the bottom of which had, at some point in its history, been enclosed by a stout wall made of wooden panels.

But I could see that one of the panels had been deliberately dislodged, and was no longer connected to either of its neighbours. The loose panel had been propped back into place over the resulting hole.

I put the little red London callbox keychain and the lunch box guitar case into the Sainsbury's bag for safekeeping. I shoved the wooden board aside, and shone my flashlight into the black void.

It smelled musty and old, like all of the combinations of mildew and rot and long-abandoned rooms you could ever imagine. The bright beam revealed a very large, upright steel drum. I guessed it was fifty-five gallons. It had a lid. And sitting on the lid was one more tiny box. It was white and it had my name on it.

I crawled into the ad-hoc storage space. There wasn't room enough to stand.

I was getting a very bad feeling.

I decided it would not be in my best interests—nor those of possible future forensic investigators—for me to have anything to do with that barrel. In fact, I shouldn't even have been there in the first place.

I picked up the box as delicately as I could, touching nothing else with my fingers.

And then I crawled out again, and sat on the floor, with my back to the wooden wall, to see what Marcus had left for me.

Inside the box was a red London Routemaster bus—made by the same toy company as the black taxi. Again, its detailing was exquisite:

a driver's compartment, with a steering wheel. Stairs going up, seats on both decks. An open platform, a silver pole. It was a Number 15, and its destination board said Covent Garden.

Under the bus, in the box, was an envelope which contained folded-up picture and, of course, the inevitable note.

The picture was some kind of PR shot showing a grinning, middle-aged guy with his arm around the shoulder of a young, spiky-haired rock star. They were evidently celebrating the signing of a contract, which was also in the picture and held up for the benefit of the photographer. I could see the two names at the bottom of the contract. Luc Horlock and Bob Winster.

I unfolded the note.

Hello Jason. You've arrived at the end of my journey. It's time for me to keep my appointment with you.

I looked at the date he'd printed at the top of the page. Monday, October 15, 2018. The same day I'd met Marcus at the top of The Shard. Had it really been less than a week?

The barrel contains the remains of Cassandra Braskey, and sand. Sand has an interesting property: it causes mummification. I expect Cass's body will still be largely intact after nearly forty years.

I'll trust you to let the police know about this, just as I trust you to return the stolen Elgar collection to the Foundation.

I'm so sorry, I thought, willing my words to be heard by Marcus's spirit, whose presence I could still feel, unaccountably, lingering nearby, in the darkness of the cellar, watching.

I would alert the police.

Assuming I could find my way out.

Cassandra Braskey did not perish in the Denmark Place fire, as her father and others have been led to believe. But she did die nearby. The fire was an unforeseen and convenient excuse.

There was a struggle. Cassandra fought hard, and tore out the earring of one of the people responsible for her death. I was directed to remove it from her clutched hand and dispose of it. I did not. It's still there, and it may still have tissue attached, if the sand has done its job. The torn-out earring also resulted in blood on Cass's blouse. I was ordered to get rid of that, too, but I didn't.

I was tasked to remove her body and sanitize the room. I found the second earring as I was cleaning up. It's the earring I sent to you.

"Give me that."

I looked up, startled. I shone my flashlight at the voice in the darkness.

It was Mary Ann Brett. And she had a knife—the one that I'd seen upstairs.

Emil had shared details of Marcus's last confession with me. I had no reason to believe that confession was false. I'd been warned about Mary Ann.

"Let me guess," I said. "Your earring wasn't stolen by an opportune thief at a Soho nightclub."

"Regrettably," said Mary Ann, "it was not."

I got to my feet. I didn't like the psychological advantage she had, standing over me. Or that knife. I folded the papers up and put them in my jeans pocket, along with the envelope. I stowed the little bus, in its box, in the Sainsbury's bag.

"I don't believe I will share that note with you," I said, stalling her. "Tell me what happened."

"The night in question was a blur to me. And I was not, as I have already explained, in my right mind. There was a confrontation which was exacerbated by Cassandra's insistence that the father of her child not only marry her—which was an impossibility, given he was already married—but also include both herself and the child as his designated beneficiaries, when the time might come to inherit. This was not well-received."

"Who killed her?" I asked.

"Marcus did, of course," Mary Ann said, holding her gaze steady, unblinking.

"But you helped him," I said.

"I was there to try and make Cassandra see sense. To try and talk her out of her insistence that my brother obey her whim—on pain of revealing his indiscretions to her own father—which would not have gone well for Marcus. But she would not relent. And so Marcus took action."

"And Cassandra was sure your brother was the father?" I asked.

"She was convinced. The child's resemblance to him was indisputable, even in infancy."

"And then what happened?" I asked.

"As I said, there was a confrontation. Marcus put his tie around her neck. I attempted to stop him. I do not clearly recall the details. Only the aftermath."

I'm not sure what Mary Ann thought she was going to accomplish by lunging at me with the knife. Or by lying about what had happened upstairs. I fended the knife off with the flashlight, whacking it out of Mary Ann's hand and possibly shattering her wrist in the process. She shrieked with pain and spun backwards as the bulk of the torch cracked bone and muscle. I grabbed my Sainsbury's bag, and ran.

Halfway up the staircase, I tossed the bag up onto the main floor landing. I could hear Mary Ann stumbling around behind me, spewing educated-sounding expletives, but she had a badly injured wrist and she wasn't going to be doing any two-handed climbing. Not easily, anyway.

I used what was left of the banister and the steps to manoeuvre my way over the gaping hole. The banister was minus its handrail and all of its upright spindles, but I planted my feet, and then my knees, and then I got a handhold around the newel at the top, and I hauled myself up.

I landed face-down on the rotting carpet, my nose buried in the dirt and decay of empty decades, my legs still dangling over the gap in the stairs. There was nothing to hang onto except the frayed edges of a hole in the carpet. Better than nothing. I wedged my left foot against a triangle of wood where the top step had once been attached, and gave myself an almighty shove forward. The wooden insert cracked apart and splintered and crashed to the basement floor below. But I'd got enough of my body onto the landing that I could use my elbows to leverage the rest of me forward. I got my knees over the void, and I was safe.

I rolled over onto my back. I like to think I'm in fairly good shape, physically. But who was I kidding? I was fifty. I could do flights of stairs—the normal way—without being out of breath. I could easily walk a mile. Two miles. And I did, often. I could haul amps and guitars and anything else that needed lugging from the back of a van onto a stage. But this particular exercise had just about done me in.

I knew Plaksin had padlocked the door, and the door was heavy-duty. I remembered, too, that the entire front of the building at street level had been covered in a solid black wall of hoarding, and all of the windows facing Denmark Street on the upper floors were boarded over.

I checked the back of the building, near where we'd come in. There was a window, and it wasn't blocked. Not by wood, anyway. It was covered on the outside, top to bottom, with a metal grille which looked like it was embedded in the bricks.

The window was divided into eight panes, four on the bottom, then a cross-beam, and four on the top. I located the piece of banister that Plaksin's guy had left behind when he'd smashed the staircase, and used it to knock out one of the bottom panes. I cleared out all the glass and then tested the grille with my hands. It was old and rusty, but it wasn't going to give. It wasn't even loose. I even gave it a really good shove with the flat end of the banister piece.

Nope.

The bricks were holding fast.

I ran upstairs to the first-floor landing, with its worn Turkish carpet and a door that opened onto a back office that had more windows overlooking the rear courtyard.

I didn't know when business had last been transacted in that room—it certainly seemed a lot longer ago than eighteen months—but the result was less-than-trustworthy remnants of flooring and, in some places, boards that were splintered and altogether missing. I made my way over to the window, which had the same four-up and four-down panes of glass as the one on the ground floor, but no protective grille. The wooden frame was as dodgy as the floorboards, and the inside sill was almost nonexistent.

But the window looked like it could be opened. And I was able, after a monumental effort, to lift it up high enough that I reckoned I could manoeuvre myself out. I shone my torch around the well created by the back of the building and the perpendicular brick walls on either side of it. I really didn't fancy jumping.

There was a drainage pipe fixed to the outside of the wall on my right. I could just about reach it if I crawled out onto the windowsill. And the pipe wasn't bolted absolutely flush to the bricks—there was enough room to get my hands in behind, and I could wedge my foot onto a branch of the pipe that was coming out of the wall at toilet level.

I looped the fabric handle of the Sainsbury's bag over my shoulder and balanced the flashlight on the sill so it was shining on the pipe. I got my left leg out of the window so I was straddling the sill, my right leg still inside, my foot planted firmly on the floor.

I was focused on the pipe, which is why I didn't hear Mary Ann entering the room behind me.

"Give me that note," she said, startling me. I swivelled around.

It must have caused her insurmountable pain to navigate the broken stairs. Her right arm and hand were hanging limp at her side. Her left hand held the knife. I could barely see her—the torch was still aimed at the pipe, but there was a yellowish light thrown up from the courtyard and it was cloudy outside and the clouds were deflecting the glow of night-washed London.

Somewhere nearby there was a police car, its blue flashing lights skimming off the overcast skies.

"No," I said, bravely. I didn't dare turn my back on her.

"I knew, when you came to visit me this morning, that the earring you showed me could only have come from my brother. And then, an urgent message was delivered to the porter at my flats. I was advised there were developments concerning Cassandra. And that it would be in my best interests to go to the building where her body had been concealed."

"So you knew it was here."

Mary Ann didn't say anything.

"Was the message written by Marcus?"

"In his hand."

"When was this message delivered?" I asked.

"An hour ago. It came by courier."

I made sure my foot was still firmly planted on the floor. I had two choices. I could make my exit—which would be catastrophic if I didn't first get a good grip on that drainage pipe. Or I could abandon the idea completely and come back inside and take my chances with that knife.

I didn't have time to make a decision because Mary Ann chose that moment to lunge towards me. At that same moment, the floorboard, where I had my right shoe planted, gave way, splintering under the pressure of my foot and Mary Ann's additional and sudden weight. Simultaneously, the mortar between the bricks supporting the bottom of the windowsill cracked and crumbled, along with the bricks themselves, pitching me sideways. I frantically tried to grab the window frame but missed. I was falling too hard and too fast to grasp what was left of the sill. I tumbled out head first and plunged towards the cobblestones in the courtyard.

I remember screaming. And the jolting crack as I landed.

And not much else.

CHAPTER TWENTY-FIVE

Am I going to die?

The voice of Harry Enfield's denouncer-of-travel-myths was rolling around in my head. That old Travelocity ad on American TV—*American appliances don't work in Europe*—and the subsequent near-electrocution of the hapless Roaming Gnome had always cracked me up.

I was feeling extremely cracked-up just then. And in serious pain, too.

But at least I wasn't dead.

Which was some kind of miracle, considering I'd landed almost face-down on the hard cobbles in the enclosed courtyard.

Fortunately, the Sainsbury's bag had got there first. And I'd crashed into its cushioning contents while—also miraculously—managing to avoid the hard-edged tin lunchbox, the London telephone booth keyring and the toy London bus that I'd stashed next to the paper bills.

Somehow, I'd landed with my legs bent, and my toes had hit the ground first. Somehow, I'd managed to roll as I smashed into the cobbles. My head smacked into the moneybag. I didn't think I'd fractured my skull. But my left leg was definitely broken—I couldn't move it. My hands were both working. I had some fairly significant cuts. I was probably going to have a concussion.

And that's all I remember…other than the line just before "Am I going to die?" which was "Oh, grow up!" as the Roaming Gnome jammed a sparking, smoking, short-circuiting plug into an incompatible wall socket.

***

"Jason."

It was a voice I didn't know.

"Just stay still, Jason."

I opened my eyes. It was a policeman, squatting on the ground in front of me.

"How are you feeling?"

"I've been better," I said.

"Can you tell me your full name?"

"Jason David Figgis," I said.

"Great. And your birth date?"

I could see his black and white name tag, barely visible in the murky light. *Metropolitan Police. Police Officer. Constable Miller.*

"May 11," I said. "1968. Am I going to die?"

Constable Miller smiled. "Hopefully not."

"Are you arresting me for trespass?"

Constable Miller ignored that question. "Do you know what day it is?"

"Sunday?" I guessed. I ought to have known that.

"And the date?"

"Can't remember," I said. Not a good sign.

"OK, Jason...ambulance on its way. Try not to move."

He stood up.

"How did you know my name?" I asked.

"I told him," said another man—again, a voice I didn't recognize.

That other man got down on the cobblestones so I could see his face. He looked familiar, even if he didn't sound it. Blond hair. Twenty-ish. Possibly younger. Where had I seen him before? I couldn't make my brain focus.

"Josh," he said. "Nice to see you again."

"Josh from where?" I said. My left leg was going numb.

"Josh from on top of Primrose Hill," he said.

"Talking Swedish?" I guessed.

"Norwegian, actually. But close enough."

"What are you doing here?" I asked, hazily.

"Following orders," Josh said. "And you. Since The Shard, last Monday."

"You were at The Shard? How did you know I'd be there?"

"Because Marc told me," Josh said.

I was trying to make my brain work again, and, again, my brain wasn't being helpful. I really just wanted to close my eyes and go to sleep. I didn't think that would be a good idea. I had to stay awake until the ambulance guys got there. It would be OK after that.

"Were you at Ardwick House?"

"I was."

"And pretending to be a courier in Hampstead...?"

"That, too," said Josh. "And you saw me on the tube."

Of course.

"Mary Ann is still in there," I said, making an effort to gesture at the building behind me. They had to be warned. "Upstairs. The window I fell from."

"Yes, the police have gone inside to arrest her. I requested they be here earlier, but they were unavoidably delayed enroute. My apologies."

My battered brain couldn't make sense of what he was telling me.

"There's a barrel in the basement," I said. "Under the stairs. Filled with sand. There's a body in it. Cassandra Braskey."

"Ambulance arriving now," said Constable Miller.

***

I was actually in and out of the hospital fairly quickly. They kept me overnight because of the very real possibility of concussion. They set my broken leg and fixed up my other injuries. I got a good night's sleep—possibly the best sleep I'd had in a week.

I was released the next day and went home in a taxi, accompanied by Rudy, my drummer, after assuring those in charge that I could take care of myself, and if I felt any need for assistance, there were any number of people I could call.

199

Taking care of myself involved first having to navigate the stairs up to my flat on Pentonville Road. Some enterprising owners have installed little lifts 'round the back of their properties. I'm not one of them. It was slow-going, but between the crutches and Rudy's drumming muscles, we got there. And I wasn't planning on leaving for a couple of days. I wasn't due back at The Blue Devil until Wednesday.

"We can always get another guest player in," Rudy said. "We've managed OK without you 'til now."

I didn't like the sound of that.

"Find me a suitable chair," I said. "I will be there."

The first thing I did after Rudy left was call my son. Igor Plaksin had taken my mobile but I had a reliable backup, one that I often used when I was investigating.

"Are you OK?" Dom said, his voice panicky. "I've been trying to reach you since yesterday. I kept getting your voicemail."

"I'm fine," I said. "Mostly. More to the point, are *you* OK?"

"I'm fine, too," Dom said. "Mostly."

"I'm sorry that happened to you. My fault. I should have been more careful."

"I'm going to relate my experiences to Aunt Angie," Dom said. "She can use them in her next book."

"She will," I said. "She's probably already put you in one of them, thinly disguised."

"She's put you in."

"So she tells me."

"You didn't recognize yourself?"

"No," I said.

Dom laughed. "Hilarious. I'll let you work out who you are, then."

"Thanks," I said. "Is Arthur Braskey OK?"

"A bit worse for wear," my son said. "They weren't kind to him. I believe he's recovering at home...as they say."

"And Matilda?"

"She's OK, too. Honestly, they didn't touch us. Just Braskey." He paused. "What was that all about, anyway?"

"They didn't say anything?" It was a stupid question. Why would they?

"They didn't speak English. Only Russian."

"OK," I said. I told him about Marcus Merritt. And everything that had happened after I'd met him at the top of The Shard, one week earlier.

After that, I took photos of the PR picture Marcus had left me, and the note.

I didn't see my beloved Cass die, so I cannot provide an eyewitness account.

I was brought in after the fact, to clean up.

The earring and the blood will provide the necessary DNA to identify my sister as one of the killers.

Cass was strangled with a necktie. The owner of that necktie will be obvious from the picture I've included in this envelope.

I looked again at the photo of Bob Winster and Luc Horlock. Winster was wearing a very distinctive tie, solid dark brown diagonal stripes interspersed with a brown and white checker-board stripe, and a third stripe composed of butterscotch and chocolate-coloured squares on a white background.

That tie is still knotted around Cass's neck. I was instructed to get rid of it, like everything else. And, like everything else, I didn't. I'm hopeful they'll be able to find some of my father's DNA on it, to confirm his role in her killing.

I believe in justice, served later if not sooner. It will be served now, since I'm no longer alive to have to deal with the consequences.

The last question you'll be asking is, of course, the identity of Matilda's father.

And the truthful answer is, I don't know.

I was Cassandra's lover—I won't deny that. And I'm sorry for the pain it caused Judy. But I was one of several. I know who Cass believed was the father, and I know who she told, and I know that's why she was killed.

To try and put the question of Matilda's paternity to bed, I joined the Generations site. I know you have a tree there too. I've looked at it. Fascinating. I did the DNA test and you'll be relieved to know that you and I are not related to one another. But if you could encourage Matilda to also do the DNA test, and upload it to Generations, that might go a long way towards sorting out the issue, once and for all.

I smiled. A final wordplay. Always in the game, Marcus.

At the bottom of the note, he'd included the login and password for his Generations account.

Thank you for everything, Jason.
See you on the other side.

I put the note and the picture back into their envelope. And then I rang the police, and told them I needed to make a statement about a cold case involving Cassandra Braskey, and that I had some documents they might find useful.

***

True to Basil's word, one month later, I received an invitation to attend Marcus's celebration of life.

It was in Newlydale, and because it was mid-November, it was indoors, in the Village Hall. The hall was at the top of the hill behind Judy and Tim's garden, and therefore it overlooked the pasture that was home to the two sheep, the donkey and the llama I'd observed during my first trip there. They were joined, on this occasion, by two curious, hardy cows, all of them looking in through the westward-facing windows as we toasted Marcus and gave him a send-off.

There were about a hundred people gathered in the little stone hall, which was all on one level, and had a pitched roof covered in moss. Inside, recent renovations had resulted in a new wooden floor, an updated kitchen with all the mod cons, and state-of-the-art toilets that conserved water and didn't look—and smell—like they'd been installed when indoor plumbing had first arrived in Derbyshire.

There were speeches and there was music—a duo from Newlydale, a young man and a young woman, she in a full black velvet skirt and he in a black velvet Renaissance cap, singing the sort of folky pop songs Figgis Green was famous for. And there was food—provided by the pub up the road—the same pub Arthur Braskey had stayed in when he'd followed me to Newlydale, the night I'd introduced myself to Matilda. Little individual pies—Steak in Ale, Chicken and Mushroom. A selection of cheeses and sliced meats and things to put them on—crackers and buns—and a variety of vegetables (roasted and raw) and pots of dips and spreads.

My leg was still in a cast, so I'd got Dom to drive me to Derbyshire. We were spending the night in a wonderful old country house in Baslow, twenty minutes from Newlydale. From there, the next day, we were going to visit Chatsworth House, which was open for the Christmas season and had been festively decorated with a "Once Upon a Time" theme, and promised twinkling lights, roaming storytellers, market stalls and even more musicians. I'd never been, and neither had Dom, but he was curious about its role as a filming location for *Barry Lyndon*, *Death Comes to Pemberley* and *The Crown*. I was content to just have a limp around its fabulous stately rooms.

I didn't recognize a lot of people at the party—they were friends and relations and people Marcus had known throughout the various stages of his life. People he had touched. A few dodgy-looking characters who stayed long enough to have a drink and a bite to eat and a word or two with Judy, before slipping away as quietly as they'd arrived.

Emil Wojeck was there, along with Polly. In fact, it was Emil who was the "master of ceremonies", if you can assign a role to the person who presents a compendium of someone's life. He introduced each person who'd been shaped or influenced or moved by Marcus, whether by his kindness and all-out generosity, or simply just his engagement in their lives. There were so many more than just those who'd stepped up to assist him in delivering his clues.

Marcus's friend from Tissington—the amateur pianist. His name was Edward and he'd come with his daughter, Tricia, who was about to go on tour with *Buddy Holly* and had changed her hair colour from blue to a more practical blonde.

Beatrix Cummings, from the old baker's cottage.

Lesley from the four-hour walking tour. Why was I not surprised?

"So," I said. "You knew Marcus too."

"My parents did," Lesley said. "In their Golden Gate days. They gave him a job behind the counter when he first arrived in London—serving up coffee and orange juice. And he used to play his guitar there, too. After he landed a permanent job with Arthur Braskey, he used to pop in regularly to make sure things were all right with mum and dad, financially. He actually helped them out when dad got really ill and couldn't work anymore. He was such a lovely guy."

Isabel. That was a given. "Not your real name," I guessed, with a smile.

"Not my real name," she admitted. "It's Liz. I work in one of the offices near Soho Square. Marc was a frequent visitor, usually on behalf of Arthur Braskey, who, fortunately, has never met me. And I do actually teach viola, on the side. My knowledge of music is quite genuine."

"I'm glad to hear it," I said.

"That list I told you about," she said. "Elgar's 'Nimrod', followed by Pachelbel's 'Canon'."

"Top of the Funeral Pops for 2012," I said.

"Number three was 'Time to Say Goodbye' by Sarah Brightman and Andrea Bocelli."

"Think I'll have the *Match of the Day* theme played at mine," I said, philosophically.

"A surprisingly popular choice," Liz said. "My husband," she added, pulling over a guy who'd been chatting, drink in hand, with Tim Galpin.

I recognized Griff, from the Heddon Street telephone kiosk.

"Were you really at Figgis Green's opening night show in Middlehurst?" I asked.

"Wouldn't have missed it for the world," he replied. "I hated how you changed the last lines of 'The Gypsy Rover' so that you sang them instead of your mum—I'm afraid I'm a bit of a purist when it comes to the Figs. But otherwise—superb concert and a fitting start to what I understand was a brilliant tour."

"Until that gargoyle nearly killed me," I said. "Everything after that was a bit of a disaster."

"Never mind," said Griff. "Do it all again next year, eh?"

"Absolutely," I said, not meaning it at all.

Florence, my dancing partner from Ardwick House.

"Not your real name, either," I said.

"Annabelle," she replied, confidentially. "Really, I'm a costumer. Currently attached to Tricia's production—you know, *The Buddy Holly Story*."

"But not an actor?" I inquired, humorously.

"Oh, that too. When required. And a dancer, of course. I'm quite versatile. But this particular production requires a younger troupe. Never mind. Next year we're doing *Four Old Broads*. I'll get my comeuppance."

"Let me know when it opens," I said. "I'll come and rattle my jewellery in the expensive seats."

I met Bulldog Dan and his owner—not George Robertson Sinclair but a guy named Jack, who, as far as I could determine, was acquainted with Josh, who'd been following me since The Shard, ensuring all the clues fell neatly into place—including, I suspected, the instructions to Mary Ann to go to the abandoned building on Denmark Street where Cassandra's body was. But Jack wouldn't tell me anything about Josh, and neither would Annabelle.

And Basil. Marcus's uncle. Who really had played the cello on board the *Queen Mary*, and really had worked with Johnny Dankworth. We spent half an hour in earnest conversation, comparing notes about our respective lives at sea. And then I made an appointment to meet him in London when I was fully mobile, so we could have a proper lunch to discuss the possibility of a guest gig at The Blue Devil—since his first true musical love was, in fact, jazz.

And finally, Albion, the clerk from the Unique Gift Emporium. Who'd only met Marcus a few weeks earlier, when he'd popped into the shop to buy a couple of toys: a red London Routemaster bus and a black London taxi. And a guitar-case-shaped black tin lunchbox.

I'd like to say I'd recovered emotionally from Marcus's undertaking, but that wouldn't have been quite true. I'd let him down. Badly. In the end, I really couldn't have done anything about Igor Plaksin, but when you've been tasked with fulfilling a dying man's wish—and he's given you a substantial amount of money to make it happen—it doesn't go down well when you fail.

And it didn't help that every single person he'd recruited to provide me with those clues wanted to meet me, congratulate me, and ask me about the Elgar Foundation, and their reaction to receiving the documents they thought had been lost forever.

I didn't have the heart to tell any of them. Instead, I lied, and said I hadn't done it yet—I was still recovering from my fall, and I was waiting until the time was right.

Mary Ann did not attend, of course. Not that Marcus would ever have invited her. She was in custody. As was their father, Bob Winster. He'd made the papers. ***Agent to the Stars Arrested in Cold Case Disappearance.*** He might have been in his ninety-third year and claiming to be battling dementia, but he still remembered enough to throw his daughter under the bus for helping to cover up his crime. Close family ties certainly weren't all they were cracked up to be.

Arthur Braskey wasn't there either. I'd heard, by way of The Blue Devil's security guy, Dev, that he was "restructuring" his business empire while he recovered from his ordeal with Plaksin. At least he was off the hook for that debt. Sadly.

Matilda was also absent, but I knew she would be. She'd let me know she'd got her DNA kit from Generations and sent her sample back. She was waiting for the results, and she promised when she got them, she'd meet me in a more anonymous location.

I understood her need for discretion. Who could have known that Marcus had recruited her to conspire against her grandfather? Certainly not me. She was a dark horse, that one.

At the end of the afternoon, everyone who was there was offered one final gift: a colourful little clay pot crafted by Edward, Tricia's dad, containing some of Marcus's ashes.

"My instructions are to ensure the recipient is comfortable with this," Emil said. "And if there is discomfort—which is entirely understandable—then I shall return the uncollected ashes to what's left in the urn, and inter it, according to Marc's last wishes."

"I'm all right with it," I said.

"I'm so pleased," said Polly, placing the little container in my hands.

"Can I have three?" I asked.

Emil laughed. "You can, and you may."

Polly gave me two more pots.

"Thank you," I said.

"He also wanted us to give this to you," Emil said.

"Not another note," I said, as he handed me the envelope.

"I'm afraid so."

"It had better not be another train problem."

It wasn't.

Hello Jason. One last thing. You may be wondering where I got the cash for your retainer and payout. Perhaps you recall that infamous robbery in Belfast, Northern Ireland, whereby on December 20, 2004, a total of £26.5 million in cash was stolen from the headquarters of the Northern Bank on Donegall Square West.

As of today, the heist remains one of the largest in the history of both the United Kingdom and the Republic of Ireland, and nobody has been held directly responsible. I'm proud to reveal that I was one of the masterminds, and it's a tribute to my breaking and entering skills, and my patience in being able to unobtrusively put my share of the money aside for sunnier days, that I was never caught—in fact, I was never even implicated.

Enjoy the fruits of my labour.

I laughed.

"What?" Judy asked, walking over with her drink.

"Nothing," I replied. "Typical."

CHAPTER TWENTY-SIX

SIX WEEKS AFTER MARCUS'S celebration of life in Newlydale, Matilda made arrangements to meet me on Level 72 at The Shard in London.

Unlike my last visit there, it was a brilliantly sunny day. And, considering it was mid-January and only about 4C outside, there were a surprising number of people up on the open-air viewing floor.

Unlike Marcus, Matilda didn't keep me waiting. She was already there, in fact, saving a place for me in one of the resin-wicker arm-chair corrals. Sitting beside her was the blond-haired guy I vaguely recognized from the pavement at the back of the derelict building on Denmark Street.

"Josh," I said.

"Hello again," he replied. I hadn't seen him since the night he'd made sure I was safely in the ambulance.

"My son," said Matilda. "He lives in Norway with his dad. We felt it best not to marry. I think he may have had qualms about my grandfather."

I sat down. Another surprise. And I was not unsympathetic regarding Arthur Braskey.

"Leg healed OK?" Josh inquired.

"All good," I said, "though I may want to take issue with you telling Mary Ann to go to that building on Denmark Street, knowing that I was going to be there as well. What were you thinking? She could have killed me."

"I'm very sorry," Josh said. "I was following Marc's instructions. I delivered the note to Mary Ann's porter. The note advised her to go to the building where Cassandra's body was concealed. It mentioned no addresses."

"Josh didn't know that's where she'd be going," Matilda added. "But he put two and two together, and that's when he decided it would be a good idea to call the police. Just in case."

"Unfortunately, they turned up a little late," said Josh. "Things sometimes don't go quite according to plan."

"No kidding," I said.

Matilda went off to the snack counter, and came back with Black Forest cake and coffee.

"You guessed well," I said.

"It's written all over you," Matilda replied. "You're a chocolate man. Those biscuits in the middle of the night in Newlydale gave you away."

"I suppose you were lurking somewhere out of sight there, as well," I said, to Josh.

"I suppose I was," Josh replied.

"So," I said. "The DNA results."

Matilda smiled. "I'd guessed, based on what you told me, that Marc might have been my half-brother—Bob Winster being the common denominator. I never thought he'd turn up as my father."

"I saved this for you," I said, presenting her with one of the colourful little clay pots, crafted by Edward in Tissington and distributed by Emil in Newlydale, that contained some of Marcus's ashes. "Just in case."

"Oh," Matilda said. She looked as if she might cry. I understood very much how she felt. "Thank you." She placed it on the table. "I loved him. Though not in any improper way. We were in each others' company a lot. Unavoidable, really—me being who I was, and he being my grandfather's driver. He must have had an inkling, all along, that I was his daughter. It all makes sense now."

"It does," I agreed.

"And thank you," Josh added, "for helping to reveal what happened to Cassandra."

"Yes," said Matilda. "That final piece of unfinished business. We didn't know the truth until Marc revealed it to you in his messages. We only knew that Mary Ann was involved. We were following Marc's instructions. I'd always believed Cassandra had run off, abandoning me.

She didn't. It changes everything." She looked wistful again, then shook her head.

"Remember the time you did spend with Marcus," I suggested, "and celebrate those memories."

"I will," said Matilda.

There was a bag on the floor. It was very nondescript, zippered black canvas, with two leather handles. She gave it a push around the cubed coffee table, so that it was beside my feet.

"A last little something for you."

I was reminded of the exchange in The Sheep and Shears during my walk around Soho.

I gave her a questioning glance.

"Don't look at it now," Matilda said. "Wait until we've left. I'm ninety-nine percent sure we weren't followed, but nowadays, you can never be truly certain, can you? Especially when you're dealing with Soho crime lords and Russian gangsters."

Mindful of her suggestion, we spent the next half hour in conversation, eating cake and drinking coffee.

And then, it was time to say goodbye.

"We'll chat again soon," Matilda promised, getting to her feet. "It goes without saying you should not mention to my grandfather that we met up today."

"Absolutely," I said.

We exchanged hugs. It seemed the most natural thing in the world to do.

"Bye bye," she said, with a hint of an impish smile.

I sat down again. I still had a few minutes before my second meeting of the day.

I checked around me, then dragged the bag up to have a look at it. Heavy. Packed with something.

Interesting.

I decided to take it to the Gents. Just to be on the safe side.

***

My second meeting of the day was with a guy named Kyle.

I'd never met him before, but he came highly recommended by my son, Dom, who shared a couple of film classes with his brother at London South Bank University.

Kyle was about thirty, with a face that was all chiselled angles. He had a head of curly brown hair that reminded me of a young Freddie Garrity—the lead singer of Freddie and the Dreamers, that pop band from the 1960s. Freddie was a bit of an eccentric, famous for punctuating nearly every song with a lunatic laugh and leaping about onstage like a madman. Kyle could have been his double—minus the horn-rimmed spectacles and the very slight build.

"Hello," he said, shaking my hand with an extremely firm grip. He was all energy and nerves, one of those people who can't ever sit still in one place for long, as if they're zipped tight in an over-packed bag, straining to be released. He was wearing jeans and a bright blue windbreaker and matching trainers, and he was carrying a knapsack over his shoulder.

"Tea?" I asked. "Coffee? Sparkling water?" I didn't think he'd want anything alcoholic.

"Nah, thanks. Best not to be sloshing around." He laughed—and there was another echo of Freddie Garrity. Not quite madcap. But verging on.

I took the second little clay pot I'd saved out of my jacket pocket, and placed it on the table. "There you are."

Kyle picked it up and prized the lid off. "Interesting," he said, inspecting the white ashes inside. "Kind of a stark reminder of one's mortality, eh?"

"Very much so," I said.

He nodded at a young man who'd just walked around the corner of the snack bar. "My mate, Bonzo." Bonzo was also carrying a knapsack. He acknowledged the nod, and kept walking.

Kyle checked his watch.

"There's Rix."

Rix was another one of his friends. All three had arrived separately, their bags clearing the security check downstairs, no suspicious articles identified, nothing to trigger alarms. Rix gave Kyle a subtle thumbs-up, then disappeared through the door that led down to the public toilets.

He was followed, a minute later, by Bonzo.

And then Kyle, who took the little pot with Marcus's ashes with him.

What happened next was something Kyle had done dozens of times before. Sometimes he managed it under cover of darkness, a solo affair that involved carrying one immense bag, evading cameras and guards, scrambling over security fences and hiking up impossible staircases that would have defeated me after about five flights. Sometimes he boldly appeared in public in the middle of the day, sorting his equipment into different bags, each assigned to one of his accomplices, all of them meeting up in the toilet for reassembly.

This was going to be one of those. A piece of cake, apparently.

Kyle emerged from the stairwell and walked briskly and with purpose to the same glass-walled corner of the viewing platform that Marcus had chosen three months earlier. He was wearing a hard helmet with a GoPro attached to its front. He was also belted into a compact parachute, with the straps running over his shoulders and around his chest and between his thighs.

I stood beside him at the window, possibly the only other person—besides Rix and Bonzo—who knew exactly what was going to happen next.

Ten seconds, and Kyle had nimbly hoisted himself up the glass wall. Another three seconds, and he'd launched himself over the top. Not head-first, the way Marcus had fallen. Feet-first—and in total control.

I watched as his tiny neon-bright pilot chute deployed, followed by the flawless blossoming of his green and white canopy. I watched as he released Marcus's ashes into the bright January sun and his dust caught the wind, drifting everywhere at once.

Safe journey, my friend.
Goodbye.
And thank you.

I turned around. Rix and Bonzo were just disappearing down the stairs, their bags noticeably empty. I knew there would be another friend on the ground, monitoring Kyle's landing, ready to help him gather up the cords, canopy and container and leap into a getaway car before anyone could be arrested. Two minutes max, top to bottom.

I took the sensible way down, in the lift.

The papers, the news on TV and all of the socials were shortly going to be buzzing with the story of the anonymous daredevil who'd just leaped off the top of The Shard. And a handful of strangers, who happened to be in the right place at the right time on the ground, who actually captured his landing on their phones, were going to be posting it on their favourite platforms. None of them knew who he was—with good reason. Kyle was an accomplished skydiver with hundreds of jumps on his CV and dozens of wins at organized BASE competitions. He sold a line of clothing on his website. And he held down a regular job as a welder on construction sites. He wore his public anonymity like a badge of honour.

I didn't feel like taking the tube home. Just as, on the morning of Marcus's jump, I wanted—needed—to be up on the surface, surrounded by life. I walked across London Bridge, just as I had the previous October. Retracing my steps, I walked all the way up King William Street, to Bank, where I caught the 43 bus that would take me to Angel tube station.

I had the upper deck almost to myself. And like a little kid, I delighted in sitting right at the front, over the driver, which gave me a privileged view of the road ahead.

It was a journey just long enough to allow me to have a second look at the contents of the bag Matilda had left beside the table for me.

She'd provided a note, with CONFIDENTIAL scrawled across the top in large red letters.

Dear Jason

Thank you so much for all the work you did to recover the Elgar collection.

Granddad confided in me about the papers when he hired me as his driver, to replace Marc.

He didn't know Marc had recruited me first, to help him. Marc desperately needed to find forgiveness during his last days.

Inside this bag you'll find the complete set of papers which Marc originally stole from the Elgar Museum for my grandfather. They're genuine. As far as I know, nothing's missing. Please fulfill Marc's wishes, and return them to the Elgar Foundation. I'd also ask that you request the Foundation keep all news of their safe return confidential. My grandfather needs to continue to believe they were taken from you by Igor Plaksin. Plaksin didn't want the collection for himself—he was working for a very wealthy, highly-placed individual in Russia.

As for the three parts that you picked up following Marc's clues...let's just say that Marc knew about Plaksin and, in spite of all his precautions, suspected he'd have the resources to track you down. So, he cleverly allowed for that eventuality.

Soho's our playground.

Forgery's an art.

And Lesley Wharton knows people who are very very good at it.

That's all I'm going to tell you. Other than this tidbit: the day before yesterday, Plaksin's Russian employer seems to have taken an unfortunate tumble out of a twelfth-floor window in Moscow, and is now dead.

Best wishes, Matilda

I put her note back in the bag.

The Elgar counterfeits were embodied perfection—as close to the originals as the samples in the replica packs Lesley had distributed at the end of her tour. Authentic papers with all the right textures. Genuine crayon scribbles and pencil marks. Food and drink stains.

I'd been fooled. Plaksin had been fooled. And it didn't matter anymore about the Russian oligarch he was working for.

As the bus continued along through Islington, I plugged in my earbuds and listened to Kenny Ball and His Jazzmen playing "Midnight in Moscow".

Angel tube station was just ahead.

I was home.

CHAPTER TWENTY-SEVEN

CODA

I'D ACCUMULATED QUITE A collection of gifts over the course of my investigation.

And I was at a loss to explain why most of the clue-givers had been asked to give them to me...other than Marcus feeling extraordinarily generous and believing that I deserved to have them.

I collected the items on my coffee table, and sat down with my cup of tea.

The Figs' 50th Anniversary Tour program.

I paged through the book, slowly, not sure what I was actually looking for—if anything at all.

About a quarter of the way through, on page eleven, there was a spread about my dad—lots of pictures and a bio and a little "In Memoriam".

There was a small white sticker in the top right corner of the page. It had a black QR code printed on it.

If I'd learned anything from my interactions with Marcus, it was that—like Sir Edward Elgar—he loved to play games.

I aimed my phone camera at the code. The code invited me to open a page on WordPress.

I did...and was presented with a musical score. Treble clef only, 4:4 time, in the key of D flat major—five flats in the signature—B♭, E♭, A♭, D♭, G♭, and an attribution: Electric Piano.

Interesting. And not a complicated piece to play. In fact, it was the same singular eighth note—B♭—repeated over thirty-six bars. Then it switched to an octave higher for ten bars, and then it ended.

There was nothing else on the page.

OK.

Next. The spiral-bound *Geographers' A-Z Great Britain Road Atlas* that Judy had given me at Matlock station.

Two hundred and eighty pages, 170 of them maps, the rest printed place names that I needed reading glasses to make out.

Where had I gone with Judy?

Newlydale, Tissington, Bakewell and Matlock.

I found the relevant page.

There was a lime green Post-it note fixed to the exact map reference square—and the Post-it had a black and white sticker on it, and the sticker contained another QR code.

This one took me to second WordPress page.

Same key, same time signature...but three staves. And three sets of instruments, all strings, playing nothing for the first six bars, then sliding in with whole notes and half notes and then very quiet quarter notes which took turns playing a little melody all the way through to the end.

Not bad, but really sounding, in my head, like some kind of finger exercise—sort-of like the version of "Bad Boy" I'd plunked out on Elton John's piano at St Pancras station on the morning I'd gone to Derbyshire.

Next.

Edward's little turquoise blue bowl with the cracked raku finish.

Not a lot of places to hide anything on that. I turned it over. Of course, it had a QR code stuck to its bottom which I'd assumed—when I'd first seen it—would take me over to a website belonging to the potter.

I'd assumed wrong.

The code took me to yet another WordPress page, and another little composition. This time it was for French Horns. Marcus was writing a symphony. It was a minute and a half long, and the horns didn't come in until twenty seconds from the end, but I could already see and hear—in my head—the effect he was going for. Not bad at all.

The Dents flat cap from Tricia's vintage emporium had a silvery polyester lining with a red and white, diamond-shaped label. One side of the label was loose. I could see a little piece of paper had been slipped into the opening. I got it out with a pair of tweezers. Another QR code? Of course.

This one was for something Marcus had labelled #1 Bass Synthesizer and it leaped in joyously with thirty seconds left in the piece and then provided sustained whole notes all the way to the end.

If there was a #1 Bass Synth, there had to be a second one. Was there something hidden inside the unusual pale blue bottle from Beatrix Cummings? There was not. But there was something on the bottom on the outside. Another white sticker, with another QR code. Which led to the notations for the #2 Bass Synth, which began immediately and continued along in a series of B♭ triplets until about halfway through, when they began to alternate between B♭ and G♭ and F and the odd A♭, and so on to the end.

What was next? Lesley Wharton's Souvenir Pack, filled with exquisitely copied and printed facsimiles. I had to hunt through every item, but there it was. Not a QR code—that would have been completely ridiculous in a package of papers replicating Denmark Street's golden years. A piece of vintage sheet music, handwritten in pencil on yellowed paper, stained with tea. Something Marcus had labelled "Calliope Lead Synth"—a series of playful semiquavers dancing all over the treble clef staves.

And he'd created a line for a pad synthesizer on a very long piece of lined paper which had been folded and then folded again and tucked between the pages of the Proms program Isabel had given me at The Sheep and Shears pub. The synths here were more like little enhancements and afterthoughts—the sorts of sounds that most people wouldn't even notice if they were listening to the piece, though their unconscious brains would register their contribution to the whole. I'd had no idea Marcus was such an accomplished musician. Or that he'd had access to any kind of computer program that would have allowed him to easily compose this stuff. And get the instruments written out on a traditional score. But then, there was such a lot I didn't know about Marcus.

My metallic balloon invitation to lunch with Emil Wojeck definitely had something hiding in behind one of the shiny circles. Again, it was only retrievable with my tweezers. And it was the score for a series of dramatic interjections with a drumset: kick drum, pedal hi-hat and crash cymbal.

The golden snake earring with the ruby blood drop that Florence had given me at Ardwick House had nothing attached to it, largely because there was nowhere to hide a sticker or a tiny scrolled up piece of paper. I even checked the white tissue it was wrapped in. Nothing.

The earring itself was probably worth a small fortune, though. And I was still waiting to hear whether the police were going to need it as evidence.

There was nothing in the Airfix Nimrod box Emil had given me—nor in the actual model plane Marcus had painstakingly assembled and painted and applied all the decals to.

Likewise, nothing on the vintage *Sapphire* postcard.

But the toy London Routemaster from the box under the stairs in Denmark Street revealed a tiny rolled up scroll of very thin paper. It was tucked inside the platform entrance, in the area reserved for bags and other stowage, beside the stairs that went up to the top deck. Again, it was necessary to employ the tweezers to extricate it. And what the scroll revealed was the score for hi-hats.

The little black London taxi from the porter in Mary Ann's apartment building also held a tiny scroll, this one hidden on the floor in front of the driver's seat. Special sound FX. Slaps and bells.

There was nothing in the guitar-case lunch box from the emporium at the OXO Tower on the South Bank, but the miniature red callbox keyring that had held the keys to the padlocked door at the rear of the derelict building on Denmark Street had a QR code stuck to its bottom. And that revealed the staves for a big bass drum inserted into the score at timed intervals.

And that left only the Shard ornament which Marcus had gifted directly to me. There was nothing on its bottom. But it had a jagged top, and the ornament itself was hollow. I shone the light from my phone down into the opening. There it was. Another tightly rolled scroll, which, after some delicate manoeuvring, I managed to extract.

This piece of paper didn't have a QR code—it had a URL for a page on YouTube. And a little printed note from Marcus:

For Jason, with my compliments. Adapt and play at will. I hereby assign you the rights.

And he'd put his signature on it.

I watched the YouTube video.

It was Marcus, sitting on a chair, playing a ninety-second melody line on a rather nice black Fender Strat. It was haunting and beautiful and it was easy to imagine the background music he'd composed to accompany him.

I watched it about three dozen times.

And then I printed off the WordPress scores and assembled the ones he'd provided on the scrolls and the vintage music paper, and I sent a text to Rudy, Ken and Dave.

***

We met at the club before our Saturday show to play it through. I'd transcribed the main bits for our instruments: tenor sax, keyboard, drums and guitar. I'd also made a backing track for the stuff we couldn't replicate in person. We'd never use anything pre-recorded for our shows—we play live, and if we can't perform something special that has some extra instruments in it, we'll invite a guest musician or two onstage to help out.

But, in this case, the extra stuff was for background effect only. And if we did decide to add the piece to our set list—as a one-time performance—we'd adapt it again, to make it work.

"Excellent guitar wailing," Rudy said, after we'd finished. "A sort-of Van Halen-Brian May-David Gilmour vibe. With overtones of Hendrix."

"Thank you," I said. I'd done my best to copy what Marcus had recorded on his YouTube video. He hadn't provided a written score.

"I like that bass line," Ken said. "It's very Afro-Cuban."

"Tresillo," Dave agreed.

"Clave," said Rudy.

"'Bo Diddley'," I said.

"It's the bloody BBC News Countdown theme, isn't it," Dave said.

I laughed.

It was.

But Marcus had rearranged the various parts so well that, in the end, it wasn't.

"So," I said. "A special addition to one of our coming-up nights?"

"One time," said Ken. "And make it a Wednesday."

"Second set," said Rudy. "Encore."

"Invite Arthur Braskey," Dave suggested, "and don't tell him who wrote it."

And that's exactly how we paid tribute to the most intriguing—and infuriating, and frustrating—but, in the end, exceptionally commendable—individual that I've ever done a job for.

And the ornamental Shard occupies pride of place on the mantle over my fireplace, standing next to the little brightly-coloured glazed clay pot that contains Marcus Merritt's ashes.

ABOUT THE AUTHOR

Winona Kent was born in London, England. She immigrated to Canada with her parents at age three, and grew up in Regina, Saskatchewan, where she received her BA in English from the University of Regina. After settling in Vancouver, she graduated from UBC with an MFA in Creative Writing, and a Diploma in Writing for Screen and TV from Vancouver Film School.

Winona has been a temporary secretary, a travel agent, a screenwriter, the Managing Editor of a literary magazine and a Program Assistant at the School of Population and Public Health at UBC. Her writing breakthrough came many years ago when she won First Prize in the Flare Magazine Fiction Contest with her short story about an all-night radio newsman, "Tower of Power." More short stories followed, and then novels.

"Tower of Power" and nine other stories can be read in Winona's recently-released anthology, *Ten Stories That Worried My Mother*.

Winona began her Jason Davey Mystery series in 2017 with *Disturbing the Peace*. Three more novels followed: *Notes on a Missing G-String*, *Lost Time* and *Ticket to Ride*. *Bad Boy* is the fifth novel in the Jason Davey series, and her twelfth book overall.

Winona lives in New Westminster, British Columbia where she is an active member of Crime Writers of Canada, Sisters in Crime-Canada West, the Federation of BC Writers, the Royal City Literary Arts Society, and Tri-City Wordsmiths.

Please visit her website at www.winonakent.com for more information.

www.ingramcontent.com/pod-product-compliance
Lightning Source LLC
Chambersburg PA
CBHW030822210726
48290CB00002B/711